A Week At Most

Nature's Crossing Series

Interior Format

A Week At Most

Nature's Crossing Series

CLAUDIA SHELTON

CCS Writings, LLC

To my grandparents—
Grandma & Grandpa Davenport,
and Mamaw & Papaw Moss

—who instilled memories of
small-town life and country living,
music in the air and swings on the front porch,
and being loved unconditionally.

CHAPTER ONE

NEWSCASTER ASHLEY LANOVAN knew she'd never forget today's date, but she still pulled up her iPhone calendar and typed TERMINATED. In the Notes section, she entered, "Said I was out of touch with my audience. Inferred that was to be expected at my age."

What did that mean? She was only thirty-eight years old.

Pressing the calendar's "Add" button, she tried to swallow back the lump in her throat. Didn't help. The sting in her eyes and uncontrollable quiver in her chin only made things worse.

She was still in good shape. Trim. Fit. A marathon runner. Up on all the latest trends in clothes. Had a makeup artist on staff who worked wonders. Even had a facial and massage every week to keep herself looking younger. She'd opened her mouth to defend herself and her show at the same time a large manila envelope had been slid in front of her.

By one o'clock, after conferring with her personal attorney, she'd accepted the new station owners' severance offer, cleaned out her desk, and headed straight to her loft condo. She'd have already moved to a more modest area if not for the three-year clause in the divorce decree. The one that gave her ex, Bradford, half the sale price if she sold sooner. At least the lucrative-severance agreement from the station would allow her to take a few months to evaluate her future options before looking for a new job.

Feeling nauseous and weak in the knees, she eased onto the closest stool at the kitchen island. "This is not supposed to happen to me."

The newscaster career she'd worked so hard to build had all been shattered in less than three hours. She picked up the manila envelope holding the agreement she'd been given. Shook it with a vengeance. Then curled it into a cylinder shape and pounded the top of the counter.

Knowing she might as well let her emotions have their way, she cried and cursed and, finally, calmed. With everything out of her system, there was nothing left but a giant hole.

Casually, she flipped the calendar to the next day's schedule. *Visit Dot and Lloyd Gregory, Nature's Crossing, Missouri.*

"Oh my gosh. I've been so busy at work, I completely forgot." Intent on canceling the trip, she scrolled to Dot's phone number. Then remembered how excited they'd been for her to visit. She blew out a sigh. "Come to think of it, I was looking forward to getting away, too."

She tucked the phone into her pocket. Might as well go since she had nothing else to do.

Tomorrow should be better. Maybe not better, but at least different. A different place. Different people. She needed this time away. Time to think about her future and try to reconnect with who she'd been before marrying Bradford.

Early the next morning, she made a list of everything needing attention, and by mid-afternoon, she was headed south in the general direction of Springfield, Missouri. Of course, she was supposed to turn off about an hour before then. She was confident her GPS would steer her onto the correct exit for the road leading to Nature's Crossing.

Secretly, Ashley hoped the Gregorys' descriptions hadn't been inflated. Back when she'd first interviewed them for one of her special event shows, Lloyd had talked mostly about their house. Dot raved about the ladies of the community, the fun monthly get-togethers, and the joy she felt just sitting on her deck in the evening. They might be as old as her parents, but they were as dear to her as her two forever friends from college, Tracie and Linda.

Cruise control set, all she had to do was focus on the road ahead. Truth be told, she was longing for a little laid-back friendliness on this trip. She wasn't sure what that even meant anymore. It had been a long time since she could just be herself.

Being past the rumble of city traffic, she opened the sunroof. The unseasonably warm fall wind blew inside, teased her hair. Felt good.

The memory of her and Bradford driving a

rental convertible through Napa Valley on their honeymoon flitted across her thoughts. Nope… enough of that.

Besides, if she ever let herself be seriously involved with another man, he'd be the kind who worked nine-to-five. Home by six. Then told her everything about his day and allowed her to share hers in return. No business trips. No fancy boats. No fast cars. And no secrets of any kind.

She flipped on the radio and let herself enjoy the passing scenery. Every time a slow song came on, she flipped to another station. Upbeat rhythms, that's what she needed. Something to make the miles disappear.

An hour into the drive, her phone rang with Dot Gregory's caller ID.

"Hello," Ashley said. "I should be there in just a couple more hours."

"That's wonderful. Lloyd and I are so glad you've finally taken us up on a visit."

"Me, too. The past few days have been hectic, to say the least. I'll fill you in once I arrive."

"That's why we're calling." Dot paused. "Here, let me put you on speakerphone."

"What's wrong, Dot? What's going on?"

"We just got a phone call from Lloyd's brother in St. Louis. His mother's been rushed to the hospital. Fell on the steps, and well…" A slight tremble in her mile-a-minute words said she was worried. "Anyhow, we need to head that way for a few days."

"You do whatever you need to do. I fully understand." Ashley's mind buzzed with what she should do next. Where she should go. "Don't worry about me, I'll just head on down to Branson and Table Rock Lake for a few days."

"You'll do no such thing," Lloyd chimed in. "We've already got everything lined up for you to stop at Red's Corner Market and stay with the owners, Janie and Patrick Horton. They're transplants from the East Coast. Been here almost a year. Nice people."

"I can't do that," Ashley said.

"Why not?"

"Because..." She tried to think of a comeback. A way around the situation. Nothing came to mind. Absolutely nothing.

Dot gently sighed. "If you'd rather, you can come on to our house. We'll just leave the key under the flowerpot. But...well..."

"Truth is, I've been looking forward to showing you around the place. Giving you all the highlights of what we've done. You know I bragged a lot on that show of yours..." Lloyd's tone held a bit of pride coupled with wanting to see if she'd feel the same way about the place they loved. "Now I'd like to see your first reaction in person. Understand?"

Ashley completely understood. That's how she always felt when her family and friends paid a visit. Always wanting to make sure everything was perfect. Needing their reaction to confirm she'd succeeded.

"Okay, you two have convinced me. Look out, Red's Corner Market. Here I come."

"Great. I'll text you their photo," Dot said. "You

can't help but recognize Patrick. He always wears a red baseball cap."

They all talked a few minutes more, then hung up so the Gregorys could head to St. Louis. Ashley laughed to herself. The three of them would be friends passing in the night on Interstate 44.

She took the next exit that listed places for food and gas. Time to refuel both herself and the car. Seeing that she'd gotten a late start, a late lunch sounded like what she needed. She'd given up on arriving before dark, so this would make a good break from the highway. After eating and browsing around the restaurant's gift shop, she felt refreshed as she walked back to the SUV. A good long shower was going to be in order once she arrived.

After a couple more hours of driving, the GPS instructed her to exit the highway. She was met with a road detour and steady rain. Darkening clouds and strong wind greeted her as well.

Slowing and trying to stay between the lines on the winding two-lane road to Nature's Crossing, she couldn't calculate how far she'd driven since the turnoff. Now a full-blown storm pulsated harder with every second. Before the detour, Ashley knew exactly where she was and how to get where she was going. Now she wasn't so sure about the GPS.

"Where the heck am I? It can't be this hard to find Nature's Crossing." The Jeep didn't answer. But her fear adrenaline answered with a swift kick. Then, out of nowhere, a sign reading "Welcome to Nature's Crossing" greeted her from the side of the road.

A little way farther, Ashley turned into a gravel parking lot at the crossroads and stopped in front of a small grocery. The area was covered in what she'd call a foggy London night. In fact, nothing showed this to be Red's Corner Market. Almost looked like it was closed.

Parking a spot away from a black BMW SUV, she flipped the visor down, opened the mirror, and wiped away any sign of smudged mascara beneath her eyes. A quick swipe of lipstick and a finger-comb of her hair completed her arrival. If this was the wrong place, she could at least get directions. If this was the right place, she wanted to look halfway presentable. Nothing like a good first impression.

She checked the photo Dot had texted her, then opened the driver's side door and stepped out. Immediately, her feet sank in a puddle of muddy water. A cold stream of wetness oozed into her loafers, surrounded her toes, and drenched her designer socks. The hem of her jeans glided on top of the puddle like a skater on slick ice, soaking the liquid upward.

"Well, that sucks." She stepped out of the puddle, shaking each foot as if that would get rid of the mess and make everything better. Not happening.

She slammed the SUV door closed and trudged to the front door of the grocery, never sure if the next step would be solid or maybe a drop off to oblivion. At least the holes weren't as deep as the city potholes she'd encountered last winter.

One dimmer-than-dim light lit the concrete pad in front of the entrance. A quaint doormat of orange and brown leaves, plus a prickly wipe-mud-here porcupine smiled up from the left. Happiness whirred to life, along with contentment and calm. Even with all the mud and yuck and potholes, she still hoped this was the right place.

A soft ding sounded when Ashley pushed open the front door. Unsure if the lights were out or they used low-wattage bulbs, she ventured cautiously. "Hello? Anyone here?"

"Come on in." From the shadows, a lady with long hair called out. "Storm zapped the lights right near the end. They should be back on any second. The generator kicked in, so we've got a little power. That's why it's so dim in here."

Tentative, Ashley moved forward until something jumped on her shoulder. She spun with surprise. The squish and bunch of wet socks in her shoes threw her off balance, and her ankle turned. With all stability lost, she grabbed in the dimness at what appeared to be one of the store's shelves. It gave way. Amid the sound of crashing cans, she fell to the floor as every light in the place popped on brighter than bright.

A man in a dark leather jacket with his back to her spun around, shoving one hand in his pocket as he held the other at arm's length in front of him like a shield. Quickly, his intense stare zeroed in on her. A second later, he blew out a cheek-puffing sigh and raised his hands in a what-happened gesture.

She could only imagine how she looked sprawled on the floor.

"What fell, Janie?" an unseen man shouted from somewhere.

"My gosh. Are you okay?" Janie darted toward her, tiptoeing through the maze of cans.

Stunned, Ashley sat dumbfounded on the floor. Elbows scraped, legs tangled, hair tousled, and any chance of making a good first impression completely lost. Besides the cans on the floor, there was also what had probably been samples of candy corn and peanuts scattered about. Frustrated, she tried to push herself up. But her hand slid across honey dripping from the lid of a crushed SueBee honey bear container and she plopped back on the floor.

"Ouch." Gingerly, she tilted to the side, then grabbed a can she'd landed on, from beneath her bottom. "That's going to leave a bruise."

Fighting to hold back a laugh, the man in the leather jacket stepped closer and held out his hands. "Here, let's get you up."

His six-foot frame looked custom made for his broad shoulders, and the smooth sound of his voice reassured her she'd be okay. The quiet power of his confident swagger, coupled with his sexy stubble, made her wish there was more to this encounter than her embarrassing fall.

Pausing, he slightly squinted, then smiled. "Ashley? Ashley Lanovan?"

Laying her hands in his, her insides twitched at his warmth. "Mark? Mark Garmund?"

CHAPTER TWO

ASHLEY TRIED TO smile as she blinked back the flutter of her pulse, then swallowed the unusual feeling of shyness. The same shyness she'd felt when Dot and Lloyd had introduced Mark to her early last year, during one of their trips to St. Louis.

"Yeah. Small world, isn't it?" Mark's dark brown hair, with just a hint of gray, accentuated his blue eyes as he pulled her to her feet.

Trying to let go of his hand, she realized that the honey had suctioned their palms together. Popping their hands apart, they both glanced at their mutually honey covered hands and laughed.

"How have you been?" he asked.

How had she been? She wasn't sure of the answer. "Oh, you know how it is. Ups. Downs." Before she realized what was happening, she'd moved her hand to rest on his arm as she stood next to him. She eased back, hoping he hadn't noticed. "Life happens. What about you?"

Glancing down at his arm, his brows pinched together in a questioning look. She quickly saw that she'd left her handprint of gooey honey, peanut, candy corn mixture on the sleeve of his leather jacket.

"Sorry," she said.

The woman, who Ashley assumed to be Janie, handed them a pack of wet wipes. "Here, let me help—"

Fast-moving footsteps sounded across the floor, and Janie stopped. Just as fast, she whirled to the side and spread her arms in front of an oncoming giant ball of fur. "No! Bandit, no. Paddy, grab the dog. Paddy... Patrick!"

The woman's long strawberry-blonde curls flashed from side to side as she blocked the dog's movement. Maybe a couple years older than Ashley, yet wrapped in a younger woman's petite figure, she was agile and quick.

Patrick hurried over and caught the dog by the collar, pulling it away from the sugary temptations. "I've got him. She okay?"

Ashley nodded.

"She's okay," Janie said.

"Good. Come on, Bandit. Let's get the broom and clean up this mess." Patrick and the dog disappeared through the doorway behind the counter.

A calico cat jumped from a high shelf and followed close behind. Ah, the culprit of the shoulder mishap. Ashley gasped as she put weight on her foot and her ankle twinged in pain.

"You sure you're alright?" Janie asked.

"I think so. Look what I've done to your store."

Ashley surveyed the domino effect of her fall. Dreadful couldn't begin to describe her klutzy outcome. She tried to put weight on her foot once again, and flinched, then steadied herself against a shelf. "Ouch. Ouch. Ouch!"

Janie cringed. "That bad?"

"Oh, yeah." Ashley clenched her teeth and quick-nodded again and again. "Oh, yeah."

"I'll get one of the ice packs from the storage freezer." Mark disappeared through the same doorway as Patrick had.

"Let's get you sat down. Lean on me." Janie braced her forearm below Ashley's. "Don't you worry one bit about the mess. Paddy will have everything cleaned up in no time flat."

Ashley let herself be led behind the counter to a stool high enough to see over the sill to the gas pumps. The lady pulled a second stool from beneath the counter and boosted her five-foot-two self onto the seat.

"I'm Ashley Lanovan, and I hope you're—"

"Right. And I'm Janie. Janie Horton." The woman's clear green eyes filled with sparkle as her demeanor bubbled with a genuine effervescence.

Ashley glanced out the front window. Now that the electricity had kicked back on, there was a bright and shiny red neon sign—Red's Corner Market.

She mustered a smile for the lady across from her. "It's been a long day. But I made it."

"You sure did." Janie smiled in return. "Welcome to Nature's Crossing."

Mark came back in with a small ice bag, then knelt in front of her to wrap her ankle. "There's not a lot of swelling, so this should do the trick. Put it on and off the next few hours. Should be good in the morning."

"Thanks. I can always get an elastic bandage if it still hurts." The feel of his fingers against her skin had felt warm and tender. Slightly embarrassing.

As he stood back up, their gazes met. Her mouth dried. And for a moment, she felt like a shy teenager again.

He didn't look away. "You know, I meant to call. But…well…my job…"

This was an awkward situation. One she would love to pursue, to find out why he hadn't called, but even he seemed at a loss for words. "In other words, life happened for you, too."

"Yeah, you might say that."

Part of her wanted this conversation to last, but who was she kidding? Her shoulders dropped a notch. He'd passed on her before. Why would their meeting be any different this time?

She smiled. "It was nice seeing you again."

"You, too." He tossed the comment over his shoulder as he opened the front door. "Maybe we'll run into each other again while we're both in town."

"Hey." Janie braced her hands on her hips. "I thought you were staying for dinner and—"

"Something came up with work." Mark pointed outside. "Gotta go see a man down the road."

Glancing back and forth between her, outside,

and Janie, he seemed nervous. Like he could hardly wait to get away.

"Really? Well, you be careful." Janie wiped invisible dust from the counter. "You know where the key is when you get back later. Make yourself at home like usual. You know where everything is."

"I told Patrick I'd see you all in the morning." Another nervous glance outside. "You've got company tonight. I don't want to intrude."

Ashley got the distinct impression she was the reason he didn't want to stay. Why, she didn't know. "Please don't leave on my account. I promise I won't bother you."

"You're no bother. I really do have an emergency at work." An awkward, peaceful silence settled for a moment before he gave Ashley a casual two-finger salute.

He quickly pointed from himself to her and made the call-you sign as he stepped outside and closed the door behind him. He'd done that after the Gregorys had first introduced them, also.

She wouldn't hold her breath.

CHAPTER THREE

SPECIAL AGENT MARK Garmund headed out of the Red's Corner Market, and all he could think about was how Ashley still smelled like magnolias. Taking the right exit out of the parking lot, he steered his new BMW X5 SUV to a familiar place. After getting permission from Lloyd and Dot years ago, he'd stayed many nights in a small clearing tucked in the towering pines that surround their property.

Peaceful, and one of the safest places he'd ever been, the hideaway seemed to welcome him as much as his home in Washington, D.C. And he'd already told the Gregorys that whenever they decide to sell, just let him know the price. He'd give them whatever they wanted.

Taking the road leading to the Gregory property, he watched for the camouflaged entrance into the pines. And just like clockwork, he eased his new BMW X5 off the road and between two imposing pines. Slowly following the path into the clearing, he knew the angles, where to turn and the branches to avoid.

The powerful machine was bulletproof, had reinforced undercarriage upgraded, and linked to a worldwide satellite. Plus, a lot more that was included in the Protection VR6 package he'd chosen. The SUV was heavier than a normal X5, but in only the few days he'd had the vehicle, he'd already mastered how to turn it on a dime. Plus, every hidden compartment he'd custom ordered to aide in his covert activities had turned out spot on. Due to the armor plating, the doors were heavy to open and close, but that hadn't surprised him.

The really special upgrades had been revamping the back so the seats could fold down and adding an independent custom-made battery operated AC/heater system. Summer or winter, he never knew when he might need to sleep in the security of his own vehicle. Especially now that he'd decided to leave the CIA and join the Park Service. At least, he was 90 percent sure that's what he wanted.

Patrick had voiced his own concerns about leaving the CIA a couple years back, so that's why he'd agreed to consult every so often. Thankful to still work with him on certain assignments, Mark could now understand why his team partner had made his decision.

There were a couple of differences in their situations. One big difference—if he took the job offer, there'd be no going back. He didn't want new CIA missions dogging him forever. And two, Patrick had been six years older when he left the agency.

Besides, it wouldn't be like Mark was giving up

government work completely. His new job might involve a few assignments with the FBI and DHS in local sites such as Mark Twain National Forest, Table Rock Lake, Bagnell Dam, and Lake Ozark in the future. Basically, anywhere a former agent with his experience might be of help in Missouri. But for the most part, he'd have his assignments in the local region.

For sure, there'd be no more long-term dark assignments out of country, except for the final CIA assignment slated for the beginning of the year. He doubted they'd let him out of that one.

Once he was parked and settled in the clearing among the pines, his mind returned to seeing Ashley again. That had been a nice surprise. She probably thought he'd left tonight because of her. And that wasn't completely wrong. Being around her scared him senseless. Had the first time they met. Had again tonight.

Also made his insides want to shout that she didn't understand who he was beneath the surface. To tell her that his much-needed vacation, the first time they'd met, had been sidelined by business the next day. How he thought she was the most flawless woman he'd ever met. That she was beautiful and sexy and… Her brown doe-like eyes, the burnished-gold highlights in her dark-auburn hair, and easy smile tagged onto his memory link as well. Maybe five-six, hundred-thirty-forty pounds, olive complexion. Long legs. Nice butt.

He remembered the night Dot and Lloyd introduced them over dinner at a restaurant in

The Hill neighborhood of south St. Louis. Ashley had made a memorable entrance as she walked over to the table, her skinny jeans and designer heeled boots making a statement. She sure hadn't been armed…where would she hide a weapon? Of course, you never knew what a woman hid in her purse. He doubted she packed anything more threatening than a tube of lipstick. Doubted she even had an inkling of all the dangers in the world. Dangers like his line of work.

He shook his head as he glanced at his phone. Even now, her phone number was still in his contact list. Sitting there. Waiting for the right moment. Problem? There just never seemed to be enough time, at least not a safe time that wouldn't put her in danger.

Very few people had even the slightest idea what Mark did for a living. For the most part, they thought he was a desk jockey with a simple government agency that pushed papers around. Ones who actually knew different were agents he'd worked with, agency staff on need-to-know basis, or agents in other U.S. security agencies. They all knew to keep their mouths shut. Ones who had an inkling usually just gave him a what-the-hell look when he left town for extended periods of time.

Maybe he should erase Ashley's number. He tossed the phone back and forth between his hands. Finally, he laid it back on the console. Nope, he just wouldn't call her. But there might come a time he needed to reach her in an emergency.

Sighing, he felt tired. Tired and alone and watching

life fly away one assignment after another. He laid his phone on the console. She'd never believe him, but he'd honestly meant to call. What was it she had said as he started to leave the grocery?

Don't worry. I won't bother you.

Not bother him. She'd always bother him. Every stinking hour of every stinking day, she'd bother him. But she'd be right about one thing…tonight he'd left Red's because of her.

Chugging down half the bottle of orange juice, Mark turned his thoughts to the impending doom prickle on the back of his neck. After four years at West Point and five years' military commitment, he'd joined the CIA. The past twelve years had involved dangerous surveillance on foreign soil. No one could ever tell him he didn't know when something felt wrong—overseas or Stateside.

He pushed his CIA boss's number on his phone.

His boss, Will Brenner, clicked into the recorder system. "What do you need?"

"Nothing really. Just checking in."

"Where are you?"

"After leaving D.C., I took a few days in Chicago to check out a couple of boats while they're in dry dock. Then headed on down here to Missouri. Figure I'll spend some time visiting Patrick and Janie."

And other people he'd made friends with, but the boss didn't need to know everything. Like the fact he was job hunting. Like the fact he planned for him and Patrick to make a road trip around the state. Like he had that strange something-off prickle on the back of his neck. The one he was usually 90 percent right about.

Trouble was, he had no idea what was eating at him. Not even a clue. Maybe he was just tied up adjusting back to being Stateside. Assignment life sometimes left an edgy feel when you came home.

"Sounds like a good plan. Listen, I can't talk long. The boss called an emergency meeting, so I gotta go."

"What's that about?"

"Been a lot of brass around today. A lot of passwords that worked a second ago don't work now." Brenner cleared his throat. "Now this meeting ASAP."

"What's your guess?" Mark sometimes asked too many questions. Questions that worked his boss's last nerve. But he also knew that was the only way to stay alive in the covert business. That, and being careful what you do, where you go, who—the prickle on his neck burned hot.

"Computer hack." Brenner lowered his voice. "Watch your six, Mark. I'll call when I can."

Watch his back?

The silence between the two men thickened. The boss hung up.

Mark rubbed his palms across the back of his neck. Pushed number one on his speed dial— Patrick.

CHAPTER FOUR

A SHLEY WAS ALREADY feeling better by the time the doorway curtains behind the counter parted with the return of the man who'd led the dog into the back. Probably six-two, and dragging a broom behind him, he wore his red cap like a crown. Before Ashley knew what happened, he engulfed her hand in a genuine handshake that felt comforting. While at the same time, his fleeting gaze seemed to see right through you, daring you not to be honest with him.

"I'm Patrick. We've been watching for you all day. Began to think you got lost."

He swept the floor and restacked the cans as Janie and she talked. Whenever they paused for a breath, he shot right in with a new stream of information about Nature's Crossing. Ashley could have lived there all her life and not felt any more welcome than she did now. Maybe Lloyd and Dot had been right about the community.

The entrance bell dinged as an elderly well-dressed man entered the store. His perfectly white wavy hair appeared soft and pristine like a waiting halo. "Anybody home?"

"We're here, Mr. Peabody," Patrick said.

"Thought the storm might have blown ye away."

The man dressed as if he'd stepped out of a 1940s ad for a local bank—pinstriped double-breasted suit, white shirt with starched collar, tie impeccably knotted, and a slightly worn felt hat with the brim smoothed to position from years of wearing. The only oddity was his pure white Reebok shoes peeking out from under flawlessly creased pants.

He quickly removed his hat upon seeing Ashley and Janie. "Oh, excuse me. Didn't know there were ladies in the room."

Janie flicked her dangly earrings in a sassy comeback and giggled. "You got that right."

"Who's this the wind blew in?" Mr. Peabody leaned on a mahogany cane, polished to a shine, with a gold guitar pick displayed proudly on the bend of the wood.

"Ashley Lanovan. The lady Dot told us to keep an eye out for." Patrick continued to replace groceries on the shelves.

"This is Mr. Peabody," Janie said.

Hand outstretched, the stately man crossed the floor. "I'm mighty pleased to meet you, Baggie."

"Ashley. I'm Ashley."

"Baggage? No, I can't carry valises anymore."

Ashley spoke a little louder in case he might be hard of hearing. "My name is Ashley."

Mr. Peabody chuckled and leaned a bit heavier on his cane. "I heard you the first time, but that's one of my favorite jokes."

She smiled at the humor of the spiffy gentleman who looked to be about seventy-five, maybe eighty.

He waggled his cane to get her attention. "Got to use this here third leg nowadays. My feet and legs aren't what they used to be. That's why I wear these here Reeboks."

Patrick walked behind the counter. "Why don't you stay for dinner, Mr. Peabody?"

"Yes, do stay. Maybe you could share the town's history with Ashley," Janie pleaded.

"I appreciate the offer, but I need to be getting on home. You know I'm not as young as I used to be." The silver-haired man gave a wink.

"Suit yourself. I've got brown-sugar ham and homemade peach cobbler warming in the oven."

The old man's expression lit with enthusiasm. "Well, now. Suppose I could stay awhile. Don't want to be rude to a newcomer in town." Mr. Peabody turned to Ashley. "By the way, Patrick, how's your partner? He hasn't been around in a while."

"He's been kind of busy with work. Got back in last week. Might even be passing through town in the next few days."

Mr. Peabody turned to Ashley. "You'd like him. Bright young fellow. Nice looking. Not much older than you."

She hadn't been there thirty minutes, and someone was already trying to fix her up. Did she look that needy? "Uh…"

Janie shot her an understanding smile.

"Tell him I asked about him. Glad he's okay," the

gentleman said.

Patrick smiled. "I'm sure he'll appreciate that."

A lull fell in the conversation. Finally, the red–capped owner cleared his throat as he walked to the front door, turned the lock, and lowered the blind.

"We'll go on over to the house while Patrick closes up. By the time he gets there, food'll be on the table." Janie opened the back door and persuaded with a voice as sweet as honey. "Paddy, bring her bags. That is if you don't mind."

From the corner of her eye, Ashley saw the husband and wife share a special look. Janie's an eyelash flutter and Patrick's a forced scowl. Why couldn't she have found that kind of love in her life instead of a two-timing cad like her ex-husband?

Mr. Peabody's air held a spark of mischief when he took Ashley's arm and looped it around his. "We might as well talk as we walk. Back in the late sixties, I started work at the local bank here in town. Ten years later, I ended up being the bank president when it merged with the bank in Henton."

"Henton's the county seat," Janie added as she followed behind them. "It's about twenty minutes away. Got some cute little gift shops."

"Oh, I might need to take a drive over there." She couldn't remember the last time she'd spent the day just strolling around shops for fun.

"I could get one of our helpers to watch the store and we could make a day of it."

"That would be great."

Mr. Peabody stopped. Looked first at Janie then

Ashley. Back and forth, following their conversation. Quiet, a bit too quiet. The slight stretch of his neck, the noncommittal set of his mouth, and his patient expression reminded her of her grandpa. Janie barely raised her eyebrows in alert. Evidently, their chatter had kept him from the rest of his story.

Smiling inside and out, Ashley turned toward the house and took a step. "Now, let's get back to your banking days, Mr. Peabody?"

He moved in step with her. "Then in 2005, the bank got bought out by the BBBs—'Big Boys of Banking'—and they closed the Nature's Crossing location. That's when I retired."

"Must have been hard to give up your career." She still had a hard time grasping that she'd never face the television camera again. Never have a mic check. Never have the pleasure of meeting viewers who shared how much they enjoyed her show.

"Oh, I still sit on a couple of the city and county committees. Like to know what's going on in the community. Keeps me busy. In fact, that's why I'm all spiffed up. Just came from the Nature's Crossing City Council meeting."

Janie scooted around them and went on to the house. "I'll leave the front door unlocked."

When Mr. Peabody's steps slowed, Ashley noticed the strain of walking and talking had caught up with him. She pretended to be interested in one of the mums blooming by the pathway to Patrick and Janie's home behind the market. Mr. Peabody slowly straightened as his breathing became even again, and they continued their journey to the columned porch.

He opened the front door, then stood aside. "We've got a small ATM in town now. Main bank is over in Henton with a branch in Surryfield. Nature's Crossing used to be a thriving community. But, what with roads moving a mile one way or the other, and the community college being built farther east, our little town has dwindled."

On their way to the table, the aroma of fresh-baked bread set Ashley's tummy rumbling. And the sight of green beans with potatoes and bacon took her back to childhood at her grandma's house for the holidays.

Mr. Peabody paused to catch his breath again, which gave Ashley time to truly admire the beautiful furnishings in the entry hall and dining room. The old-fashioned atmosphere of the grocery was not reflected here. These rooms were filled with stylish custom-made furniture and occasionally an expensive antique.

Janie finished putting food on the table just as Patrick walked in from the store. "I'll get the tea and we'll be ready to eat."

Patrick stood behind his seat. "Couldn't get the suitcase. Car's locked."

Mr. Peabody slipped his suit coat off and hung it on the back of his chair.

Before Ashley could stop herself, she lightly snapped the man's money-green suspenders.

He jumped. Janie dropped the spoon from her hand. Patrick hung his head in disbelief.

"Oooooooooh, I'm sorry." She fidgeted with

Peabody's straps, straightened them, patted his shoulder. She'd let her memories move her fingers. "My grandpa used to wear suspenders, and I just couldn't resist when I saw yours. I'm really sorry."

"You're forgiven. Besides, you're just lightweight. I've had them popped by stronger hands than yours and lived to tell the tale." He chuckled and pulled out the chair for Ashley.

"Thank you." She sat down and placed the linen napkin in her lap. What had happened since the storm ended and she stepped out of her Jeep? Her soggy socks had warmed with the warmth of these strangers. Felt nice. Felt homey. Felt peaceful, like the town's name.

The old gentleman seated himself, hanging his cane over his jacket on the back of the chair. "Thank you for allowing me to escort you to dinner, Ashley Lanovan. And for popping my suspenders."

"It was my pleasure, Mr. Peabody," she replied with a giggle.

"By the way, you may call me Peabody."

In less than an hour, she'd made three new friends. Now she understood why the Gregorys had told her she'd love Nature's Crossing. Too bad she was only there for a few days. A week at the most.

CHAPTER FIVE

AFTER DINNER, ASHLEY stood at the front window watching as Patrick got out of her Jeep. He'd walked Peabody back to his car and took her keys so he could drive the SUV over to the house's driveway. She'd offered to help him with her suitcases, but he'd made it very clear he could handle women's suitcases. Okay, by her.

The phone rang, and Janie answered. "Hi, Mark... Are you sure you won't come back and spend the night?" Her face lost some of its shine as she listened to the conversation. "I understand...I really do... No, I'd never stop answering your calls." She laughed as she opened the front door. "Hold on a minute. Hey, Paddy, Mark is on the phone. Said something about camping."

"Tell him I'll be right there."

Janie relayed the message and then put the phone on hold.

"Did I hear you mention the name Mark?" Ashley asked as she stared out the front window.

"Yes. Mark Garmund."

"Ah, I figured as much. Can't be that many

Marks in one town."

"I got the impression you two have met before."

"Yes. The Gregorys introduced us when they invited me to dinner on one of their trips to St. Louis." Ashley squinted at Patrick standing at the back of her SUV, the tailgate up. He jerked his hands in the air and viciously shook them, then plopped them back down against the sides of his pants. "What is he doing?"

Janie smudged at the window. "I don't know. Looks like he's picking stuff up out of the mud." She turned on the outside spotlight, and he flashed a look in their direction.

The women stared in disbelief as he snatched sweaters, jeans, and gowns from the wet rocks of the driveway. As he shoved them back in her suitcase, more items fell out. He stuck his hand into what looked like a mud abyss and pulled out bras and panties, along with sticks and leaves.

Janie giggled, then pointed to the two-way speaker by the door. She motioned to be quiet as she turned it on.

"What have I done now?" Patrick's voice came through clear as a bell. "Boy, that Ashley lady's gonna be mad about her clothes."

Ashley held her one hand over her face to keep her laughter from being heard, the other arm around her belly. Half the stuff still hung out of the suitcase when he wrapped his arm around the bag to hold it closed. He bent again. A flimsy pink item fluttered from his hand once he straightened, and a gust of wind toppled his hat into a puddle.

They should help him. They really should. The two women grabbed hold of each other, laughing as one as they hid behind the curtains at the side of the window. Poor Patrick.

"I know you're in there listening, Janie Belle. I better not find my pillow on the sofa tonight." His red cap rescued, he shook the water out and slapped it back on his head. "This was not my fault."

His wife giggled behind her cupped hand.

He grunted and tramped toward the house. Halfway there, a clap of thunder rumbled through the trees. Lingering clouds opened with a monstrous downpour.

Patrick hitched the suitcase tighter under his arm and looked to the heavens. "Give me a break!"

He trudged to the house and dropped Ashley's suitcase, hand-carried items, and mud on the floor in the front hall. Without making eye contact with either of the women, he kicked his boots off and said, "Are men the only ones who realize zippers have a breaking point?"

Water dripped down the side of his pants, and a trickle of mud made a path around his ear. Leaving a water trail down the hall, he stomped to the room where Janie had answered the phone. "Mark and I have some business to talk over, so don't bother us."

Ashley and Janie stared at the muddy mess Patrick had dropped on the floor in front of them before he stomped down the hall and slammed the door behind him.

"Guess I overstuffed the suitcase a tiny bit. Trouble is, I didn't know what all to bring. Besides, it zipped." Ashley tried to hold in a smile. "After I leaned on the top to get it closed,"

Janie laughed out loud. "Men don't know how hard it is for women to travel. I think they'd wear the same thing every day. Clean or not. Women require more options. We're more creative."

"What you might call spontaneous." Ashley flipped her hands above her head, snapped her fingers, and spun around a couple of times. Just like with Tracie and Linda, she felt completely at ease with Janie.

The two women laughed till they cried, their hands clasped to their chests amid gasping for air as they knelt on the floor, sorting through the gunk-filled clothes. After they started one load in the washer, Ashley moved the other stack to the laundry room, and Janie cleaned the foyer.

"Don't worry about the clothes," Janie said. "I'll dry them in the morning. We're always up early, so I'll stack them outside your door before I head over to the grocery."

For the next thirty minutes, Ashley and Janie snacked on leftover cobbler at the kitchen counter. Ashley even felt at ease enough to share bits about her divorce. And when Janie mentioned watching her show every so often, she took a deep breath and told how she'd lost her job yesterday.

"That is just not right," Janie said. "And since they mentioned your age, I'm sure you'd be within your rights to file a lawsuit."

Ashely shrugged. "I suppose so, but can you imagine working for people who don't want you there? That would have been unbearable."

"True. But still…"

"Besides, not only did I get a very nice severance package, I also kept the rights to the name of my show." She was very proud of herself on that front. Proud that she'd planned ahead years ago.

Janie's expression lit. "How'd you do that?"

"I'm the one who came up with the name when the show was first developed. I had a very good attorney who insisted they add a clause for my ownership of the name in my contract." Ashley nodded to herself. "And as they say in the business—that's a wrap."

The two women clinked their coffee cups together, agreeing that called for another bite of cobbler. Every so often, as they sat talking, Janie would glance in the direction of Patrick's phone call.

"How did you meet Mark?" Janie asked.

"The Gregorys introduced us a couple years ago when they were in St. Louis for a weekend. In fact, the four of us had dinner together." Ashley scooped another spoonful of ice cream and pie in her mouth. "I don't really know him, but I take it he's a friend of yours."

"He and Patrick are what you might call business partners plus"—Janie poured them fresh coffee—"best friends. Why?"

"No reason. You just seemed upset by his phone call."

"I'm not upset, I'm just… Well, Patrick is trying to ease out of the business they're in together. He'd like to retire permanently." Janie glanced at the room down the hall one more time. "But Mark's calls about camping usually turn out to be one more job for my husband. I worry, that's all."

"If Patrick won't say anything, then why don't you tell Mark to back off?" Ashley cozied her mug in her hands. If she ever saw him again, she planned to tell him exactly that.

"Oh, Mark is the nicest man I know outside of Patrick. He works hard. Cares about his job." Janie smiled. "Patrick couldn't ask for a better partner. And I couldn't ask for a better man to watch my husband's back. I just get a little irritated sometimes."

"Speaking of irritation, I'd say he's rating an eight on my irritation scale."

Janie's apple-cheeks rounded as she smiled. "Is that good? Or bad?"

"I can't decide." Ashley felt the heat rise in her cheeks. "He is hot-as-heck in a sexy, tingly sort of way. And until tonight, I'd only met him once."

"So…"

"So, he's had my number all that time and never called."

"Maybe he was busy."

"For over a year? I don't think so. I've decided he's right not to call. We probably just don't click. But nothing says I can't make him a figment of my imagination." She glanced around and lowered her voice. Why? She had no idea except it felt like sharing a secret with a childhood friend. "Maybe I'll make him a bad guy in disguise. Someone Patrick doesn't know as well as he thought."

Janie laughed out loud. "I doubt that. My husband makes it a point to know the people he works with."

"All I'm saying is that, well…" Ashley sipped her coffee, "One of my friends is a cop, and something about Mark gave me that same feel. What did you say he and Patrick do?"

"They aren't policemen."

Ashley noticed her new friend didn't elaborate, so she wouldn't ask directly. Didn't matter. Just seeing him tonight had stirred something deep inside her. Something she hadn't even realized she'd locked away after her divorce. Maybe it was time for more than just a change of location.

"Well, I still wouldn't be surprised if he carried a gun."

"Hey, don't forget; good guys carry guns, too," Janie said.

Ashley scrunched her face. "True. But, since I'm turning Mark into a figment of my imagination, I can make him whoever I want. But he'll always be—"

"Irritating." The two women laughed in unison.

Still no sign of Patrick, and it was getting late; Janie said he probably got to talking and lost track of time. She appeared nervous, with her frequent glances at the door down the hall, but maybe that was always her reaction.

Ashley tried to stifle a yawn. "If you don't mind,

I think I'll go to bed. It's been a long day, and I'm a little tired."

Janie laid out one of her gowns for Ashley to wear while explaining the alarm system in the house. "Patrick is always telling me I'm safe here. No need to worry."

The assuredness with which the pert strawberry-blonde spoke of her safety triggered a why question. Not one Ashley would voice, but one that nagged for a moment. Of course, owners of a grocery probably needed to take extra precautions. What else could it be for? From what Lloyd and Dot said about Nature's Crossing, she couldn't imagine anything serious lurked about.

The clothes Ashley wore all day were now smudged from the laundry sorting. She really should take a shower, but she was tired beyond belief. It could wait till morning. After she changed into the offered gown, she handed the dirty clothes out the door to Janie.

"I'll toss them in with the last load. If you need anything else, let me know," Janie offered.

"I'll be fine. Thanks for everything."

After listening to "Up Where We Belong" from the music box on the bedside table, Ashley crawled into bed and snuggled under a warm blanket topped with a new Dutch Doll quilt. Exhausted, she slept without a care, except for once during the night when the muffled sound of a phone ringing interrupted her sleep.

Unsure of the exact fantasy she'd been dreaming before it vanished with the disturbance, she longed for at least the feeling, the desire, to return to sleep. She nuzzled close to the other pillow in the four-poster bed and draped her arm across the sweet-scented sheet. An ache filtered through her body, eyes drifted closed, and her breathing slowed. Her hand clung to the quilt as her half-awake dreams embraced the intense man with blue eyes.

"Ummm…" She could get used to him real fast. Too bad he'd never called her.

CHAPTER SIX

MARK GLANCED AT his watch—six forty-five a.m. The few hours of sleep he'd got last night had not been enough, but he was still ready to get on the road for their so-called camping trip. After talking to Brenner, sleep had been hard to come. Once he woke this morning, he'd headed straight over to the grocery.

Patrick continued to double-check everything around Red's Corner Market, creating one commotion after another.

"I know Janie can do all this," Patrick said, "but I don't want anything to distract me once we're on the road. Like, did I send in the gas payment?"

His friend was a man of routine who made the same statement every time they started out on an assignment. Of course, this time wasn't so much an assignment as Patrick showing him around Missouri landmarks and parks and lakes and forests. Their cover would be they were just looking for hunting and fishing sites.

Content to stay out of the way, Mark waited patiently, keeping his attention tuned to one of the national television early morning shows. If nothing showed up there this morning, then the CIA might have put a stop to whatever had been rumbling last night.

Patrick was probably thinking the same. Might even explain why he was stalling to leave. The two of them had been partners long enough, they knew each other almost better than they knew themselves. The best thing to do right now was leave his pal alone.

"You know, Janie wasn't very happy about this," Patrick said.

"I could tell by her tone. In fact, if I were in her spot, I'd have hung up the phone after telling me to take a long hike off a short dock. She actually told me that once." Mark ran his fingers through his hair. "Scary part is, I think she meant it."

"She knew what came with the territory before we got married. Wouldn't have it any other way," Patrick continued.

Mark gave him a look that said, "you're stone-cold crazy if you believe that makes a difference."

"You know what I mean." Patrick shoved shaving cream and razors off the counter into his overnight bag, along with half the suntan lotion. "She understands."

"You almost forgot your dessert." Mark tossed a bottle of Tums to his friend.

"Oh, yeah. Give me that other bottle, too. I'm getting way too old for this."

Mark picked up on a restlessness in his partner's tone. Knew he should make some smart remark to lighten the mood. Knew he should point out that his pal was barely fifty. But all he could do was stand there and clench his jaw. For the life of him, he couldn't think of anything to say. But the words had hit a nerve.

Patrick brushed his fingers across the photo hanging on the wall behind the cash register. The one of Janie and him fishing at the lake. "Way too old."

Ashley's internal clock woke her at seven, and she reached for the pillow next to her, hoping to hold onto the man from her dreams. He'd felt warm. Her pillow was cold. Sighing, she rolled out of bed and shuffled to the bedroom window.

Last night in the dark, she hadn't been able to see much in the yard outside her window. Now, the early-morning sun gave a clear view as squirrels scurried about burying acorns from the tall oak tree. She saw flower beds laced with steppingstones and a manmade fountain waterfall cascading into a small pool, while small benches and bistro table sets peeked from beneath nearby trees.

Later, she'd make time to take a cup of coffee outside, along with one of the books she'd seen on the living room bookshelves, and let herself get lost in the setting for a bit.

Ready to clean up, she shampooed and showered in the guest's en-suite bathroom, then left her wet hair wound on top of her head in a towel as she slipped back into the borrowed gown. Cracking the bedroom door slightly, she checked for her clean clothes. They were nowhere in sight, and when she called out for Janie, there was no answer.

Running low on options, she opened the door to the bedroom closet. A stack of neatly folded clothes with a note on top reading the items were for the local charity, sat on a shelf. Not much there, but maybe she could find something to wear. Surely, something in the pile would get her to the laundry room and back.

She tried on a pair of Janie's jeans, but to get them zipped would require she lose ten pounds and develop slimmer hips. That left a pair of Patrick's khaki pants. Lost inside them, she rolled up cuffs, tied a scarf through the belt loops, and tried to walk. The pants were big-time baggy, but she could at least leave the room.

The only top available was one of Janie's black tanks. Ashley shimmied into the stretch knit and then turned to the mirror. She winced at her reflection. No bra and a way-too-small top made for a bad combination. Oh well, she'd go with the flow until she found her clothes. At least the black tank was wearable. Besides, who would see her except Janie?

Finally ready to face the world, she opened the bedroom door and started down the hall leading to the kitchen. Halfway there, she stubbed her little toe on the side table and cried out in pain. A man's heavy footsteps sounded against the kitchen tile, heading in her direction.

"Who's there?" she asked.

"It's me. Mark."

Quickly, she turned, trying to hobble back to her bedroom as her toe throbbed in pain. Every time she bumped it against something hard, the toe always popped out of its socket. Then the pain. The swelling. She knew the routine. Knew what she needed.

"Ashley. Ashley!" he asked from a short distance behind her. "You need something?"

She turned around, bracing her hand against the wall to steady herself. And there he stood at the edge of the kitchen doorway. Of course, last night, Janie had said Patrick might be going camping with Mark. Him being here in their house made perfect sense. But why did it have to be now?

His leather jacket had been replaced with a fishing vest. In fact, he looked like he could have just stepped out of a *GQ* magazine spread featuring the latest on what to wear in the woods.

For a moment, they stood staring at each other, then his gaze momentarily lowered to her top. His lips parted a second before he turned his head and stared at the picture on the wall.

"I asked if you need something?" he said.

"No, I—" She took a tentative step. Cringed. Yelped in pain once again.

"Is it your ankle from last night?"

Shaking her head, she might as well admit it. She needed his help. "Uh…I kicked the table. My toe popped out like it always does, and…" She tried to take another step then swiped away the tear forming in the corner of her eye. "I need to sit down."

He was beside her before she blinked. "Can you walk?"

"I don't think so."

Instantly, he scooped her up and headed to the living room. Leaning against him, she eased her arm over his shoulder. As if he'd done triage before, he sat her in the chair by the front window and lifted her foot on to the ottoman.

"This happen a lot?"

"No. Maybe once a year. But this time it really hurts." She tried to bend her toe. No luck. "I need an ice cube."

"Just one?"

"Yes. Please." For all that was holy, the man needed to get a move on. The faster she got cold on the toe, the faster she could pull it back into place. Because if it swelled too much, she'd never be able to get her shoe on.

He stepped into the kitchen, and she heard the ice cube maker rumble. Then returned holding a glass. "Brought you two. Just in case."

She dumped a cube in her hand and reached for her foot, but the baggy pants got in her way. Mark grabbed the ice from her and held both pieces tight against her toe.

Janie appeared in the doorway. "What happened?"

"Breathe," Mark said. "Breathe."

"Long story." She gulped in a couple of deep breaths. Again, he had his fingers against her skin. They needed to stop meeting like this.

"Breathe." He popped the toe back in place and

the pain subsided.

Five minutes later, he'd taped her toe to the ones beside it. Her shoe was on. And she was able to walk to the kitchen as Janie poured three mugs of coffee.

"I'd better get back over to the store and make sure Patrick's ready to go. But I'll take this with me." Mark picked up his mug and opened the back door. He braced his hand against the doorframe and paused as if thinking. "Ashley."

"Yes."

"I am sorry that I never called. After leading you to believe we'd have dinner the next evening, I can see where you might be upset." His voice was soft, quiet, neutral. And when he turned to face her, the forlorn look in his eyes was almost painful to watch. "I hope you'll accept my apology."

Apology? Here? Now? Okay, whatever he wanted. But this conversation was going to go two ways. She'd stopped being a doormat the day she found her ex having a play-day on their cabin cruiser with his assistant.

"Now, let me make sure I understand why you're sorry. Because you didn't show up for dinner the next evening after the Gregorys introduced us? Or the fact you never even called to say business had come up?" Unsure of how bare she wanted to leave things between them, she considered her next words. "*Or* when, because you didn't show up at the restaurant, I sat there for two hours—by myself—eating all the appetizers while the waiter took pity on me and kept bringing bread. Do you know how embarrassing it is to be stood up and everyone around you figuring out that's exactly what has happened?"

In her peripheral vision, she noticed Janie standing at the sink. Staring out the window. Washing and rewashing a spoon. Moving quietly back and forth from one foot to the other.

"Yeah, I think I do." He fidgeted with the doorknob. "Let's just say I had my reasons for doing that."

"Reasons? Like what?"

His demeanor changed in an instant as he lifted his chin, squared his shoulders, and determination flashed across his expression. "Maybe I'll tell you the story one day. Today, all I can say is I'm sorry."

Caught off guard by his apology, she tried to think of a quick, sassy comeback. Nothing came to mind. For some reason, his rejection of not showing up and not even calling had been the catalyst of awakening her emotions again, because she'd been hurt. Feeling sad and lonely and not worthy. Even now, her insides ached at what had happened.

But his apology sounded sincere. Like he'd felt the pain also. She'd learned long ago that rejection and words ran deep, sometimes for everyone involved.

"Apology accepted." She lifted her mug in recognition and nodded once. There had to be a lot more to what happened, but for the time being, she was satisfied with the fact he'd tried to make amends. She wiggled her foot at him. "And thanks for the ice cubes."

Staring at each other seemed to last forever.

Janie cleared her throat. Hummed. Dried her hands. "If you all will excuse me, I'm going to head on over to the store and—"

"No, you stay here. I'm going to go keep Patrick company. Maybe get him to move a little faster at packing," Mark said. "So, are we good, Ashley?"

She sucked in a deep breath until her entire body felt the tension release, then exhaled slowly. "We're good. For now."

"Hey, I forgot to ask. How's your bruise?" Stepping outside, he grinned and, slowly, pulled the door closed behind him. "By the way, I like your top."

Glancing down, she had ample view of the impression her bra-less breasts were making against the stretchy tank top. She grabbed the dish towel from the counter and jokingly threw it at the door, but he was already gone. "Just when I think he's a nice guy, he turns out to be irritating again."

"I thought it was kind of sweet." Janie topped off their mugs, sat a small platter of cinnamon rolls on the kitchen island, and slid onto the stool across from her. "Kind of flirty, too."

Nibbling the icing on the roll, she had to admit he looked just as good in the fishing vest as in the leather coat. And just as good coming or going. "Flirty. Sexy. For the life of me, I can't figure him out. Where did you say Patrick and Mark are going camping?"

CHAPTER SEVEN

STANDING BESIDE A fishing supply pegboard wall in Red's Market, Mark fingered the bags of different size weights and hooks. Eyeing the colorful jigs, trying to figure out how in blue blazes a fish could ever be fooled by wires and feathers, he tugged a package labeled "scented purple worms" from a hook. He sniffed. Smelled nothing. Did fish even have olfactory capabilities?

The first thing Patrick and Janie had done after buying the store was order a complete update of the basic equipment, then had the market's atmosphere renovated to a 50s look and feel. Black-and-white floor tile. Energy efficient nostalgic coolers. Tin signs and old baseball pennants on the walls. The only two modern items were the bright lights Janie insisted on and the cutting-edge refrigeration system Patrick had demanded.

Mark still loved the look of his gift to his friends, a modern digital cash register with all the necessary apps to make finances easy to track. Plus, he'd had it anchored beneath the shell of an ornate antique 1800s register.

Townsfolk were amazed at the amount of money shelled out to refurbish the store. Even more surprised by the no-nonsense speed that completed the project. Little did the locals know that Patrick's friends and contacts from the CIA had pitched in simply because it had been for two of the nicest people around. Sometimes who you knew mattered. And, sometimes what they owed you was even more important.

"Hey Mark, I'll be back in a second." Patrick's voice blared through the special walkie-talkie system on his cell phone. "Tell the customers to wait."

Mark looked around. What customers? The morning rush had already happened. Now the lull before the lunch rush had set in.

He turned his attention back to the rods and reels, wire baskets and metal stringers, and nets. They were useful tools. They were things he knew how to use. He lifted a long-handled net from the wall, twirled it, side-stepped, twirled it again, side-stepped again, twirled and twirled, then slammed it to the floor. They were all improvised weapons he could use in a pinch. He balanced the net on his fingers. Nice weight, easy to move.

He eased it back into its place among the fishing equipment, then moved on to an ancient-looking yet brand-new refrigerator in the corner. A sign on the front read, "BAIT!" He opened the door, saw the neatly stacked Styrofoam containers of worms, got a whiff of moist dirt, and promptly shoved the door closed. One time, he made the mistake of asking Patrick about the worms and proceeded to receive a lesson in proper usage of nightcrawlers and little wigglers.

As far as bait in Red's Corner Market, Mark liked the metal aerated minnow tank. He picked up the tiny net from the side of the tank and chased the tiny fish. Grinning, he caught a minnow, only to release it back into the water the next moment. Here at the minnow tank, he didn't need worms or crickets, just focus and agility. He had a lot of that. Came from years of experience in his job.

The front door opened, and he glanced up. At least he could let the customer know there was someone in the store. No way he'd try to ring something up, though. To his surprise, he had nothing to worry about on that side. The so-called customer was Ashley.

Wearing a tan loose-knit cable sweater over a pair of tight denim leggings, she looked as if she'd dressed for a getaway weekend with friends. Or a lover. He wouldn't mind spending a weekend showing her the area. Here. There. Anywhere. Trouble was that his vacation had evaporated with a call from his boss.

He kept track of her in the corner security mirror. She seemed intent on seeing the store and wandered from aisle to aisle, with only a slight pause every so often to roll her foot from side to side. One time, she even slipped off the leopard-patterned flat and rubbed the ball of her foot. Guess her toe still ached. No way he could fix that.

She surprised him when she headed in his aisle's

direction. Trying to grab a handful of fishing items to make it appear he'd been shopping, he knocked them all on the floor instead.

"Who's there?" she called out.

"It's me. Mark."

A couple seconds later, she stood next to him as he picked everything back up.

"I didn't see you when I came in. How long have you been in the store?" she asked.

"All morning." One by one, he shoved the fishing lure packets back on their appropriate hangers. "I mean…except for when I was over at the house… with you. That whole problem with your foot."

She reached out, snagged a packet he'd put on the wrong peg, and proceeded to find the spot where it belonged. Even straightened a few others. "So, you saw me when I came in? You knew I was here all this time?"

"Yeah. Looked like your toe might still be hurting."

"Yes, my toe still hurts." She glanced toward the door, but of course, it couldn't be seen from where they stood. Her brow crinkled when she couldn't see the door, even while standing on the tiptoe of her good foot. "How could you tell?"

"When you took your shoe off and rubbed your foot." A bolt of you-just-screwed-up lightning hit him broadside. He was in so much trouble.

She crinkled her brow again as she glanced two aisles over in the direction she'd been standing at that time. "And just how did you see…" Slowly, her head tilted upward at the corner of the store.

Straight at the security mirror. Jerking back to face him, her mouth and eyes were wide open as she sucked in a deep, deep breath and blew it out loudly.

"Spying?" She pointed at him fiercely. "You were spying on me. All the time I walked around the store. Why?" She got right in his face. And she was mad. Mad enough she poked him in the chest. "Why would you do that to me?"

"Don't you think the word spying is a bit harsh?" What could he say? That she was beautiful. Smart. Confident. That her body made his do things he had no control over when it came to her. But he couldn't tell her that. He also couldn't tell her she had him wound in knots so tight he couldn't look away.

But spying? He wouldn't call it spying. He'd never call it that, but… He sighed. Yeah, he could tell where she'd get that idea. He was in trouble. So, damn much trouble on so many fronts. Yet the more he saw her, the more she became his primary problem.

"My ex has enlisted the help of someone else in my condo complex to send him reports on anything out of the ordinary happening at my place. And I've learned to tolerate it. To play their game." Her voice had gotten softer and softer, quieter and quieter. She briefly stared at the floor, then back into his eyes. "But I won't stand for anyone else spying on me ever again."

The room seemed to stand still at such a fierce yet sad statement. He couldn't tear his eyes away from her, and it took every ounce of willpower he had not to reach out to her. Tell her he was sorry he'd made her feel uncomfortable. That her ex was a jerk.

Patrick cleared his throat loudly. When the hell had he come back into the store? "You two gonna stand there all day staring at each other?"

Mark turned back to the rods. "I'm thinking about a new reel. Got anything good over here?"

"You do a lot of fishing, do you?" Ashley bent, studying jars on the bottom shelf.

"Quite a bit." Glancing to the counter, he caught his partner's attention.

Patrick rolled his eyes and glanced at the ceiling. No help there. Mark needed to have a serious talk with his friend about backing him up when faced with a smart, sexy, sassy woman.

He tried to focus on something else besides the way she moved. Could she be any more the right size, the right look, the right...? *Stand up, lady. Damn it, stand up.*

Mark inhaled deep, shifted from one foot to the other. Ashley finally stood. Good. She leaned in front of him, stretched upward, and grabbed a package of treble hooks. Then she jogged around him and reached the checkout area in time to block his escape to the front door. A fake, cutesy smile flashed at him before she laid her items on the counter. Staring at him all the while, she ripped open the package of three-pronged hooks and took one out. "Okay if I pay for these when I get my purse?"

Patrick leaned back against the wall, crossed his arms, and nodded.

Mark felt his jaw clench. Wherever she was headed with this, he wasn't going. He walked to the back of the aisle and came up one closer to the door.

She blocked his way again. "You know, when I was growing up, my family used to fish. Especially for catfish. Did you ever eat catfish, Mr. Garmund? Probably not. I imagine you're more of a trout guy."

Trout guy? Yeah, he liked trout. Catfish, too. So what? Mark never backed down when challenged, and she was treading on thin ice. "And you, Ms. Lanovan, probably never spent a night sleeping on the ground under the stars."

"So?"

He laughed. "That's what I thought. Did you even bait your own hook?"

She huffed her indignation. Guess she baited her own hook.

Patrick shook his head, then headed out the front door. "Janie and I will meet you out front."

"He'll be right there," Ashley shouted, watching the door close behind the owner. The second the door clicked, she turned on Mark. "How dare you?"

"I don't know what you mean." He liked her banter, liked her sass, liked her everything if he was honest with himself. She'd become a nice momentary diversion in his life.

"I'll have you know, I'm not a naïve young girl. I've traveled the world. Met and made business deals with important people." She took a breath and then exhaled slow and long. "I know why men stare, Mr. Garmund. I know why men spy on women."

He could deny her accusation, but why. Instead, he winked. Why the heck this woman made him want to wink at her was beyond him. Wait… What just happened? Had she winked back…or at least started to. The two of them were standing so close, she had to bend her head backward to look into his face.

Her look questioned what she might or might not have just done, but instincts told him she wouldn't back down from whatever she had planned in retaliation. Instincts also told him his only chance was to toughen his stare and wait, that he could put her in her place. Shatter her confidence. Make her blink. He'd win. He always won with his adversaries. Funny, that wasn't what he wanted this time.

His body eased with the brief lull in the conversation, and he chuckled. "I'm sure you do, Ashley."

She straightened her shoulders ever so slightly, and the twinkle gathered in her eyes reached the corners of her mouth. For a moment, he saw humor flick across her face, almost like someone with a squirt gun full of water tucked away. Waiting for just the right moment to use their secret weapon.

This might be the calm before the storm. And as the tempest brewed, he realized escape was his only hope of rescue from whatever she had planned.

"Much as I'd like to continue this discussion, Patrick is waiting," Mark stated emphatically.

The tone he'd used was usually greeted with capitulation from his adversaries. Of course, they were mere enemies compared to her. Didn't take him long to realize she never read that page of the surrender manual. His mind careened through the different styles of negotiation, but he was so captivated he couldn't concentrate.

Ashley held up the hook she'd taken from the package. "Before you go, here's a lesson on how to catch catfish. First, they don't bite on jigs, they bite on treble hooks like these."

Mark's heart pounded, and his right foot tapped the floor until he compelled it to stop. He decided to try a different approach. One he sensed would not go over well with her.

"Thanks for the offer, but I don't need one. But I do need to leave." He crooked his finger and gave her chin a quick upward tap. "It's been nice, sweetie. See you later."

Ashley shoved his fingers aside. "Sweetie? No one calls me sweetie."

Guess that technique hadn't worked. Appeared he'd really opened the powder keg now.

"One second, please." Her voice became so calm, so soft, he could barely make out what she said. He leaned in to hear better. "This is called stink bait. Catfish love it. Want me to show you how to bait the hook? Of course, you do."

Mark was outnumbered by this woman. Outmaneuvered. And out of his comfort zone.

Where was his backup plan? His escape routes. Through the front window, he caught sight of Patrick and Janie standing by the BMW. His partner shot him the walking fingers signal, meaning time to go. He had to agree.

"I really need to leave." He assumed his best I'm-the-authority persona.

Meanwhile, she took the lid off the jar, and the pungent odor saturated the space, seeming to be a cross between a skunk and who knew what. For a moment, there were no magnolias as her fingers dipped the hook into the goop.

"Don't you want to take this one, at least? It's already baited. That's probably all you'll need anyhow." Ashley reached out, took his hand in hers, and held the hook above his palm with her other.

"No, thanks." He quickly reversed her hold on his hand, to his on hers.

As she jerked to get away, she fell off balance, and her other hand braced against his fishing vest. He dropped his hold as her fingers fumbled at his vest.

"Ouch!" Grabbing her finger in pain, she glanced back and forth between his chest and his face. All the while, her eyes rounded wider and wider.

He glanced downward, and in unison, they both stared at the stinky baited hook dangling ominously from the pocket webbing of his vest.

"Oooooh, I'm sorry." She leaned closer, trying to untangle the mess, but the stinky goop smeared in an ever-widening circle on the tan material. The closer she got, the more her hair brushed against the bottom of his chin. The more she bumped her fingers against his chest, trying to make things right. The more his dick rose to the occasion. Never mind the fact, she suddenly smelled like magnolias and musk combined.

"Here, here…" He gently pushed her hands aside and straightened her away from him.

Holding her now stinky hands out to her sides, she focused on the floor. "I really am sorry."

"Last night, you smeared honey goop on the sleeve of my leather jacket. Ten minutes ago, you accused me of spying. And now this." He pointed at the dangling hook and sighed heavily. "Have I done something to you?"

"Yes! I mean no. I mean…" Her chin quivered, her expression softening with some deep realization. The fight appeared to drain from her body as she looked up at him.

Their eyes met, and his world shifted. He felt it. No, not going to happen. His middle name was control and duty. He knew his duty. His life. He could have taken control of this situation at any time. Brushed her aside and walked out the door. Why hadn't he? There were no shifts in his world. No changes. No him and her. No future. Time to leave.

He stepped to the counter, removed the hook, then grabbed a wet wipe from the open box by the register to clean his hands. Grabbing the pack of wipes, he returned to Ashley. He cleaned her hands. Took extra care to clean off the blood on the finger she'd stuck on the hook. Through everything, she hadn't moved, hadn't looked up at him. He eased back in front of her, tipped her chin up till her eyes met his.

"You've got some of that stuff on you." He wiped her cheek with a clean wet wipe, resting his palm resting against the smooth skin of her face for a second, maybe three…maybe five.

Her hand covered his as she leaned into his touch. Lips parted. The warmth of her skin against his palm reached all the way to his gut. Without thinking, he leaned in her direction, letting his mouth be drawn to hers. He should stop. Not an option…not an option.

Ashley's eyes centered on his lips, her own waiting openly for his touch. And he kissed her as light and tender as a butterfly landing on a petal. Then she blinked and lightly pushed his hand aside. Shaking her head, she covered her lips with her hand before stepping back from him.

"Goodbye, Mr. Garmund. I'm sorry about your vest." She glanced out the front window to the gas pump area. "Be careful you don't get that stuff all over the seats in your nice BMW."

Not bothering to look at him again, she turned and walked out the curtained doorway behind the counter.

Unfamiliar emotions surged through his body. What had he done? He steeled himself against the thoughts struggling to break free. The woman had shut him down. He hadn't offered himself to a woman in a long time. Hadn't wanted one. Now, Ms. Ashley—Ashley Lanovan had twisted his mind and body into hot, sultry heat with her sassy mouth, tight top, and stink bait. Then shut him down. Shut. Him. Down.

Even if he did deserve it, he didn't like the feeling. He stomped out the front entrance and banged the door closed behind him.

"Hey, watch that. Doors cost money, you know," Patrick yelled.

Janie and Patrick stood by Mark's black BMW SUV, talking low and close. Mark stopped and gave her a quick, friendly hug.

"Patrick is only on loan. Understood?" she whispered, stepping back as she held her hand over her nose.

"Understood." Mark nodded before he climbed into the driver's seat of his BMW.

"Whew, what is that smell?" Patrick asked after sliding in on the passenger side.

Mark jumped back out and removed the fishing vest. After cleaning out the pockets, he tossed it in the trash barrel by the pumps before sliding back into the seat. He glanced once again at the storefront. Was Ashley standing there? Watching him? Didn't matter. He was gone. Duty. Nothing else……ever. Least of all some brown-eyed woman full of herself.

A movement just to the right of the "Open" sign in the window caught his attention. Fingers braced against the pane—her fingers. A tiny smile tugged at the corners of his lips, then the CIA operative in him slid behind the wheel and turned the key.

Yep, didn't matter if the top was snug or the jeans were tight, Ashley Lanovan was one classy, full-of-sass woman. Too dangerous for a man in his line of work. Way too dangerous for his way of life. Self-preservation mode kicked in as he turned the ignition.

Patrick rolled his window down. "Did you hear me? What's that smell?"

"Magnolias." Mark slammed into gear. "Rotten magnolias."

CHAPTER EIGHT

ONCE THE BMW sped away, Ashley walked to the trash barrel and peered inside. She glanced at Janie who raised her eyebrows and shrugged.

"Dang it all." Ashley braced her hand against the inside edge to keep from tumbling in as she leaned over and retrieved the stinky vest. "Looks like I'll need to borrow your washer again."

Janie stepped away from her as the two women walked toward the front door. "Whew. What is that?"

"Catfish stink bait. Guess I got a little carried away." Ashley held the vest at arm's length out to the side as she made the trek. "Before I put this in your washer, I'll take it around back and rinse it off at the faucet I saw earlier."

"I'd better get to the register before the lunch rush starts." Janie walked inside.

Ashley washed the vest as best she could, then headed back to the entrance.

Tires squealed to a stop at the gas pumps, and a man jumped from a dark-gray truck. Staring at Ashley, he stalked toward the front door of Red's

Corner Market. A black Missouri State Highway Patrol SUV pulled in the lot and parked near the right-side exit. The state trooper got out, talking on his phone, and walked over to one of the grocery's picnic tables for eating beneath the orange and yellow leafed maple shade trees.

The man from the truck glanced backward over his shoulder, then accidentally walked into Ashley. She stumbled, grasping at the ice chest to keep her upright. He grabbed her wrist and yanked.

"Let me go." Ashley jerked her arm away, slamming the still-wet vest into the man's face.

The man quickly released her and jerked his hands in front of himself. "Wait up there, little lady. I was just trying to make sure you were okay."

The trooper, maybe early thirties, pocketed his phone and glanced in their direction. "Everything alright over there?"

Ashley nodded once, then stepped through the entrance where the truck guy was holding the door for her. He followed her inside, then walked the aisles as if looking for something.

"Can I help you?" Janie asked.

"No… Uh, yes." The man ambled over to the counter, smiled. "I was supposed to meet a fella to do some fishing over at the lake. For the life of me, I can't remember which store he said to meet him at. Or even which road to take."

"Happens sometimes." Janie straightened the newspapers on the counter. "What's his name? Maybe I can help you."

"I don't even remember his name. He's a friend

of a friend of a friend who fixed it up for me to do some fishing while I'm in the area. Only met him once." The man leaned against the counter, invading her personal space. "But he drives one of those fancy black BMW SUVs. Can't be many of those around."

"No. Can't say as I've seen that around here. But I'm not too good on car brands." Janie never batted an eye. Never flinched. Never lost her trusting expression. "Maybe you got the wrong town."

The man whirled around to face Ashley. "What about you? You ever seen that BMW around here?"

"No." She lied without reservation. "I'm new in town."

She bent to straighten a row of cans on the bottom shelf. He stomped his foot next to her fingers. A flash of a chill raced up her spine, and she tightened her grip on the can she kept in her hand as she stood back up.

"Don't mess with me, woman." His tone was menacing as he pointed his phone in her direction. "What about this man. Have you seen him around?"

"No." Ashley shook her head as she stared at a blurry photo of Mark on the phone screen.

Janie cleared her throat, and the man turned back to face her. She slid a pen and paper in his direction. "If you'd like to leave your name and number, I'll give it to him if he happens by. We get a lot of people in to buy bait."

The man shook his head, pushed the offer away as the policeman stepped inside the grocery.

"Can I help you with anything else, sir?" Janie

asked.

He narrowed his gaze to the cop, then back at her. "Yeah...yeah. I was looking for a restroom."

"Sorry, it's being remodeled. There's a bigger convenience mart a few miles down the road." Janie kept her eyes trained on the man as if she were taking a photo for future reference. "They have one."

The tall, ginger-haired trooper ambled toward the counter. His shoes polished to a bright shine. "Maybe I can help you, sir. I'm headed in that direction."

"No. No, that's okay. I can't believe I made the mistake of stopping at the only grocery store around without a working privy." The man fast-walked back to his truck, then revved the engine and sped down the road.

"You two okay?"

"We are now." Janie sighed a relief. "Ashley Lanovan, this is State Trooper Wheat McIntosh. She's visiting the Gregorys and staying here till they get back."

"It's nice to meet you, Trooper McIntosh," Ashley said.

"Just call me Wheat." The trooper tipped his hat in her direction, then stared down the road, watching the gray truck out of sight.

She glanced at Janie. "What do you think that guy really wanted?"

"He wanted Mark." She and the trooper exchanged a glance.

"My hunting buddy Mark Garmund?" Wheat

asked.

Janie nodded.

"Think I'll make sure the man in the truck moves on down the road."

"You might want to know that he showed me a picture of Mark. Asked if I knew him."

Wheat scribbled on his notepad. "What did this photo look like?"

Remembering the fierce look on Mark's face in the picture sent a chill up Ashley's spine. "Kind of blurry…gritty-looking. Must have been on one of your hunting trips."

"What makes you say that?"

"His face was dirty, like when you've been repotting flowers and you wipe the sweat off your forehead and cheeks." She realized she was talking with her hands to describe exactly what she meant.

"That all?"

"Oh, he had on one of those camouflage suits like you guys wear on hunting trips." Her insides held a question, maybe even questions, but she wouldn't ask any. "Funny thing, though, his wasn't green camo. It was…beige. Kind of like what the military wears in the Middle East."

"Thank you. That's very helpful." Wheat turned to Janie. "Patrick around?"

Shaking her head, her friend straightened with a strength she hadn't seen before. "Mark and him went camping for a few days. You've got his cell number, right?"

"His and Mark's. I'll give them a call if I think there's a problem." He eased out the front door. "In fact, I'll take a few extra loops by your place for the next couple days. You know what to do if you need the police."

"Sure." Janie stowed the pen and paper away. "Let me know if you think there's anything to worry about."

He closed the door behind him, leaving the store quiet. Alone now, the two women stared at each other across the counter.

Janie reached for her cell phone. "Think I'll give Paddy a call." She held the phone to her ear, then ended the call. "Guess they're in a dead cell zone right now. I'll call again later."

A tense silence filled the air.

"You have a working restroom, right?" Ashley asked.

"Yes, I do." Janie's fingers trembled as she fidgeted with the papers in front of her. "And you know the man in the BMW. Even recognized his photo."

Ashley nodded as she watched the police cruiser disappear down the roadway. She had an uneasy feeling about the man in the dark-gray truck. Evidently, Janie had the same feeling when she lied about remodeling the restroom.

Why had she lied about knowing Mark? She shivered. Something about the past few minutes made her antsy. She didn't know him well enough to know if he was a good guy or a bad buy, yet she'd lied for him. The man had a strange effect on her even when he wasn't around.

"Does Wheat live around here?" Ashley noticed the parking lot filling with an assortment of highway worker's trucks.

"Just about a mile down the road from the Gregory place. His family's been in the area for over fifty years." Janie moved a box of cookies to the front of the counter. "Mark used to be his boss years ago, but Wheat decided he'd rather be closer to home, to help the family, so he became a state trooper."

The front door opened, filling the store with workers in bright orange and yellow vests from the road construction crew, so there was no more time for questions. Her friend went into her hello, smile, can-I-help-you mode. Friendly and laughing, the men tackled the coffee pot or the donut display or headed to the deli area. Lunch rush had evidently started.

Ashley replaced the can she'd picked up from the bottom shelf, and, at the same time, bumped a couple over, scattering them across the floor. She had to stop doing that. The lunch group side-stepped the mess as she apologized and raced to pick the cans up. A couple of the men made jokes about Patrick being a bull in the china shop, too. The door opened again, filling the store with a mother and assortment of preschool-age kids in tow. They scattered through the aisles, each with their own mission.

Unseasonably warm weather had blown in with the rain from last night. The outdoors was inviting. And Dot called mid-morning to say she and Lloyd should be home in a couple of days. They were anxious to see her. She was excited to see them, too, but she loved getting to know Janie, also.

The store stayed busy for the rest of the morning, and Ashley found she enjoyed the small-town community atmosphere. She learned a lot about Nature's Crossing by listening to the friendly questions and answers that transpired between Janie and the customers.

Once the assistant manager and part-time help came in to work at eleven, Janie and Ashley retreated to the house for their own lunch. After which, the women shared ice cream and laughter and secrets. She even opened up more about the emotional strain of the divorce.

"The final straw was when I found him on our boat, making sure his client had everything she needed. And I don't mean legal advice." Ashley noticed the twist in her stomach wasn't as painful as it used to be. "And it appeared to be a clothes-optional business meeting."

"Your ex sounds like a royal jerk." Janie poured herself a cup of fresh-steeped apple-cinnamon tea. "I'm really lucky to have my Paddy."

"That was the last straw. Except for the nasty divorce." Ashley scooped another bite of ice cream. "Was tough dividing things. Especially mementos from our travels. Gifts family and friends had given us through the years. But I stood my ground and battled over the one thing I was determined to own."

"The house?" Janie asked.

"No. The boat."

"Oh. That probably would have been the last

thing I'd have wanted." Janie carried the dirty dishes to the counter. "Why did you find that so important?"

She heard no condemnation in Janie's words, just a simple statement. A simple question. No one, not her parents or friends or even business associates, had ever questioned her making a stand at owning the boat.

"There was no way I was going to live the rest of my life knowing he'd be entertaining all his lady friends on it." Her chest tightened. "No way. Just knowing he still owned that boat would have been a constant memory of the day I found them there. A reminder of what ended our marriage."

Janie leaned back against the counter. "But the boat didn't end your marriage. The jerk of a husband you had ended that. So, have you made some new memories on the boat?"

"No. The last time I saw the boat was the day the divorce was finalized. I kept it in dry dock. Finally sold it this past May." Thank goodness she wasn't still paying monthly fees on dockage.

But she didn't regret anything about the battle she'd waged. Or the money spent. That had all been worth it. Just remembering the look on Bradford's face when she hadn't allowed him back on the boat to retrieve his personal items was priceless. She'd packed his things up and set them on the dock next to the boat that day. He'd looked shattered… or had he? She really couldn't remember.

She swiped a couple of uncalled-for tears from

beneath her eyes. What was wrong with her? Maybe losing her job and the trip and meeting someone who had questioned her reasoning…maybe all of that had tangled her emotions.

In hindsight, though, the wise decision would have been to fight for complete ownership of the condo. Instead, she'd fought for the boat just to spite Bradford. Maybe she should take a closer look at other iffy decisions she'd made with her life before she laid out a plan for her future.

Here she was, almost thirty-eight years old, and— "I'm a failure."

"Don't you dare say that! Look at all you've done on your own the past few years. The great career you had in St. Louis. Anybody would be proud to have done all that." Her new friend engulfed her in a quick hug then stepped aside. "And look how you've been given a whole new slate to lay out your future. You're not a failure. You're just finding the next you. And this road trip is the first step. Right?"

Ashley couldn't believe how simply Janie had put everything. "Right. You're absolutely right."

"So, let's get started." Janie grabbed her purse from out of the pantry, applied her lipstick, and scrunched her hair. "Now, what say we go for a drive? Dot and Lloyd will give you their version of the area from having lived here for close to thirty years. Let me show you around from a newcomer's viewpoint." She laughed. "Let me fill you in on

some of the new gossip and the old shenanigans.

You may be surprised."

"Now that sounds like a plan."

CHAPTER NINE

MOST OF THE time since Mark had pulled the BMW out of Red's Corner Market, silence filled the air between him and Patrick. Miles had passed, and the little they spoke concerned work or maybe a short-lived view. Red's Corner Market and Nature's Crossing were far behind them at this point.

"Do you remember there being this much driving when we first signed with the government?" Mark asked.

Patrick shifted in the passenger seat. "Nope."

"You've been kind of quiet. Anything wrong?"

"Just thinking. By the way, Janie was none too happy about your call this time."

He quickly picked up on the concern edging into his friend's voice. "She okay taking care of things back at the store?"

"Sure. She's nervous this time, though. Got one of her feelings." Patrick appeared to be deep in thought, his fingers tapping time to the country station. "Especially once the morning news had a segment on a possible leak of CIA agent names."

"Did you tell her Brenner said they got it stopped before the leak had full steam?"

"Told her right after you called last night. But somehow seeing it on the news, for the whole wide world to see..." Patrick's words were pounding through gritted teeth, "...made her think our boss might not be on the level. What do you think?"

Unsure himself, Mark had spent half the night trying to calculate what actions would be needed if his real name surfaced. The alias he used on assignments would be bad enough. "I think I'll stand my ground no matter what. Starting with this new line of work I'm considering."

He glanced in the side mirror and merged onto the interstate. They had a comfortable partnership and read each other well. Too well.

"Hey, thanks again for taking time to show me around Missouri. Working for the Parks Service sounds like I'd be stationed in this region, but I figure I should see what other places might pop up."

"No problem." Patrick glanced in his direction. "You've paid your dues. Given a chunk of your life to keeping the country safe. Time you made a life you can enjoy."

"For the most part, I've enjoyed my life."

"Really?" Patrick turned to stare at him this time. "And when exactly was that part? I seemed to have missed that."

Mark sighed heavily. Tried to think of the times. There was... He tapped the top of the steering wheel. "I enjoy being at my home in D.C. Enjoy visiting Nature's Cross."

Patrick looked away. "And how often do you get to do those things?"

Not often enough, he wanted to shout. Not often enough.

"That's what buying Red's Corner Market is all about for Janie and me. Life! Having friends and neighbors. We deserve that. Seems like the CIA didn't hear the word retirement when I said I'd do some occasional consulting for them. They just keep calling." Patrick adjusted his seat back and forth, ending up back where he started. "Just because I'm fifty doesn't mean I can't retire from one career and start another." Patrick's tone had grown serious, almost like a professor trying to mentor a student. "You deserve that, too."

Mark stayed quiet. Patrick had said everything there was to say.

The two men glanced at each other. Agents learned that when the doubts edged in, having your thoughts out in the open helped. Helped get your head straight. If the doubts didn't stop, then a desk job or out of the agency entirely were options. Good agents knew their limits. Knew not to ignore those limits.

More miles passed while Mark's mind replayed the episode back at the house. Ashley had felt perfect in his arms when he'd carried her to the sofa to see about her foot. He'd never forget the way she'd leaned against him, with her arm draped across his shoulder.

"What are you smiling about?" Patrick asked.

"Nothing," Mark said. "I wasn't smiling."

His partner grabbed a book from his duffle. "Think I'll catch up on my reading. Let's stop for lunch soon?"

"I'm not hungry. We can stop later."

"Well, it's way past lunchtime already, and I'm famished. Besides, I've got seniority in age, if nothing else. I need nourishment."

Mark turned the country music to a jazz station.

Patrick sighed and shook his head.

He ignored his friend and concentrated on trying to keep the baggy jeans and tight tank top of Ashley's out of his mind. He lost.

"I should have said something," Mark mumbled.

Patrick looked up from his reading. "What are you talking about?"

"Ashley. That's her name, right?"

"Don't play dumb with me, you know that's her name. Hey, you just drove past a perfectly good diner." Patrick tossed his book into the back and took a quick glimpse at his watch. "By the way, you cost me a dozen roses for Janie."

"How?"

"She bet me you'd bring up the subject of Ashley within the first five hours of our trip. I told her you were too smart to be distracted by a woman."

Mark flipped the music off. "I think I take offense at you two wagering on my personal life and—"

"Personal life? You wouldn't know one if it hit you over the head. Now, that sign said there's a rest stop a mile ahead. Pull in and I'll drive for a while. Seems like the only chance I've got to eat is to be in control of the steering wheel."

Patrick donned his red hat and checked the visor mirror, then repeatedly jabbed his fingers in his friend's bicep. "And you should have let her know you were still in the store. Of course, maybe you didn't want her to know. How's that for a thought?"

His thoughts were stuck on the way she walked. How each step seemed to start on her heel and slow roll to the ball of her foot. Smooth and simple and unaware of the vibe she was sending him. And, oh, those hips. They were like a magnet to his eyes. Of course, that little black tank top earlier today had also got his attention.

Damn, what was wrong with him. He needed to stop ogling her. That's not who he was. And that's not the type of woman she appeared to be. But she knew how to stand her ground. For a moment, he hadn't been sure she was going to accept his apology.

Sassy, too. Not that he ever had time, but if he did, he'd like a woman who could be intelligent and mature, but also a little impertinent every so often. Someone who could keep him on his toes long enough to forget his other world for a while. From what he'd seen, that was her. Poised and proper with a touch of sass.

In his mind, his hands rested on her shoulders, thumbs looped under the thin straps of her top. Her auburn-gold hair would brush the side of his face when she leaned to whisper in his ear. Whoa—stop right there.

"I don't know why she was so upset," Mark said.

Patrick opened the console and retrieved a piece of gum. "I take it we're still talking about Ashley.

"When I went over to your house this morning, she didn't seem to be wearing her own clothes. Got any idea why?"

"Janie washed all of hers and they weren't dry. That was the mud I was talking about last night on the phone. I figure what she had on was Janie's and mine from the guest closet in her room." Patrick fiddled with the brim of his hat.

"Strange, she only had one set of clothes with her?"

His partner yanked his hat off and tossed it in the back, alongside the book. "If you must know, I dropped her suitcase in the mud. Most of her things were a mess by the time I got them in the house."

Mark burst out laughing before he could stop himself.

"Wasn't funny. If it hadn't been for me leaving on this assignment today, Janie would have made me sleep on the sofa."

Wiping his eyes, Mark couldn't stop laughing. No matter what else happened, Ashley's presence had given him a range of emotions he hadn't felt in a long time. "Did you notice the scent of magnolia?"

"Of what?" Patrick asked.

"Never mind."

Mark pulled into a drive-thru spot at the rest area. He and Patrick had exchanged seats so many times before on assignments, they knew the routine by heart. Each walked halfway around the car in a clockwise direction, slid inside, and buckled up as if just taking a breath.

"Did I ever tell you about the summer I spent an entire month with my grandma and grandpa on their farm?" Mark asked.

In the driver's seat now, Patrick shook his head as he merged onto the highway.

"I would have been thirteen. They slept with the windows open, so every morning I woke to the sound of birds. Grandma would already be up fixing a big breakfast. She made the best French toast I've ever had."

Mark rolled the window down to enjoy the wind in his face. "My grandpa and I would spend the day working in his garden or piddling in his woodshop. But they also made sure I had time to just be a boy. Nights we'd all pile in his pickup. Head to town for ice cream or a movie. Sometimes we'd even go down to their pond and fish."

"No kidding, you actually know how to fish?" Patrick said.

"Yeah, but mostly I sat and watched the bobber. But once I tried out his plastic scented worms for bait and he taught me the secrets to bass fishing, I never used live bait again. We never catfished, or I'd have known what stink bait was all about."

The two men laughed, then drove for a while in quiet again.

Mark hung his arm out the window, his palm fighting the wind. "Grandpa had me mow the grass once a week. Had an old John Deere riding mower. I thought I was king of the world on that thing. Although, one day, I got distracted and mowed down a patch of Grandma's flowers."

"Bet you got in trouble on that one."

"No, Grandpa told her the rabbits had been in her garden again. She side-eyed both of us and went back inside." He'd give anything to be that kid again. Anything. "I picked up all the flowers that still had a stem attached and put them in a vase."

The men once more shared a laugh and a few miles.

Mark rolled the window up. "Once the rest of the yard work was done, Grandma brought some cold lemonade out to the front porch. The three of us sat there on the front porch with a tray of cookies, enjoying the smell of fresh-mowed grass and magnolias. Best time I ever had."

"Was that the same year your dad talked to you?" Patrick asked.

"Yeah. We talked the next month."

Quiet, Mark relived the day his dad had told him he worked undercover for the government, just like Grandpa and Great-Grandpa and even further back had done. He'd talked about freedom and hope. The world. How people had to think of more than themselves. Said just because the USA wasn't involved in a war at the moment didn't mean we could let our guard down.

No specifics; Mark learned those on his own years later.

He might have only been thirteen, but sitting with his dad at the Lincoln Memorial that day, he'd felt like they were talking man-to-man. His dad had apologized for not being around all the time, His dad had told him how proud he was to call him son. His dad had said he loved him. Next morning his dad was gone again. Came home in a box a few months later.

"You're awful quiet. You okay?" Patrick angled up the off-ramp.

Mark rubbed his palm down his face. "Yeah, I'm okay. Just thinking. Still wish I could remember the end of my dad's conversation."

"Probably wasn't as important as you've made it out to be in your mind."

"Maybe. I do remember Washington was having one of those stifling summer heatwaves. It was hotter than blue blazes that day." Mark turned to stare at the passing scenery. "That's why we stopped to get an ice cream from one of the vendors. Mine dripped all over my hands, so we threw our wrappers away and walked over to the Reflecting Pool."

They'd sloshed their hands in the water, then went to sit on the steps in front of Lincoln. "I remember Dad put his arm around my shoulder. Hugged me against his side. Said I shouldn't worry about the future…my future. Asked me what I wanted to study in college. What I wanted to do in life."

Patrick stayed quiet like he always did when Mark mumbled this story. And there were stories his friend told that he also stayed quiet on. That's what men did. That's what friends did. That's what partners did. He appreciated that about his friend.

"Said something about the price being paid… that it would be a steep price to pay, but he didn't mind as long as I was happy. And free…" Pay the price, a final price. For what? What price? He must have been talking about the ice cream or college or… But what about the free part? What about him being free had to do with a price?

He mulled the conversation over in his mind again and again, reaching the same not-remembered conclusion. Maybe someday the fog would clear, and his father's words would be there in full. Of course, what did it matter? Patrick was probably right. It wasn't important anyhow.

Tears stung Mark's eyes. He blinked. Swallowed hard.

Then again, how could anything his dad said that day not have been important?

His phone rang with Brenner's ringtone, and he pushed the speaker on. "Yeah?"

"The leak is real. The list is out. Your alias is blown."

"Damn! I hope you've caught the traitor." Mark felt a jolt of adrenaline hit hard to his system.

"Working on it."

Patrick straightened in his seat. "What about me?"

"Your alias is blown, too. Nothing else." Patrick turned into the next strip mall, looped around, and headed back in the same direction they'd just come.

Why had his boss said Patrick had nothing else? Brenner was usually precise in his words. Why hadn't he said the same to him?

Mark felt a jolt of adrenaline hit hard to his system. "At least, tell me *something* good."

"That was your good news, Mark." Brenner sighed. "Bad news is that a couple of your undercover photos have surfaced on the dark web."

CHAPTER TEN

A COUPLE HOURS LATER, Ashley sat in the passenger seat as Janie drove the two of them to Henton, the closest town of any size in the area. First, they'd stopped by the store to let the assistant manager and part-time staff know Janie would be gone for the afternoon, but to call if there were any problems.

Once they arrived in Henton, they said hello to Peabody as he strolled on the sidewalk around the town square. Grabbed a bite at Della's Dream Tea House. Then took in some of the shops lining the outer perimeter of the town square.

Ashley made eye contact with a portly gray-haired man watching her from the front window of a real estate office. He nodded as she passed. She smiled and nodded in return, keeping step with Janie as she turned to enter the gift shop on the corner.

"Who's the man in the window?"

"That's Chadwick Andrews. Why?" Janie replied.

"He seemed to be extremely interested in mine and Peabody's conversation. Kept staring at us. In fact, he seemed to be watching everything on the street."

Janie scooped up some note cards. "Oh, that's an understatement. You might say his thumb's on the pulse of the community, and his eyes are on the deals."

When the two women got in the car, Ashley noticed the man in the real estate office hadn't moved from his perch. "Who is this Chadwick Andrews anyway?"

"Investor, real estate broker, town elder, and other names I won't repeat. Owns a good portion of properties in the county. Most of the locals believe he's made bad investments. Me and Patrick think he's waiting for the right time to make a killing in sales." Janie navigated the car through traffic at the stoplight.

"But why would he be interested in my talking to Peabody?"

"I'm sure word spread you're the news lady from St. Louis."

"So? I'm just visiting."

Janie navigated down the highway headed back to Nature's Crossing. "Doesn't matter. To him, you mean outside money. Outside thinking. As far as his interest in Mr. Peabody, that goes back a long way. Peabody bested Chadwick in sports during high school. Got the scholarship he'd planned on receiving. And ended up marrying Della, the girl who'd spent years turning down Chadwick's advances."

"That sounds like a story just waiting to be

written." Ashley figured there were lots of people in the world, just holding on to an old grudge to explain the way they thought. Really, everyone made their own paths in life. Something about that thought troubled at her.

"Oh, there's lots more." Janie slowed at the flashing yellow light before driving on down the street. "You see, Chadwick didn't take kindly to being let go from the bank years ago. No one ever knew for sure, but talk has it he got caught loaning money on properties that weren't worth half the value. Seems he and the owners would split the difference through finagling the price on a tractor, a car, or whatever he sold to them."

"Wouldn't he have been caught by bank auditors?" Ashley had heard about this scheme previously in other parts of the country.

"This was decades ago, when a town could absorb its scandals without the world's influence. Back then, things were swept under the table. Evidently, the president of the bank at the time decided to sweep everything under the table, but since Mr. Peabody was the supervisor who discovered the cover-up, it fell to him to take care of the loose ends. He's the one who had to inform Chadwick he had three choices: Be fired, resign, or end up in jail. Next day, he resigned."

"Well, he's got no reason to think I'm here to mess up one of his real estate deals." Ashley contemplated what an evening news story would look like if that happened nowadays. Would be the headline for days, and everyone the man knew would be questioned. And if a reporter got too close to the truth, they'd be fearing for their safety. That was why she'd stayed on the lighter side of the newsroom.

"And, then there's the fact Chadwick loved Della, but she chose Peabody." Janie set the cruise control, then raised her eyebrows a couple times. "That's a story for another day."

"Wow." Ashley's imagination ticked into overtime. "You may not have lived here long, but you seem to know a lot about the community workings. How's that possible?"

Janie smiled. "When you own the only grocery in Nature's Crossing, you hear everything. With lots of different versions. Now, I have a question for you."

This sounded serious. "Okay. I'll answer if I can."

"Since you've met Mark up close and personal, do you still think he's irritating?"

Ashley's lips parted as a smile tugged her insides before she reclaimed her composure. Did she? Did she really find him irritating? No. The way his blue eyes seemed to penetrate all the way to her soul floated through her senses. She'd need to be careful this week, or he might be more of a problem than simply a disturbance. Maybe his camping trip would last till she was gone.

And his voice? If she weren't careful, his voice could spin her insides around and lure her right into his arms. Worse yet, make her drop each barrier she had worked so hard to build. Her chest tightened with a tiny hitch, and she felt a warm blush, followed by a heat tickling all the way to her core.

"I think I'll take the fifth on that." She redirected the car's A/C vent in her direction. "One thing for sure, though, the next guy I'm serious about will be a nine-to-five guy. The kind that comes straight home every day and we share our workday over dinner. No late-night business meetings. No going out of town on work. No secrets."

"That's quite a list," Janie gave a fake are-you-kidding-me laugh. "Anything else?"

Ashley brushed her hair back with her fingers. "No secrets. Absolutely no secrets."

CHAPTER ELEVEN

THE NEXT MORNING, Ashley rose bright and early, eager to see the Gregorys. Late last night, Dot had called to say Lloyd's mother was better and they were almost home.

Patrick had called about fifteen minutes later, saying he and Mark were cutting their trip short. After a long conversation, with Janie listening for the most part, she'd finally convinced Patrick to at least spend another day camping before they headed back. Janie had double-checked the locks at the store and home…maybe even triple checked. Sensing something had her friend on edge, she'd decided to stay with her one more night.

Now the sunny October day promised to be another beauty. Still an unseasonably warm one, this could be exactly right for another adventure.

Janie gave her directions to the Gregory house. "Seeing that the campers will be back tomorrow morning, you should stop back by then. We can see how their fishing trip went."

"I can hardly wait to see what they catch." Ashley slid into her Jeep, opened her sunroof, and programmed her GPS with the Gregory address.

"Maybe it's one of the fishermen you can hardly wait to see."

Warmth rushed to her face as she tilted her head, widened her eyes. "I don't think so."

"By the way, where's that clean fishing vest?"

Ashley bit her lower lip for a moment. "In my suitcase."

"Alrighty then. I'll know where to tell Mark he can find it when they get back." Janie smiled, and her apple cheeks rounded with a glow. "And don't forget to drive by the older part of Nature's Crossing while you're here. You'll like the feel of the old buildings."

"I've got my camera right here." She patted the passenger seat. "In fact, if you think it's safe, I think I'll stop on my way over to Dot's."

Her friend stepped back from the Jeep. "What's not to be safe in Nature's Crossing?"

Waving, Ashley drove away, happy with the way her visit had turned out so far. She thought over the past few days and decided all-in-all everything had gone smoothly, except for the suitcase incident. Plus her clumsy entrance the first night. And her ultimate fiasco—Mark and the stink bait issue.

Years ago, she would have pursued a man who caused her heart to flutter. Wiser now, her feelings would need to wait till she found a settled, little-on-the-boring side, so-so looking, nine-to-five man who put her first. Heart flutters would have to take a back seat in the future. Last night, as she lay beneath the colorful quilt, she'd rethought the way Mark made her feel and decided there'd be no crumbled barriers…for her…with him.

That was the safest thing to do. The proper thing to do.

"Dang, I should have turned back there." Ashley slowed at the next street and made a left. Since the day was so nice, with a good amount of sunshine, she wanted to snap a few photos of the original town. Who knew when the weather might change?

A couple of connecting streets should get her back to the center of old town Nature's Crossing. The road she took angled left, and before she knew it, she missed the first left turn. After crossing what looked like out-of-use railroad tracks, she missed the second one, too. Finally, she came to a T in the road and shook her head. She'd never been good at maps. And all Siri kept telling her was how to turn to go to the Gregory place.

She shrugged. "Well, at least I can't miss this left turn."

Empty lots gave clues to structures that once stood there—a few brick chimneys, outlines of block foundations, a couple cellar doors with no houses attached. Making another turn, she passed an old grain mill still in operation as a feed store. On the right, a long row of freshly painted connected cinder block buildings with decorative stone inserts lined a crumbling sidewalk next to the street. A sign above a couple of the windows read "Nature's Crossing Volunteer Fire Station" and contained modern overhead doors in one raised section.

After crossing over the railroad tracks, she passed a modern-day library, and a softball field on the opposite side of the road. To the back of the field stood an aged and shuttered school next to a park with up-to-date cedar swings, slides, and a jungle gym.

Like a developing country, this area was like old meets new.

She parked at the intersection where the row of white buildings began and ventured out to shoot a few pictures. Crisp air mingled with the scent of get-the-chill-off morning fires burning someplace. The fallen leaves, still damp from morning dew, struggled to swirl around her. And the sun's caress made the earthbound yellows, reds, and oranges sparkle beneath her feet.

Heavy footsteps trounced behind her, closing fast. Automatically, she clutched her keys in her palm, sliding one protruding key between her fingers. But before she could turn around, a morning jogger raced by, nodding a greeting as he passed. Okay, she needed to remember she was in Nature's Crossing, not unknown parts of the world.

Still, maybe an update on self-protection should be on her agenda. She strolled onward, kicking at the leaves and acorns strewn across the sidewalk.

A loud, growling wolf whistle shot through the air behind her.

"Well, look who it is. All the way from St. Louis," a man's taunting voice called out.

Ashley whirled around as the tone bristled across her shoulder. Maybe this hadn't been such a good idea after all. At least, she should have been watching her surroundings, but the jogger had thrown her off her safety routine.

A tall, blond man, mid-thirties she'd guess, leaned against a silver Jaguar parked by the side of the buildings she'd just passed. "Didn't mean to scare you. It's a beautiful day for a drive, isn't it, Ms. Lanovan?"

"Yes, a beautiful day."

The man pushed off from the car and sauntered toward her, his legs eating up the ground in a slow, calculated, purposeful strut. She felt her breathing increase. Don't panic. Think. Stay smart and think.

He knew her name. How? Had she met him at the grocery? Why did his attempt at friendliness leave her on edge? Ashley had been in a lot of iffy situations out on television shoots. She could handle herself, but this man's demeanor gave her pause. Especially since he knew her name. She'd felt so safe in the community, she'd let her woman's alertness falter.

"I'm sorry, have we met before?" A chill settled across her hands that had nothing to do with the weather.

"No, but word travels fast in these parts when anyone new comes to town. Especially someone like you."

Like her? "I don't know what you mean."

He was close enough she could smell his exaggerated use of expensive cologne. "A classy act from St. Louis. Used to have been some type of reporter. Right? Of course, no one told me what a looker you are."

Ashley tightened her grip around her keys, primed to jab in defense. She tried to judge how far it was to her Jeep. Wondered if anyone would come if she pushed the panic button on the key.

Narcissistic self-importance permeated this man's attitude and attire, from the expensive brown loafers to the gold necklace. His steps continued in her direction, slow and measured like a tiger stalking its prey.

"Flew in through St. Louis myself not long ago. Spent a few weeks in the Bahamas. You ever been there?" The smoothness in his voice seemed cunning, controlled.

She wanted to run, but her instinct told her she should stay planted for the time being. "Do I know you?"

"I'm Chase Andrews." He sneered and reached a hand toward her face. "You've got a leaf caught in your hair. Here let me—"

Ashley smacked his hand away. The leaf tumbled to the ground. Andrews? Where had she heard that name before? "Sounds like you already know who I am."

He leaned straight-armed against a tree near the sidewalk and looked down at her. "Bet you'd look good in a swimsuit. One piece? No. I see you in a hot little bikini."

She didn't give him the satisfaction of a rebuttal.

Chase snickered. "Like I said before, didn't mean to scare you. Uncle Chadwick said a news lady named Ashley Lanovan had come down from St.

Louis to look around Nature's Crossing."

"Uncle Chadwick?"

She needed to get to her Jeep. This man had danger written in his attitude. Mark's face flashed through her mind. Why wasn't he here? He'd take care of her. Protect her. But Mark wasn't there. She needed to take care of herself. Ashley backed up a step.

Chase squatted and picked up a piece of straw, taking time to eye her legs. His gaze then oozed a path up her body. "Chadwick Andrews. Figured you'd heard of my uncle. Biggest real estate agent in the county. Probably the whole state."

Her pulse picked up its beat, in sync with her tensed breaths. That Andrews, the one who'd been standing in the window in Henton, looked nothing like this man. However, this man showed the same look of arrogance she'd seen through the uncle's real estate window when he nodded.

Standing, Chase twirled the straw in the corner of his mouth. "Learned everything I know from him."

"I think I might have seen him yesterday."

A car pulled into the library parking lot and parked. A gray-haired woman stepped out, grabbed a satchel from her back seat, and moved to the front door. After unlocking, the lady glanced over her shoulder at the two of them.

Ashley waved as if she knew her, hoping the lady would walk over to them. No such luck. Instead, the woman went inside and closed the door behind her.

Chase crept a few steps closer. "You ever need a real estate agent in this area, I'm your man."

"Thanks, but I'm not looking to buy." He was close. Really close. Closer than she wanted.

"Really?"

Her skin itched, and the back of her neck tingled as she started down the sidewalk towards her Jeep. "I'm here to visit the Gregorys. In fact, I'm late. I missed the road and got sidetracked."

Small talk chattered out of her mouth. Maybe that would end their conversation. Keep his mind off other things.

He took one smooth step to her quick two. "Thought sure I saw you drive through twice. Maybe I was wrong."

Her insides gripped. He'd been watching her.

"No, you weren't wrong. Janie Horton suggested I stop on my way to the Dot and Lloyd's place. She knows I'm here." Hopefully, that would make him back off. "This must have been a nice town at one time."

"Guess it was years ago. Uncle Chadwick seems taken with it. Me, I like contemporary. How about you, do you like modern?" Chase's arm brushed against her arm as he caught up to her once again.

"Modern?" She inched away until her feet hugged the edge of the sidewalk.

"You know what I mean. Condos, villas, shopping centers, golf courses. A big-city developer could make a tidy sum here with the right incentives."

Did he think she was a real estate developer? A speculator?

She sensed the glance he gave to gauge her reaction. If all he wanted to do was accost her with real estate banter, she'd be more than grateful. But she really wasn't in the mood for his sing-song mansplaining.

The man continued to keep pace with her. Deliberately leaning into her arm every time he brushed against her. "Smart person could buy up this whole place. With the right permits and zoning, this old part of town could be demolished. Flatten it to the ground." He smiled in satisfaction at the thought. "Maybe build one of those new planned communities. You look like a woman who'd like those kinds of places."

"What places?" She pushed the unlock button on her key fob. The lights flashed a welcome beacon, and she cherished the fact that only the driver's door would have unlocked. Angled toward the street, her pace picked up speed.

"Planned communities," he said sarcastically, stepping between her and the SUV door.

"Yes, I've seen them." Ashley felt he wanted to say more before he'd let her in the car. "It was nice meeting you, Mr. Andrews."

"Chase. Call me Chase, and I'll call you Ashley."

"Like I said, Mr. Andrews…Dot and Lloyd are probably worried about me by now. I better go."

He opened the driver's door and bowed, but his hand gripped the top rim and held. The straw continued to spiral between his lips. She slid inside and reached for the door's armrest to pull the door closed. He held tight.

"Wouldn't be hard to get." He leaned toward her and smiled. Might be early, but his breath greeted her with the scent of whisky.

"What wouldn't be hard to get?" Even she heard the tremble in her voice.

"Incentives! Don't you listen, lady?" Anger flared in his voice and expression. Just as fast, his eyes hooded and he stretched his neck, tilted his chin upward, and sighed. He appeared to have regained his composure. "Remember, honey, I'm your man if you need anything while you're in town."

She jammed her finger against the starter, and the engine roared to life.

"Anything at all, Ashleeeey." He pulled the straw through his lips and tossed it on the ground. His tongue trailed a slow circle around his lips. "Anything."

With adrenaline-induced strength, she jerked the door closed, locked it. Sped away in a blink. Her deep, panting breaths echoed through the interior. Her heart pounded in aerobic mode. She glanced in the rearview mirror. Good, the man hadn't moved from his spot. She was safe. Safe.

Her nerves calmed. Her breaths quieted. Her heartbeat simmered its staccato flutters.

What had just happened?

When Chase mentioned developers and planned communities, she understood what he meant. But the rest of the conversation had been difficult to piece together. Or maybe she'd been a little frightened. Little being an understatement. She shivered.

Besides, why bother to tell her? She was just here to visit friends. Then it dawned on her; he thought she'd come to town to pull the rug out from under his uncle's deals. From under his own deals.

Must have big plans.

Ashley shivered and made sure to turn toward the Gregorys' house. The community seemed nice, and the little town held a welcome feeling. Still dignified even in disrepair. Shame someone like him thought of the place only in terms of money.

Or was there more to his thinking? Revenge? Spite? Power?

Someone should stop him.

CHAPTER TWELVE

THE GREGORYS GREETED Ashley with the same affection she'd felt from them the first time they'd met at one of the events she'd been covering for the station. They were a good thirty years older than her, but that was only in years, not attitude.

Lloyd and Dot both seemed to be cut from the same pattern—short, gray-haired, friendly, and generous with their welcome. Dot's rosy cheeks complimented her button nose, whereas Lloyd's face crinkled with his contagious laugh.

"We planned this house for years before we started to build." Lloyd led the way from room to room, pointing out the walnut, hickory, birch, and pine covering the walls. "I researched trees, stones, slate. In fact, I think I researched the whole dang environment."

"He was like a sculptor searching for the image within the stone. Even oversaw the cutting of the trees for the lumber." Dot laughed and tapped his shoulder.

"Darn tootin'. Nature should be seen at its best.

And this house was designed to be part of the natural surroundings."

"Well, you did a good job. This is truly a beautiful home." Ashley's hand glided over the massive rustic oak mantel adorned with wonderful photos of the Gregorys' lifetime. "And I love the pine trees surrounding your land. They seem to reach to the heavens."

She remembered their only child had died from leukemia years ago. After that, the couple had used their money to travel, donate to charities, and acquire beautiful artwork. Rare books lined the shelves bookending the fireplace along with classics and titles she recognized as current best sellers.

The three navigated the stairs to the lower level, where a cherry stone fireplace accented one end of the family room.

"My gosh, I don't know which I like better. Upstairs or down here." Ashley stood at the patio door, gazing at the ground-level view, out the rear of the house. "The pines look even taller from here."

Lloyd eased onto the arm of the sofa. "I planned the main living area upstairs—"

"Complete with the circle drive in front of the house." Dot patted her husband's cheek.

"She had always dreamed of a circle drive, so I gave her one." He lifted his wife's hand to his lips. "Then I planned this downstairs more for the guys. That way, no one has to worry about messing up the main floor with muddy boots or trails of grass."

"Enough about the house. How about lunch?"

Dot asked. "Thought we'd take it on the deck. You can look out over the land from there."

"Sounds great to me," Ashley replied.

Lloyd held onto the stair rail, pulling himself upward with each step. "Later today, we'll take a walk around the property."

"Let her eat and have a little rest first," Dot said.

"I know, I know. In fact, I'm gonna take a short nap after lunch, too." Perspiring, he opened a couple of windows on the front side of the house. Then headed to the front door.

"Where are you going, dear?"

"To get some air." He stepped onto the front porch and called through the open window. "When you get a chance, honey, could you bring me a glass of raspberry tea?"

"Sure will. You okay?"

"Need to relax after this past week. Well, will you look who's pulling in?"

The blast of a car horn announced the arrival. A few moments later, a car door slammed, and Ashley's curiosity got the best of her. Glancing out the window, she saw Peabody rounding the front of a vintage black Trans Am. Lloyd held the door, and the two men walked inside.

Peabody broke into a grin as he entered the kitchen and caught sight of her. "If it isn't the sneaky suspender snapper."

"I may have to snap them again. You didn't tell me you owned such a snazzy car," she replied.

"Not just one, either. Got four classics over at my place. You'll have to stop by my house and let me give you the tour one day."

"Sounds like a plan." She leaned against the counter. "You know, I showcased a car club on my television show once. Loved every minute of it. Almost bought a little red truck to restore that day."

"Why didn't you invest in one?"

"Money to buy the truck. Money to store it. And money to pay someone to do the restoration."

"You could have done a lot yourself."

"Maybe. But I was still married at that time, and he didn't want to be bothered with the idea." Besides, it would have only been fun if there'd been someone to work on the truck with her. Someone who had the same dream. "Maybe someday."

He smiled, then tapped his cane on the floor and chuckled. "You're gonna fit in fine around here."

There wouldn't be time to fit in, she was only there for a short visit. People didn't seem to understand. Did she look like a lost waif? Maybe she felt like one at times, but in St. Louis, no one saw through her veneer.

"We're just sitting down to lunch. Would you care to stay?" Dot offered.

"Most times I would." Peabody grabbed a mint from the bowl on the table, then pointed at the hostess. "She's the best cook in the state."

"I don't think your sister, Eloise, would take kindly to hearing you say that."

"Oh, she's the best cake and pie maker around. Got it natural, you know." He chuckled and laid a pink flyer on the counter. "As you can see, I'm on a mission today. Out and about delivering reminders of the Halloween dance. Want to make sure we have a good turnout at the VFW."

"I plumb forgot," Lloyd said.

Peabody spun his finger in the air above his head. "These two people can make the dance floor come alive."

"Not sure we'll make this one. It's been a long week, what with my mother being sick." Lloyd dabbed perspiration from his brow.

"You take care of yourself." Peabody patted his friend's shoulder. "There'll always be another dance."

Peabody meandered back to his car, blew the horn, and headed farther down the road on his dance mission.

Lunch on the deck had turned into an afternoon of laughs, followed by an insightful conversation in the living room. Ashley listened with interest to the ping-pong of conversation between Dot and Lloyd.

"Ten years ago, we updated inside the house," Lloyd said. "Nowadays, what's cutting edge one year, can be outdated the next."

"He's always looking ahead. Comes from him being an engineer. Always thinking of the next thing to design." Dot smiled and patted the seat beside her. "Me, I'm more of a past person. If it still works for me, why should I change?"

Lloyd eased onto the chair arm and took a sip

of tea. "Because new usually means better. Got to keep up on things. Besides, we're here to make the world a better place for the next generation. The future's in the children, and we need to support that. Can't live in the past, you know. Which are you, Ashley? Future or past?"

"You're the first person to ever ask me. I'm not sure how to answer."

She walked to the triple picture window that overlooked the freshly mowed acreage. The majestic pines surrounding the property swayed like agile ballet dancers in the breeze, giving backdrop to the serviceberry trees in bright orange-red plumage.

"Truth be told, three years ago, I'd have said I was a past person, or at least a leave it as it is person. A lot has happened since then."

Two hawks circled on the breeze, and Ashley envied their ability to float on the air. Free to fly at the whim of the wind and the tilt of their wings. She longed to possess the same freedom. To reach out and grab the world. But her foothold on the future had been shattered by her ex-husband, the man she'd trusted.

Now she'd lost her television career, too. The ladder to her future was steep and shaky at this point. Yet, for some reason, she felt as if she'd made progress just by taking this trip. One thing for sure, there'd be no turning back.

She replied honestly to the Gregorys, and to herself, "Future. Definitely future."

Before long, Lloyd headed to the bedroom for his afternoon nap, leaving Dot and her to catch up on what had happened between now and last time they'd had a chance meeting in Florida.

When Lloyd didn't wake from his nap like he planned, Dot decided to fix them some light appetizers of cantaloupe, grapes, cheese, and crackers. With the main entrée being a bowl of soup fresh out of the can as she referred to it. She convinced Ashley she didn't need any help and to go enjoy herself on the deck.

Enjoying the briskness of the approaching evening, Ashley grabbed an afghan from the sofa and took it outside with her. She tucked it across her lap, leaned back, and got lost in the view. For a moment, she thought she saw something, a person or animal, start to step out of the pines about three-quarters of the way down the ten acres. But when she blinked, there was nothing there.

Her phone rang. Caller ID only showed a number. One she didn't recognize. "Hello?"

"Ashley?"

The voice sounded familiar, but that wasn't possible. "Yes. Who's this?"

"Mark Garmund. I just called to make sure I had the right phone number."

Okay, this was odd. "Where are you?"

"Patrick and I are still camping. But we'll be back tomorrow."

"Caught any fish? Or are you starving?" The quick, light-hearted comeback she'd given surprised even herself.

He laughed. "I'll have you know we had fish for dinner."

"Well, that's surprising." Why had he called?

"Yeah, there's this place down the road called a diner. Got a nice menu. You order. They bring you the food. Easy as lightning. And you don't even have to clean the fish. Hold on a sec." He mumbled something to someone. "Okay, I'm back. Where was I? Oh, yeah. And dessert…let me…"

By the time he finished embellishing the meal, all the way to the blackberry cobbler and paying, her sides hurt from laughing. She swiped a couple of laughter tears from the corners of her eyes. When he finished and the quiet set in, she missed the sound of his voice.

"Why did you call?" she asked. "I know it wasn't to share your dinner menu with me."

"I called because…I was thinking about you." His tone was serious. "Wanted to see how long you may be in town."

"A week at the most." Warming up fast, she tossed the afghan aside. "Right now, I'm sitting on the Gregorys' back deck while Dot finishes fixing dinner."

"They're good people."

"Yes, they are. Uh—"

"Oh, I've got to go. Patrick's motioning me it's time to leave." He lightly cleared his throat. "Alright if I call you again?"

"That would be nice."

"Okay, then. Talk to you later, pretty lady."

"Bye." The line went blank, and for a moment, she wondered if she'd only imagined what he was saying. Going through it again before she forgot, she felt even warmer.

Unable to sit still, she paced back and forth on the deck alongside the house until she couldn't stand being alone any longer and headed in to help Dot. Together, the two women finished cooking the light dinner. Ashley carried the appetizer platter to the table on the deck as Dot filled their bowls with soup. Then, together, they settled in on the deck, lighting a scented citronella candle off to the side.

Dot picked at her fruit, glancing at the bedroom through the open patio door. "Lloyd hasn't been feeling well. Even in Florida, he complained of being short of breath."

"I noticed, but thought it might be normal for him," Ashley said.

Dabbing her cheeks free of tears, Dot continued, "This place has become too much for him. He used to love to mow the grass. Lately, it's more like a chore. Oh, look at me. I'm ruining your visit."

"No, you're not."

"Let's talk about you." A smile enveloped Dot's wrinkled face. "We were so excited to get your call. What made you finally decide to come for a visit?"

"Partly because I needed a change. Losing my job has made me rethink what I've been doing with my life. Think about it, I devoted thirteen years to my career. Ten years to Bradford, fourteen if you count the four years we dated." Ashley shook her head. "I feel like this is a crossroad in my life. A new slate. A starting point for me. Trouble is, I don't know where to start."

Dot scrunched her brow. "Maybe you don't have to *start* anywhere. Maybe you just need to *be*. The future will always find you as long as you don't shut your doors to change."

"But I'm already missing my news event show. I really like talking to people. Learning new things." Maybe she should think about starting an online blog. Maybe a podcast.

"Nothing says you can't keep doing that. You'll find Nature's Crossing has a great history." Dot laughed. "And lots of people who'll happily give their own version."

"You know it was just last year, I did a show on finding your new tribe. Widows. Divorcees. People losing their jobs. Being transferred. Or just hoping to reconnect to their dreams from decades ago. Now here I am in the same boat." She gave an embarrassed grin. "I should have paid more attention to their suggestions."

The two women laughed, then quieted to listen to the rustle of leaves among the swoosh of the pines against each other. The melancholy hoot of an owl in the distance floated on the air, along with the smell of fallen leaves mixing with the dirt.

"The other day on the phone, my wise mother coaxed me to not worry about who I used to be," Ashley said. "Said I'd never find her. She suggested I find who I am now and enjoy life."

"Sounds like a smart woman."

"What if I don't like the new me?"

"How do you know if you never give change a chance? Why, I can go for months, even years, doing the same thing. Then, out of the blue one morning, I look at things different." Dot smiled. "That's when I know I'm on the verge of a new adventure."

A lonely whippoorwill's song drifted through the night, pinching Ashley's heartstrings.

"My mother also told me I should find myself a new man." Ashley could feel the warmth rise in her face. "Even Janie said I should."

"Why, you're blushing." Dot shook her finger in a wise, all-knowing manner. "There is someone, isn't there?"

"Let's say, this trip has been interesting." She wasn't ready to share that Mark had called. Having that between just the two of them felt kind of nice for now. Besides, she might be making too much out of what he'd said. He was probably just being friendly.

"What could have possibly happened in this little town to make you blush?"

Ashley leaned across the table. "You'll think I'm being silly. I ran into Mark at the grocery."

Dot patted her chest in mock palpitations. "My goodness child, if I was young like you, I'd be blushing and fidgeting and…and I don't know what all."

Felt good that someone thought she was still young. Guess everything is in perspective of where one is in their own life. Age. Experience. And openness.

Dot turned at the sound of the bedroom door opening. "We're on the deck, dear."

"Well, what do you know, the tour guide missed the tour." Lloyd chuckled, ambling out through the door to the deck. "Tomorrow morning, while the dew's still glistening, we'll all take our coffee and walk the grounds."

"Wake me when you get up. I can be ready in five minutes," Ashley said.

"I've got a better idea," Dot said. "When the coffee's done in the morning, you two take your mugs and wander around. Meanwhile, I'll make homemade cinnamon rolls with extra icing. Maybe squeeze some oranges for juice."

"You know the way to my heart." Lloyd encircled Dot with a hug, placing a kiss on her brow. "What were you two girls giggling about when I came out of the bedroom? Looked like a conspiracy to me."

Dot peeked at Ashley. "Well, if you must know. She mentioned meeting Mark."

"Nice man," Lloyd said.

Ashley's heart palpitated with a mind of its own as she pushed her empty plate away and fiddled with the handle of her cup. "Sometimes yes. Sometimes...aggravating."

"Mark? Actually...he's kind of shy until you get to know him. Wait till you see him again to pass final judgment."

Ashley couldn't believe she was in the midst of a conversation about a man who'd called less than an hour ago. "I'll have you know he made no impression on me whatsoever."

Dot smiled. "Really?"

"Yes, really." Embarrassed, Ashley laughed. "Oh, you two!"

"What about those blue eyes you mentioned earlier?"

Ashley felt herself soften. "They were blue, that's all. Kind of like a sky, when there's only a couple of small white clouds sailing along, but with a hint of silver. Kind of… Anyhow, it doesn't matter."

"You could always come for another visit," Lloyd said.

Ashley walked to the patio door, combing her hands through her hair. The reflection of Dot and Lloyd in the glass pane tugged at her heart—two people still in love after decades of being together. Would she ever have that?

Her insides ached with the thought. Might be she had no one to blame but herself. When Mark had leaned toward her at the market, she pulled back, turned away. What was she so darn afraid of? For a moment, the woman in her had emerged from the self-inflicted abyss and grasped for the surface. Tingles had shot to pulse points like a match sucked to a pilot light. Feelings like those could get her in trouble.

No, Mark was not the man for her. The perfect man for her would be a little henpecked and subdued. That sure wasn't him by a long shot. She shoved her raw emotions back down.

"I'm just not ready for complications in my life." Ashley turned, closing her eyes. Definitely not ready for a complication like Mark Garmund. "I guess if he's half as nice as the two of you think, then maybe he's not all bad."

Lloyd raised his cup of coffee to Ashley. "Well, finally. Here! Here!"

"I'm still not interested, though." Although seeing him again might be nice. If nothing else, she could tell him about meeting Chase. Get his take on the man. And Chadwick.

CHAPTER THIRTEEN

ASHLEY FLIPPED OFF the alarm on her phone, drug herself from the warmth of the bed to a warm shower, then scrambled into a fleecy sweater and jeans.

"Ready or not. Tour leaves in thirty minutes," Lloyd cheerfully called from outside the guest bedroom door.

"I'm almost ready." She brushed back her hair and added a dab of color to her lips. Thankfully, there were only the three of them, so she didn't have to bother with makeup this morning. As she stepped into the kitchen, the background noise from a local radio station caught her attention. Must be one of the morning short-range radio programs that not only tells you the local news, but also hosts crop reports, trade and sells, community meetings, lost pets, and lots more.

"Where's that radio program originate?" Ashley asked as she poured herself a cup of coffee.

"From over in the Jefferson City area," Lloyd replied.

"No, dear. I think that one's from Springfield or

Rolla." Dot busied herself at the kitchen counter.

"Might even be Branson." Lloyd shrugged. "Don't matter. They start you off on a good foot for the day. Did you know Jefferson City is the state capitol?"

"Sure did." Ashley sipped her coffee. "And Columbia is where the University of Missouri is located. Home of the Mizzou Tigers, I believe."

His face lit with joy. "Gooooo, Tigers! They're having a good year."

"You'd think he was the one who graduated from Mizzou instead of me." Dot rested her palm against his back. "Truth of the matter is, he graduated from Rolla. But he's adopted all the Mizzou sports teams."

After some discussion of the football season, Ashley poured herself another cup of coffee. "I'm glad we called Janie last night and invited her over for breakfast. I feel like she and I have been friends forever instead of only a few days."

"Come here. Quick." Lloyd coaxed from the living room while pointing to the back acreage.

The two women rushed to his side in time to see five deer nibbling on apples beneath the apple tree toward the back of the property. He motioned for Ashley to look through the land telescope positioned at the triple-picture window.

Two of the larger deer stretched their necks, ears perked, and glanced at the house. When she looked through the scope, she saw up close the most peaceful faces and large, soulful eyes. Seeming content with the surroundings, they returned to their food and eventually wandered off into the property's surrounding pine trees.

"Aren't they something?" Lloyd asked.

"They're beautiful," Ashley said. "Do they come to the tree often? Because I thought I saw something move at the edge of the pines yesterday about dusk."

"Might have been. When they're not holed up in the brush, the deer wander around. I knew you'd enjoy them. Are you ready for our walk?"

She'd worn her warmest sweater this morning, along with a pair of super warm socks and her loafers. "Sure. Let me get my hat and gloves."

"You'll need more than that. There's a nip in the air this morning. Afraid our nice weather is coming to an end." Lloyd opened the hall closet and retrieved one of his insulated parkas for her.

To placate the good-natured man, she donned the coat and tied the drawstring hood in place beneath her chin. She cringed when she caught a glimpse of herself in the hall tree mirror. "Good grief. I look like a blimp. But…I am warm. That's what counts."

"Alright, here we go," Lloyd said.

"Take your time. I'll have breakfast ready when you get in," Dot called out as they left.

For the next hour, Ashley followed Lloyd like a small child on her first day of school. She listened while he told her the names of trees and bushes, at times picking up a leaf for her inspection. Paths through the pines revealed hidden clearings and glades. In one clearing, rocks and fat chunks of wood offered a place to rest around a rock surrounded, charred fire pit.

"We've hosted many a hot dogs and marshmallows roast out here," Lloyd explained.

He paused to catch his breath, and the two of them watched squirrels scamper across the ground, storing their winter nuts. A few minutes later, Ashley and Lloyd moved on, a little slower. Another nook contained deer tracks and a couple of spots where the soft grass still held their shape from having bedded down earlier.

Lloyd pointed to a bench near the pines, just a bit past the apple tree. "Let's take a rest before we hike on up to the house."

She noticed he moved even slower than yesterday. And even though there wasn't a hill to get to the house, there was a gradual incline, one you'd never notice most days. One that would grab your attention if you weren't feeling well. "I think this is the most peaceful place I've ever been. Just exquisite."

"What about those beautiful places you've traveled to for work." He groaned as he eased onto the seat.

"No comparison. This place outshines them all. You and Dot have such a wonderful life. You're very blessed."

"Yes, we are. But to tell you the truth, I don't know how much longer we'll stay. Lots to keep up, and believe it or not, I'm not as young as I used to be." His voice cracked. "Can't do those somersaults anymore."

She started to laugh, but he motioned her to stay still and pointed across the open ground to the tree line. Try as she might, she couldn't see what he was wanting her to see. That had always been one of her drawbacks.

Lloyd patted her hand. "Look at the pines. Zero in on the one to the left of the bright yellow-orange leaves on the maple tree. Now take the trees out of the picture."

With his directions, she narrowed down to the area he wanted her to see. At the edge of the tree line, she finally saw four deer. Little by little, they edged out, into the grassy area, on pencil-thin legs that looked like they'd break in a stiff wind. Their tails twitched behind them.

"Earlier weren't there five?" she whispered.

"Other one's a buck. He's not so trusting. Kind of a loner. Always on guard. If you're patient, though, he'll show himself when he's ready." Lloyd lightly shook his head. "He needs to feel secure. Kind of like people do sometimes."

They lingered awhile before deciding they were cold and hungry. Slowly, they started toward the house. She huddled farther into the parka, then, about halfway to the house, she looked back. The deer were out in the open and nearing the bench now. Nibbling at grass and apples along the way. They seemed to know there was safety in this tiny bit of the world. Still no sign of the buck, though.

Lloyd paused for a couple of deep breaths before going on. He glanced back and forth between Ashley and the deer. "Usually, it's just me and Dot the deer seem at ease around. But they aren't afraid of you, either."

"I'll never forget this morning." Ashley smiled to herself, storing wonders into her memory. She hated the thought of leaving in a few days. If she stayed patient, maybe the buck would make a showing before she left.

"I smell bacon." Lloyd quickened his step. "There was a day when I'd have raced you to the house."

"I think you could win even today."

Janie dashed out the door and across the grass to meet the pair and took them arm-in-arm. "Dot says you better get in gear. She's already popped the biscuits in the oven."

Lloyd chuckled, "I'm in gear. Low gear."

Ashley enjoyed the feel of friends. Laughter for the sake of enjoyment. No worries. She squeezed Janie's arm. "I'm glad you came for breakfast."

"Me, too. It was kind of lonesome once you left yesterday." Janie turned and walked backward.

"You look like you've got a secret, Janie girl. What are you up to?" Lloyd asked.

"Guess who pulled up before I started over here. None other than the two camper guys." She pointed at the woodpile, and there stood Patrick.

"Figured you'd want a fire downstairs." He hoisted another piece of wood on the stack in his already full arms.

"You're a lifesaver. I've dreaded bringing in wood all morning." Lloyd ambled in Patrick's direction.

"Here, I'll help, too," Janie yelled and ran ahead.

In one quick motion, Ashley pushed her hood

down and shed the coat. She knew how she looked, and the thought wasn't pretty. Not when there was a chance… Releasing her hair, she tried to secretly scan the yard.

"Looking for someone?" Mark's strong voice came from the deck above.

Her heart skipped a beat when she glanced up to where just last evening, she'd shared thoughts on him with Lloyd and Dot.

Arms crossed on the rail top, he leaned forward and captured her with his stare. She couldn't move. Dot had been right; he really was something. Ashley hoped her soft moan was completely in her mind. It was bad enough warmth had flooded her cold face.

"No." She hoped he'd think her cheeks were red because of the cold. "What are you looking for?"

He glanced across the yard, then at her. "I like watching the deer."

Their eyes continued their connection until she felt hers lower across his shoulders, then return to his lips. She blinked. What little self-control she managed to hold onto was rapidly fading.

"I can hardly wait to taste those warm cinnamon rolls Dot was making," she said.

Suddenly, Mark's concentration moved farther down the land. After a bit, Ashley realized she'd lost his full attention.

"Fine," she muttered to herself.

"Far be it for me to tell you what to do, but if you want to see something majestic, take a look at the apple tree by the salt block." Mark's gaze stayed in the distance, his voice a whisper. "Slow and quiet, if you can."

Feeling that he'd spied on her again, she had no intention of being bossed by him. Her voice raised a notch above normal deliberately when she replied, "What is it you want me to see?"

He straightened. "Too late."

With that, she spun around and true to his words, she was too late. All she saw was a fleeting glimpse of a six-point buck disappearing into the thicket.

"That was so beautiful, so…" She looked up at the deck, but he wasn't there. Maybe if she stood absolutely still and waited, the buck would return.

"You going to stand there all day and freeze, or come in for coffee?" Mark asked. "Up to you."

She jumped at the sound of his voice and turned in that direction. He was standing outside the patio door, leading to the family room, in the lower part of the house, and she couldn't imagine how he'd gotten there so fast.

"Think I'll come in, thank you very much."

"Probably a good idea, in case it snows later. Of course, watching you out there on the land, you looked like you were dressed for the hundred-year blizzard." He winked. "I must say, you do wear the most interesting outfits. My favorite is still the black tank top."

She smiled in spite of herself as she shoved the coat in his hands. "You make me so mad."

Tossing the coat inside, he laughed and stepped aside for her to pass. As he did, she caught him off guard with a teasing push. He tumbled backward over the wood stack by the door. She reached out to catch him, then thrown off balance, she tumbled forward, causing them both to fall. He pulled her toward him, sheltering her from crashing into the woodpile. Hitting the ground, flat-on-his-back, he cushioned her fall.

Suddenly, she was on top of him. Not only on top of him, but molding into his body's chest and muscles. Her breasts heated with desire, and she found herself pressing against him with her uncontrollable arch. In turn, his undeniable erection pressed against her. Their bodies meeting, talking. Like a puzzle where the final pieces had slid into place. Not the best for a lady trying to keep her distance.

"You okay?" he asked.

She nodded. "Good thing you were there."

He gently curled his fingers through her hair, strong and sure. "Anytime."

"Ummmmmm." She'd uttered the longing out loud. Her body reacted against her will. Really, really not a good position.

His delectable I'm-so-innocent smile surfaced for a moment, followed by an all-male look that relayed intimacy. "Did you say something?"

"No." Doomed, that's what she was. Doomed.

"Funny. I could have sworn you did. Kind of like at the grocery."

Condemned to a place of embarrassment so deep she could feel the insides of her toes. "Let me go."

He slid his arms from around her and stretched them out beside his body. Lost in the lure of his eyes,

Ashley could swear their lips were getting closer. He hadn't moved. She had. So close, her breath fluttered his hair. His cheek muscles twitched with the parting of his lips.

"I can't do this." She lowered her forehead against his. "I can't."

"Can't what, Ashley?" His breath whispered across her ear.

Raising her head to face him once again, she whispered, "Please, let me go."

"I'm not holding you," he replied softly, his gaze centered on her lips. He skimmed his fingers across her cheeks, then slipped them loosely in her hair once again. "You can get away any time you want."

Legs still tangled from the fall, she attempted to roll from his chest. Yet, the more they tried to separate, the more ensnarled they became. And the scattered logs seemed to barricade them closer together.

With one swift kick to his knee, she broke their intertwined hold on one another.

"You want to watch where you're kicking?" Mark growled and rolled to his side.

Janie ran over from the yard, followed close behind by Patrick. They grabbed Ashley's hands and pulled her up.

"What are you two doing on the ground?" Janie asked.

Ashley brushed herself off, her hands trembling. "We fell."

"You pushed me. And then kicked me," Mark countered, rubbing his leg as he lay on the ground.

"Did not." She hadn't meant for any of that to happen, but she had to admit her part in the catastrophe. "Well, if I did, he deserved it. Sorry about your knee."

Mark quickly jumped to his feet on his own. Then retrieved her coat from inside the doorway as she started up the stairs. "Don't forget your blizzard jacket."

Unbelievable. He was worried about the coat. She glanced back just as he tossed it to her, and she caught it mid-air.

What did he want from her? She turned away for a few seconds before looking back to see he hadn't moved. His eyes still watched her. Still waiting. Were her friends right? Had she become stonehearted and cold? No, they were wrong. She was afraid of feeling again. Of caring and then being betrayed. The pain of betrayal had put a hole in her, one she'd steadily built back, one that still had cracks.

"Thanks. We'll have to do this again sometime." Had those words come out of her mouth? Was that an invitation? "Uh…I mean…"

He grinned. "Any time. Any time at all."

Halfway up the stairs, she heard Patrick laugh. "Mark, I've told you over and over and over again, you've got to brace yourself against the unknown. And there's nothing in this world more unknown than a woman."

Within a few minutes, everyone was gathered around the dining room table. Dot's breakfast—from the table setting with sugar on the orange juice glasses to the French toast sprinkled with confectioner's sugar—felt like dining at a five-star bed and breakfast. The morning flew by with good food, friendly conversation, and laughter.

"When are you guys headed out again?" Lloyd asked.

Between bites, Patrick replied, "Next week. Need to find a better fishing spot."

"That means you'll have time to take Janie to the VFW dance this evening."

Janie encircled her husband's arm and batted her eyes. "Could we? Please, please, please."

Patrick kissed her cheek. "Well, a guy can't hardly turn down begging. Especially from such a pretty thing. We'll go. But no costume."

Janie turned to Mark. "What about you?"

"Think I'll pass. Thought I might drive up to the lake later today. Give you two space," he replied.

"Lloyd, it was your idea," Janie asked. "What about you and Dot? Then Ashley would have to come."

Lloyd rose and stood behind Dot's chair. He gently touched her shoulder. "We told Peabody we'd need to pass on this one. I'm not feeling up to it. But look out for the Christmas Ball."

"Ashley, you come with us," Janie urged.

"Think I'll stay here, too. In fact, this evening, I may sit on the deck and read like I did for a while last night."

Once the food had been devoured, everyone pitched in to tidy the kitchen. Except Lloyd. He excused himself to take a nap. Ashley kept an eye on Mark to make sure she moved in the opposite direction of him. Unable to trust herself at this point, she needed time to think through what happened before breakfast.

Once cleanup was complete, the group stepped outside for some fresh air. Patrick and Janie decided to take a hike around the property before taking over at the store to relieve the part-time help.

"See you two tomorrow," Mark called to the couple as they started their walk then turned to Dot. "I'm going to head on out, too."

Leaning against the split rail fence surrounding the patio, Ashley soaked in the sunshine. The sun had reheated the air, and she no longer needed a coat. And the warmth wrapped her in a soothing cocoon.

Mark headed to his BMW. "Dot, thanks again for breakfast. It was nice to be included."

"You know you're always welcome. Maybe you need to think about settling down here in Nature's Crossing. We'd all like to see more of you." Dot waved and went inside.

He opened the driver's side door and hopped on the runner to get in, then stopped. Instead, he propped one arm on the car door and one on the roof. When his gaze traveled to Ashley, she figured, what the heck, flirt a little. She might never see him again. After all, two could play the same game. Slowly, she pushed the windblown strands of hair from her face, bit her bottom lip—and winked.

"I see I've grown on you." He looked down and shook his head. "Took long enough."

When he looked up, a grin covered his face before he gave his two-finger salute to her. She returned the gesture. He was right. Him and his wave or whatever he wanted to call it had grown on her. Not only was it unique, it was sexy as all get out.

Mark maneuvered the BMW along the long, winding driveway. At the entrance, he stopped, opened the driver's side door, and stood on the runner as he had before. Ashley watched him run his gaze over the land and the house, settling on her. He didn't look away, and she didn't move.

What was he thinking? Had Dot's words prompted an idea? Her mind raced at the possibilities. Reactively, Ashley's feelings threw up their shield, and she blinked. Her mind told her she barely knew him. Don't take chances with trust or commitment or maybe. Maybe could shatter a person's heart. She swallowed hard the lump that crept into her throat. Once in a lifetime was enough to be shattered.

Suddenly, he reached back inside the BMW. When he stood back up, his stance conveyed he was on the phone. In less than a minute, he slid behind the wheel and sped away.

Him and his phone. Why should she worry about the two of them becoming anything more than friendly adversaries? He always had someplace he had to be. Always something he had to do.

CHAPTER FOURTEEN

DOT AND ASHLEY drove around most of the afternoon. As they toured the area, Dot offered town history. "Most of the people can tell you stories from their childhood about the way Nature's Crossing used to be. Some can even trace the town to their grandparent's and great-grandparent's time."

"Must have been an important place. Do you know what buildings were on the vacant lots?"

A white SUV pulled out in front of Dot, and she swerved to miss the rear bumper. "I've never seen that one around town before. If I had, I'd give him a talking to."

Ashley smiled at the older woman's courage.

"There was a big building housing the post office and a printing company on one corner. Of course, they built a new post office years ago. The opposite corner lot held one of the grocery stores," Dot replied.

"I forgot to tell you. Yesterday while I walked around town, I ran into— No, let me rephrase that. Chase Andrews made it a point to introduce himself."

"You be careful of that one. Him and his uncle are two of a kind. Their scruples are lodged between shrewd and ruthless. I'll admit, Chadwick has a few good points. He's more polished about his business dealings, but Chase is one to be leery of."

"So, it wasn't just me." Ashley shuddered at the memory.

"What do you mean?"

"I mean he's creepy. You know that uneasy feeling women get around certain men? The kind that says something isn't right."

The gray-haired lady nodded.

"He made me feel like that." A flash of a tremble shot through her. "He even held on to my car door when I tried to close it. I know it sounds silly, but for a moment, I felt trapped."

Dot pulled to the side of the road and stopped near the corner of the two vacant lots. "One of these days, his uncle will take him into his confidences. When that happens, no telling what kind of business transactions will take place around here. Lloyd and I have noticed he seems to be around Nature's Crossing quite a bit lately."

Ashley opened the car door. "I'll be careful. Now, do we have time for a walk? You can fill me in on the town up close."

The women lost track of time, and the light had begun to fade before Dot wheeled the car down the driveway at their house. "We'll go another time and take Lloyd. He loves to share the history of the churches and cemeteries. The local libraries appreciate the work he does on the old births and burials in the county."

Dot spied her husband as they rounded to the back of the house. "There he is now, planting more daffodil and tulip bulbs. I don't know what I'd do without him."

Alone on the back deck after dinner, Ashley nibbled on grapes as the owls soothed the night air. Lloyd had retired for the evening, and Dot was working on a puzzle in the den off the kitchen. Felt good to be alone under the clear, dark sky lit with bright twinkling stars. No smog or city streetlights to dull the view made the feeling even better.

A chill in the air forced Ashley to find the afghan from the night before, and she tucked it over her lap. Fall would soon lead to the beginning of winter. Too bad she'd miss seeing the deer skipping through the snow. She picked up her phone and dialed her parents' number, half-hoping no one would be home.

Her mother answered, "About time you called."

"Sorry. The day seemed to get away from me. Anything new there?"

"We got our flu shots. Now your dad's in bed with a fever. I think he wants attention. What have you been up to?"

Ashley filled her in on the past few days since she'd arrived in Nature's Crossing but steered clear of the strange encounter with Chase. No need to worry them.

"Sounds like a lovely place. Make any new

friends?"

"Were you listening to me?" Ashley sighed and combed her fingers through her hair.

"Yes, I was. The people sound friendly, Dot and Lloyd sound like people your dad and I would like. And you may have found yourself a new friend in Janie. Now, any interesting male friends?"

This wouldn't stop until Ashley shared.

"So?" her mother prodded.

"Let's say, I may have forgotten how to play the game. I made a fool of myself in front of a very interesting man. Three times. Hold on a minute." Ashley saw a glimmer of lights headed down the long driveway. She leaned over the deck rail and caught a glimpse of the black BMW as it passed one of the pole lights that lined the drive.

"Speak of the devil. It's him. I've got to go," she whispered. Without waiting for a reply, she ended the call.

Ashley raced toward her bedroom, sticking her head in the den to get Dot's attention. Hurried, she pointed to the deck. "Mark is out there. Don't let him leave."

"Certainly, dear." Dot put the puzzle piece in her hand down and toddled to the deck doorway.

"Oh…don't tell him I said that."

The gray-haired lady smiled. "I'll tackle him flat if he even hints at leaving."

The vision caught Ashley off guard for a moment, and she stopped. Laughed. "I can actually visualize you doing something like that."

Dot waved her away. "Go get pretty. I know what

to do."

In her room, Ashley changed into a butter-colored silk blouse. Buttoned to the top, she undid one of the buttons. Oh, heck. She undid one more. Perfume spritzed on her pounding pulse points and gold earrings added, she frantically brushed her hair. A quick dab of blush and mascara. A bit of lip color, blot.

She heard Dot ask Mark if he'd like to come inside. He said he'd been passing by. Just on his way back from the lake. Couldn't stay long.

Liar. No one just happened to pass by at this time of night.

Deep breath…open the door…walk to the deck.

Dot smiled at Ashley when she appeared at the deck doorway. "Look, we have company."

"Who?"

Arms folded across his chest, Mark leaned against the fence rail and barely glanced up. He shifted his stance and studied the tree-line in the dark. "I think you know who."

What could she say to that? He might have seen her leaning over the deck as he drove in. Considering how off-balance he made her, her best bet was to keep quiet. See where this went.

"Well, isn't this nice?" Dot cleared her throat. "If you two don't mind, I'll go back inside. I'm kind of tired. Think I'll settle in for the night. Make yourselves at home. You two know your way around."

Ashley winced at the words. That was just the problem. She didn't know her way around.

"Good night, Dot," he said.

The elderly lady padded softly inside, closing the door behind her.

Mark stared at Ashley until she blinked and looked up the stars. When her gaze returned to him, he was still focused on her. Those all-seeing sensual eyes of his would be her downfall.

"From what I can see in this light, you look beautiful," he said.

"At least I look better than this morning."

"You were pretty this morning, too."

"Was that before or after I knocked you down?" The moment it was out of her mouth, she felt the heat rush to her face.

Mark's head tilted, and his face filled with that little-boy grin. His look teased. Did he always look that darn sexy? Maybe he remembered the moment his self-control faltered? Or hers? For the moment, she needed to regain her own self-composure.

He walked to the BMW and braced against the hood with his elbows. "Want to go to the dance?"

The rise and fall of his leather jacket had her mesmerized, inside and out. Her heart hammered harder and harder as she looked down from the deck to where he stood. "Thought you were going to be busy this evening."

Mark stared at the pines and shoved his hands halfway in his jean pockets. Finally, he shrugged. "Got done early. So here I am. You didn't answer my question. Do you want to go to the dance?"

"It's kind of late, and I'm not dressed for it."

"Good."

"What does that mean?"

"Costume dances aren't tops on my list of entertainment." He turned around and leaned back against the BMW's front grill, bending his knee to shove one foot against the bumper. He acted like they'd done nothing more than discuss the latest football score.

"Well, I love to dance when someone asks me in a decent amount of time." Not liking to dance was a flaw in her book for him. Maybe he wasn't perfect, after all. His evasiveness frustrated her. Another flaw. Before long, he might not appeal to her at all. Doubtful. Real doubtful.

"Didn't say I didn't like to dance," he said.

She brushed her hair back from the tickle on her cheek. "There you go with your semantics. By the way, I've noticed you're real good at evading questions you don't want to answer, too."

He glanced up. "Are we going to keep word fighting like this?"

Ashley sucked in a breath of reality. Blew out a breath of being alive. A woman and alive. She shook her head. "Could have fooled me. I thought you were flirting."

Biting the side of his lower lip, he looked a little embarrassed. "Let's agree I might have been. So why don't you come down here? We can sit and listen to music on my phone. I even brought a bottle of wine. Just in case."

A smile crossed her lips. "In case what?"

"What?"

She grabbed a leftover grape from the patio table and flung it at him. He caught it on the fly and popped it in his mouth. "Thanks."

Maybe she did remember how to tease after all. "I'll bring wineglasses from the kitchen, unless you happen to carry those around in that monster-machine of yours."

"Glasses would be good. You got anything else to eat in there besides grapes?" He headed to the woodpile.

"I'm sure there is. I'll be down in a second."

Ashley put together a platter of fruit, cheese, and salami, then tossed crackers in a bowl and finished off the tray with two glasses. The klutz in her feared she might trip on the stairs, so she lowered it through the dumb waiter, retrieving the food once she was down the steps.

As Mark opened the patio door for her, he took the tray as she stepped out into the back yard that had become a wonderland. Flowers sprouted from a watering can placed on the picnic table, lanterns cast a warm flickering glow, and soft jazz floated in the air. Two chairs bordered the wood-filled fire pit. He'd been busy.

"I don't think you were planning on going to the dance." Ashley marveled at the finesse he showed in lighting the wood.

He shrugged and poured them each a glass of wine. "You'll never know, will you? You said no."

"By the way, don't forget to take your clean fishing vest. I can get it from my suitcase."

"Thanks. But I'll pick it up the next time I'm

through town."

She wouldn't break the mood by telling him she'd be gone by this time next week.

His grin told her his question even before he asked. "Why's it in your suitcase?"

What was she supposed to say? That she'd hoped he'd come for the vest? She wouldn't dare tell him she tried it on twice. Already his flirty tone played with her. "After I washed it three times and got the stink bait smell out, I needed to keep it someplace."

The cold night air overtook her. She shivered slightly. A sweater instead of the blouse would have been a smarter choice.

"Are you cold?" he asked.

"No." She shuddered again. "Maybe a little."

"Won't take long for the fire to get going. You'll warm up fast then." He pitched more wood on the blaze.

Her teeth chattered together lightly.

Mark removed his leather jacket. Facing her, he wrapped it around her shoulders. "There, that should help."

It had been a long time since she felt lost in a man's coat. A long, long time. She smiled as the fresh aroma of his ocean breeze cologne, mingled with the scent of leather against her skin.

Their breaths intermingled, and chemistry sparked. They'd more than invaded each other's space and she couldn't quite focus. Stay in control. Stay in control. Stay in… How could she when his coat carried his scent and tempted her senses.

"I can't take your coat. You'll get cold."

"Not a problem."

Gently, he drew her into the circle of his arms. Before she realized she'd relaxed, her head rested against his chest and the warmth of his body. The kiss they'd briefly shared at the market had only made her want more. Something she'd avoided during the past three years. But something about his kiss, and the way he'd touched her cheek, had her insides feeling again even before this morning's compromising position on the patio.

His cheek eased against her hair, and they swayed with the melody. Eventually, his hand found hers, and she moved her arm to rest on his shoulder. She continued to follow his lead as they danced among the scattered patio furniture, moving as one until the song ended.

Neither of them drew apart. She was apprehensive, and her pulse relayed her nervousness when his lips brushed across her forehead, soft and inviting. She flinched with uncertainty. Why? She knew how to kiss. How to caress. How to whisper and lean and hold. Question was, could she yield?

Mark's gentle embrace stayed solid. "Did someone hurt you, Ashley?"

"I think I'd better…"

Tender, his lips skimmed her temple, her cheek. He loosened his hold and tipped her chin up, seeming to lose himself in her face. "I'd never hurt you if you were mine. I'd never let anyone else hurt you, either."

"I really need to…"

Another melody encircled them, and he pressed

his fingers lightly to her lips. "Shhh."

She regrouped in his arms, moved once again with the music. Her hand returned to his shoulder a moment before her fingers slowly caressed the back of his neck. The two of them slowly stopped moving, and she gazed into the warmth of his weathered face as his fingers tangled through her hair. Captured in their hold, she surrendered. Light as a butterfly's breeze, his kisses inched down her cheek toward her lips. She leaned in to capture the sensation, her heart ached for what might be.

"Ummmmm…" Her response was unintended.

"Do you know how beautiful you are?"

His lips brushed hers, and she leaned toward him. His lips caressed, and hers separated. His lips parted, and her resistance faltered. Before she could think about stopping, they were embraced in a timeless hold. Latching them into the heat of the other, each one grasped to hold on to this moment. And their kiss tingled all the way to her core. Made her ache for the man holding her as if he'd never let her go.

She eased lips away from his kiss, and he let her rest her cheek against his chest. Breathless. Unsure. Frightened at the rush of a feeling she'd pushed aside, she stayed exactly where she was.

"I'm sorry, but I…" Anchored against someone she wasn't ready to accept, or ready to release, she needed to explain. "I just can't do this. I barely even know you. We're not even friends. And to answer your question from before. Yes, I've been hurt. Never physically. But when someone you thought loved you betrays that trust…it hurts. Hurts more than you can imagine."

"Then we'll take things slow. If we're meant to be, everything will happen in its own time." For an instant, she felt the resting of his cheek against her hair. "You have my promise, I'll never push you. Never."

"Thank you." Glancing up as they fell back into the slowness of the music, she honestly believed what he'd said.

Suddenly, a salsa blared from the radio, and he stopped moving. Stepped back. "Let's take a break."

"No. This is my kind of music." Swinging her hips from side to side, she couldn't stop herself from spinning and dancing and teasing to the beat.

Laughing and lost in the song, she cha-cha'd backward, wiggling her fingers in a follow-me gesture. He bit the side of his lower lip then smiled all the way to his eyes. Brushed his palms back at the sides of his hair and readily fell into step to the beat. Each on their own, they covered the patio with their steps. Never touching. Yet at times close as a breath away. Locked in each other's moves. They swirled. They shouted. They stomped and swayed. Sexy and sensual. Faster and faster. Around and around and around. Closer and closer. Hotter and hotter and—

The deck door slammed open, and Mark quickly jumped in front of her. His arm held her behind him. Solid and protective.

Dot leaned over the rail. Panic in her eyes. "Come quick. I think Lloyd's having a heart attack."

CHAPTER FIFTEEN

ASHLEY AND MARK rushed to the bedroom, where Lloyd clutched his chest, gasping for air. Perspiration covered his forehead. Immediately, Mark took control and shouted orders first to one of the women, then the other. Dot called the ambulance but dropped the phone when Lloyd went into cardiac arrest. Ashley grabbed the receiver and conveyed information to the dispatcher.

She could tell this wasn't the first time he'd resuscitated someone. He pulled Lloyd to the floor, glanced at a smartwatch on his wrist, and started CPR. "Hurry. Heart stopped. Time, 2250:14. CPR in progress."

Dot wrung her hands, tears rushing down her cheeks until, in a calm voice, Mark told her to get dressed. She obeyed.

He yelled out more specifics for Ashley. "One minute down. CPR still in progress."

Focused, Mark kept the pump rhythm going, he never slowed. Sirens grew louder. Resuscitation was nonstop. He pounded on Lloyd's chest at one point. "Don't give up, Lloyd. Fight, damn it! Fight.

Two minutes down."

Dressed and trembling, Dot knelt next to her husband. She took his hand in hers, being careful not to interfere with Mark's movements. "I love you, my darling. Please stay. I need you."

Finally, Lloyd's chest rose. He took a breath of air, then another and another. Mark stopped the CPR, felt the pulse. He looked at his watch again. "Heartbeat and breathing returned."

He looked at his watch again. "Time 2252:35. Good."

Sirens stopped in the front drive, and Ashley ran to open the door for the paramedics, then followed them back to the bedroom. The medical personnel gathered around Lloyd, opening bags and the AED. Mark stood to the side, conveying information from the past few minutes to an EMT.

Dot took his hand, pressed it to her lips, and whispered, "Thank you, Mark. Thank you."

He patted her hand in return and handed her off to Ashley. Jaw clenched, he walked to the front door and went out into the night. Who was this man who spoke in military time? Who walked with authority? Who had just saved Lloyd's life?

Once stabilized, the medics loaded Lloyd into the ambulance. Hooked up to oxygen and an EKG machine, he looked frail, but he gave a thumbs-up before they closed the doors. Where was the chuckle she'd heard on their walk?

Ashley helped Dot with her purse, keys, and jacket. Then settled her in the front seat of the ambulance where the paramedics had said she could ride. "Mark and I will be there as soon as we lock up the house."

Dot squeezed her hand and nodded. The emergency crew's lights started flashing, and the siren wailed when the ambulance turned onto the road.

Ashley said a short prayer before searching for Mark. She found him seated on a bench on the back patio, elbows rested on his knees, head bowed into his hands. She slid quietly into the spot next to him, content to wait. After a moment, she lightly placed her hand on his tensed shoulders.

He jerked at her touch, as if he'd been in a faraway place and hadn't even seen her. She noticed the wetness on his face. Sweat? Tears? Relief? He leaned back and placed his arm across her shoulders.

"Where did you learn how to do all those things? To stay so calm?"

His other hand reached out and took hers in his. He didn't answer her question.

"We better go. Dot will need us," Mark said.

They doused the patio lanterns, locked the house, and drove to the hospital. On the way, she called Janie to let them know the situation.

Dot was in with Lloyd when they arrived at the hospital in Surryfield, but in a bit, she came out to let them know the doctors had placed him in ICU. Mark answered Dot's questions on the different types of equipment in Lloyd's hospital room. Meanwhile, Ashley listened with a zillion questions floating in her own mind. Before long, Janie and Patrick arrived from the dance.

"We left soon as you called." Janie looked at her watch.

"What time is it?" All she knew was that it was dark outside, with only a partial moon. She'd lost all track of time. And the kiss on the patio seemed a million years ago.

Patrick glanced at the smartwatch on his wrist. "0120:32."

Mark ran his fingers through his hair as he watched Ashley and Janie walk away to find coffee. His deep sigh cleansed the tension from inside. This night wasn't supposed to end in a hospital waiting room.

Patrick glanced around the waiting room. "After talking to one of my paramedic friends making the run tonight, sounds like it was a good thing you were at the Gregory place. By the way, why were you there?"

"Minding my own business," Mark replied.

"That's what I figured. In fact, that's exactly what I told Janie on the way over here. She came up with a wild story about the possibility of you and Ashley." His partner sat down, picked up a magazine. "Yep, that's what I told her. Minding your own business."

"Okay, I get the point. By the way, Brenner called right before I headed over to the Gregory place. Seems the big brass want me to make myself visible in some places around the country that I'd be recognized by my alias. Some of the others on the list are being asked to do the same."

"Why?"

"They say that will give them an idea of how much traction the leak caused for me. See if they got it locked down fast enough."

Patrick rolled his eyes. "So, let me get this straight. The CIA didn't do their job protecting your identity. And now they want you to do their work seeing what the fallout will entail?"

Mark felt the same way. So did the other agents whose cover had been blown. But there weren't many alternatives. "That's the crux of it. They asked if you'd be my backup on the project since you'd know some of the people, there'd be a better chance of one of us catching anything out of the ordinary."

He paused. Gave Patrick time to think. He wouldn't blame him for saying no. In some ways, he hoped he did. But knew deep inside that his partner would do just what he would do for him in return.

Mark watched Ashley and Janie walking back toward them, coffee cups in all hands. How could he let his friend do this? If something happened, he'd never be able to face Janie again. "Listen, tell them you won't go. Don't worry about me. I'll be fine. You've got to think about your wife. About the future you've—"

"I'll go. For you, I'll go. Because you'd do the same for me. But you tell— No, I'll call Brenner myself," Patrick said. "This is the last time. No more. I am out for good after this. And they better scrub all signs of me out of their system."

Mark placed his hand on Patrick's shoulder. "Thanks, man. Your backup means a lot to me. A whole hell of a lot."

"When do we go?"

"They're still getting the route set up. Our final destination will be Washington, D.C. But each night when I check in, they'll give me the new location to head." Mark glanced at his partner. "I figure we need to head to New York by this afternoon. Okay?"

Patrick nodded. Straightened. "Janie and I will be going for a walk now."

Ashley gazed out the third-floor waiting room into the darkness. The dance on the patio flitted through her mind, and her hand brushed across her cheek when she remembered Mark's kisses. What would have happened? She wasn't sure, never would be. Unthinking, she followed the progress of Janie and Patrick as they walked around the hospital parking lot.

"Janie looks upset. Why?" Ashley asked.

Mark crossed the empty waiting room from the opposite end of the wall of windows. "Patrick probably told her we're going to head out for some serious camping. Heard fish are biting big time a few states to the east of here."

Camping? Fishing? How could he think about having a good time after all that had happened in the last couple of hours? Lloyd might not even make it through the next twenty-four hours, and all Mark could think about was fishing?

He took a step toward her. "This isn't what I hoped for this evening."

She stepped back. "Seriously? You are seriously leaving to sit around a campfire while the man whose life you just saved is hooked up to every machine known to mankind."

"Trust me, I wouldn't leave if this trip wasn't more important than—"

"Than what? Fishing?" How could she have been so blind? The man she thought might pull her from her shell had turned out to be the most superficial man she ever met. "Being there for a friend is more important than catching the big one or sleeping on some cold, wet ground. You're just like my ex. He always had a business trip to go on. A business dinner that kept him late."

"I'm not your ex, Ashley."

"The only difference is that you use fishing and camping and who knows what else, all to cover your tracks." Her insides were breaking, but she couldn't be fooled again. Never again. "I shouldn't have trusted him. And I refuse to trust you. Now or ever."

He took another step toward her, and this time she stood fast.

"Are we going to argue again?" Mark reached out and stroked her hair.

She shoved his hand away. "No. A person has to care for it to be worthwhile to argue."

"Not necessarily." Mark straightened, and his

voice conveyed harshness. "You're right about one thing, though. There are a lot of things more important in this world than fishing. More important than me. You. Or us. Whether you like it or not, I leave today."

"Go ahead. Nobody's stopping you."

"Ashley, I have a job to do, and—"

"A job? I thought you were camping, or did you forget your story?" Her throat tightened as she fought to keep her voice even, tears pooling in her mind, then her eyes. Lost in her emotions, she realized meeting him had made her feel again. By feeling, she was vulnerable. She'd built her barriers for the past few years. Letting them fall scared her.

Other women she knew had divorced around the same time as her, and they were already remarried. She wasn't built that way. She barely dated. Hadn't slept with anyone since Bradford. Maybe it was time she figured out why, but not tonight. "I've already had one man in my life with secrets. I don't want another."

His voice softened as he took her hand. "There are things you don't understand."

"Then tell me." Tugging her hand away, she continued. "What would make Janie cry about a camping trip? Why was she crying the other morning before you two left?"

A touch of steel gray touched his blue eyes. She anxiously searched his face for the man from the patio dance, but she couldn't find him beneath the sharp demeanor.

His shoulders straightened as his expression

melded into seriousness. "Aw, hell, I don't need this, Ashley. Not now. Not ever."

She glared at him, and her heart began to ache. "Neither do I. Leave any time you want. Doesn't matter to me one bit."

"I hoped it might. At least a little." He walked to the other end of the room and stared into the dark night sky.

What had happened to her perfect evening?

An hour crept by while they each stayed at their own end of the waiting room. Patrick phoned to say Janie and he were heading home, to call if there was any change. Eventually, the nurses and Lloyd convinced Dot to go home. And Ashley promised to drive her back whenever she wanted. Mark pulled the BMW to the entrance and helped Dot into the front seat while Ashley climbed in the back. Quiet. Alone.

At the house, the emotion of the evening caught up with Dot as they helped her to the master bedroom. Ashley offered to change the sheet for clean ones, but Dot said no. Said she'd feel closer to Lloyd this way, so Ashley straightened them.

Dot took Mark's hands in hers. "Thank you again. Without you, this evening might have turned out differently."

"Get some rest. Tell Lloyd we'll make a few more trails when he's better. Sleep well." He bent and kissed the top of her head.

Ashley helped the suddenly feeble woman change into her gown and snuggle into bed. She kissed her forehead before turning on the night light and closing the bedroom door.

"Guess I'd better be going." Mark retraced the path to the front door. "We'll have to finish our dance another time."

She stepped aside. Opening the front door, she hoped her steadfast look conveyed her message— no more dances. He braced the door with his hand for a moment, determination still in his stance and his eyes. There was also a dejected look on his face that tugged at her heart.

"Ashley, I…"

"I can't do this. I can't be with someone I know is keeping secrets right from the start. I just can't." She shook her head. He could keep his secrets. "But I do want to apologize for the way I acted back at the hospital. We clearly are not in a relationship. And evidently, I'm not ready for one, so I have no right to expect anything of you. I have my past… and you have yours."

There wasn't much he could say. The secrets he carried couldn't be shared with her. Sighing, he stepped out the door onto the porch. "Good night, Ashley."

"Goodbye, Mark. Goodbye."

CHAPTER SIXTEEN

B Y THE LIGHT of the moon, Mark drove to the first place he could turn around past the Gregorys' property, then turned the lights off and drove slowly back to the pull-off he and Lloyd had cut into the pines a couple years ago. Once past the outer trees, a secluded clearing opened. No one could see him there. He and Lloyd had planned it that way.

After dinner a few years back, he'd mentioned stopping at the rest area about twenty miles down the interstate. Truckers and travelers made good use of it for layovers. Lloyd said he had a better idea for the future and would have it ready in a couple of weeks.

Weeks turned into a few months of duty before Mark had returned. When he did, though, Lloyd could hardly wait to show him the area he'd cleared. Told him, day or night, to pull in and no one would know. With the help of a few bushes, mulch, and gravel, even the tire tracks seemed to disappear.

Also, Lloyd's standing invitation to come down

for breakfast any time had made Mark feel more than welcome—like part of the family. He'd taken him up on the invitation a few times when the smell of bacon frying wafted across the land. Most times, he merely pulled in, rested, and moved on. Most times, he doubted they even knew he'd been there.

Tonight, the camouflaged view of the house through the firs and white pines would work to his advantage. Plus, he would hear if anyone went down the driveway.

He cracked a couple of windows to hear the morning sounds better, and a chilly breeze stirred the treetops high above, sending a slight rustle through the wind. There was no need for him to stand watch over the ladies, but he would anyhow. He had no place else to be. The weariness of the night wore on him, but sleep wouldn't come. It was hard to sleep when he was always on alert.

Tonight, he needed to shake off his thoughts about Ashley. The way she looked. The way she smelled. The way she felt in his arms. If he had any guts, he'd walk right down to that front door and…and what? She'd said it herself—she couldn't get involved with a man who kept secrets. And he for sure had secrets. Some even he'd forgotten.

How had he gotten himself into this mess with her? He could crawl into an enemy camp to rescue someone and come out unscathed, but he was no match for this woman.

Readjusting the seat, at least, made him more comfortable, but he needed to get some sleep.

Sleep to lose himself in. Sleep to pass the hours. Sleep…and rest. Lately, there were days he felt like turning forty–two had skewered his entire mind, body, and outlook.

Trouble was, he'd grown tired of doing the same thing year after year. He needed something new. Maybe this new assignment with the FBI and Department of Homeland Security would put everything in perspective. At least his insides felt invigorated again.

Besides which, he was looking forward to sleeping in his own bed in his own home in D.C. The one place on earth where security, familiarity, and peace welcomed him any time he wanted. In fact, those had been the exact words his mother had written into her will.

He'd always realized she came from a wealthy family but had no idea, until the probate attorney read the will, just exactly what all and how much that entailed. She'd left everything to him. Said she understood he'd chosen a career of commitment to defend the United States just like his dad. Said she also understood he'd need a base to come home to and rest. And that even though he was seldom there, she hoped he didn't sell the family home there in Washington. She'd even mentioned that one day he'd find his own life and understand how much he needed a base. She'd been a very smart woman.

He'd kept the house, and he enjoyed the few times a year he made it back to D.C. to sleep in his own bed. He breathed deep then sighed long and slow. Yes, he was tired. He needed to go home. Go to base. Ashley was right. He had secrets. Secrets he couldn't share…ever.

CHAPTER SEVENTEEN

ASHLEY'S VISIT TO the Gregorys had quickly turned into an extended stay when Lloyd needed more tests, possibly surgery. His brother had insisted he see a top-notch cardiologist in St. Louis. Even drove to Nature's Crossing to pick them up. But since they had no idea when they'd return, Lloyd insisted on finding a house sitter before they left town. And when everyone had turned in her direction, Dot had said please, and Lloyd had sagged with worry, she'd agreed to stay.

Her one-week trip had turned into two, now going on three, and here she was still enjoying herself. She'd had time to check in with a number of local radio stations about the process for proposing a new segment on their broadcast calendar. Plus, fall had turned out to be a perfect time for enjoying the change of scenery. And the change of menu.

Fridays at Red's Corner Market meant barbeque, Patrick's specialty, but he was out of town with Mark. Evidently, the first time that had happened after they'd bought the store, Janie had taken on the job. The customers had told her that as much as they loved her lunch salads, she lacked a certain finesse when it came to barbeque.

Now, when Patrick wasn't there, the previous owners, Lorna and Gus Wills, always volunteered to take over the grilling. Ashley made a special trip to the store just to see what was on the special menu for today. Of course, she'd done that every day since the Gregorys left town. If she ate much more fattening food, she'd have to join a gym while she was in town. And from what she'd seen, there was no such thing around. That meant driving over to Henton or Surryfield.

The other reason she came was to ask Janie some questions. And she planned to get some answers. Answers on Mark. He might not be here in person, but the man was driving her crazy in her dreams. Dreams that always ended with uncertainty. Doubts. Questions.

Day or night, his blue eyes were always a blink away. Last night, she woke tangled in her sheets, and the pillow clutched against her had been heat and muscles in her dreams. That was when she decided to get some answers.

Such as why had Mark and Patrick both worn the same type of smartwatch. One she'd never seen before. And why did they both tell time in the same military jargon?

Ashley waved to Gus in passing. "Smells so good, I could stay here all day."

"We'll make sure to put you a dinner aside this evening. Chicken or pork steak?" Gus asked.

"My waist says chicken, but my tummy says pork steak. Surprise me."

"You got it."

"Where's Janie?"

"She stepped over to the house. Give her a buzz on the intercom."

Ashley went inside to the two-way system on the wall and pressed the button. "Ashley calling Janie. Anybody there?"

"You bet I'm here. Come on over."

Janie met her halfway there, and arm-in-arm, they made their way to the front door of the house.

"I'm so glad you're staying at the Gregory house for a while," Janie said in high spirits.

"So am I. What are you up to? You're on cloud nine," Ashley asked.

"I talked to Patrick. Whenever he's out-of-town, I wait by the phone about eleven each day to see if he gets to call. And he did."

"How many fish have they caught?"

"Fish?"

"Yeah. You know. Camping. Fishing. I wondered how many fish they'd caught." Ashley tried to sound nonchalant.

"We didn't talk about fish. Just some personal stuff and the store. You know how it is. Always something going on. Patrick being Patrick, he wants to keep on top of everything. This place is his pride and joy." Janie paused for a breath as they entered the kitchen. "He loved retiring here."

Ashley sat down at the kitchen table. "What did Patrick do before he retired?"

"How about some lemonade and snickerdoodles? Eloise Collier, Peabody's sister, sent some over with him yesterday."

Janie avoided questions almost as well as Mark.

"Sounds good to me."

Janie placed a platter of cookies on the table, then cocked her head to the side and scurried down the hall. "Excuse me a moment."

"What's wrong?"

"Nothing. I have to get the phone."

The phone on the wall wasn't ringing, but a faint sound came from elsewhere in the house, and Janie disappeared into the room at the end of the hall. Just like Patrick had done Ashley's first night in town. Whatever was in that room had become a mystery she was intent on solving. Of course, she'd never dare open the door. But no one said she couldn't ask questions.

The first camping trip had come into play right after the call from Mark that night. Ashley's instincts told her there was more to the phone calls than a couple of men fishing. More to the men than fishing. But what? What could be so private?

While she waited, Ashley examined some of the beautiful antiques scattered through the hearth room. Having attended some of the traveling antique shows, she knew some of the items were rarely found in such original mint condition. Must have cost a top-of-the-line dollar, too.

One of the glass display cases held teapots, cups, and saucers. Another cabinet held an assortment of pewter and one more, a collection of steins. The dining room table, hutch, and buffet appeared to be English, from the 1800s. A Davenport desk in the entry hall was probably 1840s. On a pedestal in one corner of the dining room was a porcelain vase, which captivated her. She eyed the piece, trying to determine the timeframe.

"Beautiful, isn't it?" Janie said, entering the room.

"When I was growing up, my parents took us on at least one antiquing trip a year. And they'd always come back with something unique." She loved that flash of memory. "Then my dad and I would spend time together researching the piece online. One thing would lead to another, and suddenly I would have learned something about the entire time period of the piece. Guess some of that need to know rubbed off on me."

"Sounds like a fun way to have learned history. Go ahead. Pick it up. Have a closer look."

"Are you sure? I can already tell this is an exceedingly rare piece." Ashley lifted the vase with both hands. She turned it every which way, peered inside and underneath, then carefully placed the piece back on the carved, mahogany pedestal. "Besides, I'm sure he wouldn't mind," Janie voiced.

Ashley laughed. "I don't know about that. Patrick probably thinks I'm one big klutz."

"I was talking about Mark."

"Why should he care?" At the mere mention of his name, stomach butterflies tickled her insides.

Janie must have seen the dumbstruck look on her friend's face. "He shipped the vase and pedestal from China a couple years ago. Said we should keep the pieces setting out. Enjoy the splendor. Kind of like an on-loan program."

Ashley smiled and nodded. "Some of your antique savvy must have rubbed off on him."

"Afraid it's the other way around. Patrick says years ago when the two of them first teamed up, he instructed Mark on the job. Mark schooled him on antiques."

"So, does he make a lot of trips to China?" Ashley monitored her words, her tone.

Janie moved to the tea display cabinet, opened the door, and picked up a porcelain teapot. She removed the top. "This was the first piece Patrick ever bought for me. It was my birthday, and he gave it to me at dinner. We were still dating then. I thought it was the loveliest thing I'd ever seen. But every time I moved it; a tinkling noise rattled inside. Patrick looked surprised, said he hoped the teapot wasn't broken."

She replaced the lid and hugged the container. "When I looked inside, there was my engagement ring. We were married a month later. Been together seven years now."

Ashley noticed she still hadn't answered her original question.

After replacing the container on the shelf, Janie closed the door.

"That's really sweet." Ashley already figured out how crazy in love Janie was, but now she realized how much Patrick must love Janie in return. A knight in shining armor. Too bad she didn't have one of her own. "Maybe I should talk to Mark about looking into some antiques for me the next time he's in Asia. Or does he travel to a lot of other places, too?"

"This desk also belongs to him. His other finds are in climate-controlled storage units." Again, Janie skillfully ignored the question. "If he gets many more pieces, he should buy a storage business. Be cheaper that way."

This time, Ashley heard the distant phone ring a second before Janie once again cocked her head.

"Excuse me." Janie dashed to the muffled sound.

Ashley gently brushed her fingers across Mark's polished writing table. She tried to imagine what had attracted him to the piece. Maybe the deep, rich grain. The lines were warm, yet elegant. Beautiful burled walnut. Undoubtedly, he'd pulled the drawers out and examined the dove-tailed corners, ran his fingers across the bottom to make sure it had been hand-planed, and looked for any signs of touch-up stain.

She wondered if he ran his hands along the top and edges the way she did to find nicks. Her body shivered with enticing tingles. Okay, enough thoughts about his hands and fingers.

Carrying a cordless phone in her hand, Janie giggled as she came down the hall.

"Patrick again?" Ashley asked.

"Nope, this time it's Mark. He heard you were here and…" Janie shoved the phone in her hand. "You can talk to him."

Ashley tucked the phone against her ear. "I'm not sure I want to talk to you, Mr. I've-Gone-

Camping."

"Could have fooled me. I mean, it's not like you threw me out or anything," he teased with a voice smooth as silk. "And, if I'm so bad, then why'd you take the call, pretty lady?"

If she knew that answer, life would be a lot easier. "To be polite."

"Just polite?"

"Just polite." Lying would get her in trouble.

Silence backfilled between them. She swallowed, sighed, smiled. "What did you want to talk to me about?"

"Oh, yeah." His voice held a soft chuckle. "What do you have on today? A parka? Flannel shirt? Maybe you've got on that nice little black tank top from before."

"You are the most infuriating man." Ashley reactively glanced at her top. "It's none of your business what I'm wearing. Or what I look like. I'll wear what I want when I want and that's that."

He full out laughed. "You are something, Ashley Lanovan. Really something."

She smiled. "So are you."

"I hear you may be around for a while," Mark said. "Next time I stop by the Gregory place, I'll bring the wineglasses."

"Maybe I won't answer the door." There she was lying again. "In fact, I think I'll hang up right now."

"No one's stopping you. But is that really what you want to do? Hang up on me?" The hoarseness in his voice, whispered with seduction. "You already pushed me out the door. Now you want to hang up on me. Before long, I'll get the hint that you really don't like me. Is that what you really want, Ashley?"

His final questions had taken on a serious tone. A serious voice.

"I don't know…I'm not sure…I…I…" She had no other answer. "You confuse me, Mark. I don't even know what you do for a living. I need answers."

He sighed with resignation. "Fair enough. Let's just say I'm a man who doesn't want to hang up the phone right now." He sighed again, slow and easy. "We didn't even finish our dance. Why don't we see where the music takes us? Can you do that much?"

Her fingers skimmed across the antique desk. Could she? The wood felt sleek and polished and sturdy. Could she take this one step at a time, risk the pain of disappointment again in her life? Mark wasn't her lying ex. Mark was Mark, not Bradford. She polished her prints from the wood with the soft material of her sleeve.

"I like to dance," she whispered.

"Good. So do I."

They talked another ten minutes about nothing before they each said good night in a civilized tone. Her wants, her needs, her mind, her body, her what-ifs were working overtime. She glanced at her top again. A loose-fitting beige sweater. Maybe she should buy her own black tank top, one size—maybe two sizes—too small. Just in case.

Enough was enough, though, and before she

allowed herself to even imagine another date with him, she needed answers. "Who does Mark work for?"

Janie glanced at her watch. "Look at the time. We'd better get over to the store before Lorna and Gus think we've deserted them."

"What does he do, Janie?" Ashley didn't move. "I'm really falling for him. I deserve to know what I'm getting myself into."

"You need to ask him yourself."

"Okay. What was Patrick's job before he retired?"

Janie straightened. "He worked for the government."

"What about now?"

"Patrick retired so we could move to Nature's Crossing. Where it's calm. Where we have good friends. And...where it's safe." A slight edge entered Janie's voice. "When you've worked your whole life to give others that life, it's nice to finally have some for yourself."

Ashley's brain pulsed to make sense of the words. From the look on her friend's face, what had been shared was important.

Janie looked lovingly at the teapot. "We're living the dream some never live long enough to enjoy."

"Are they really fishing?"

"You might say that."

"I don't understand." With her soft sleeve, Ashley gently wiped her palm print from the desk once again.

Janie paused at the security panel, waiting for Ashley to go outside before she engaged the alarm.

"Why do you always set the alarm at the house?" Ashley asked.

"Comes with the job."

The chilly breeze made them walk briskly toward the grocery, while a strained silence filled the air. Ashley lagged behind. Thinking.

Janie stopped, shook her head, and turned to her friend. "Sometimes when people retire, they still consult with the company they leave. Patrick is an occasional consultant. As far as Mark is concerned, you'll have to ask him."

Ashley's thoughts raced as fast as her pounding heart. She felt her friend spoke something meant only for the breeze. "I don't know what you mean. Please help me understand."

"Do you like Mark for more than hello-goodbye?"

"I don't know. There's something about him...I... I don't know. He could be a drug runner for all I know."

"What would make you think that?"

"He's full of secrets. He's always got a job. And his phone is a very important part of his life."

"First off, he's not a drug runner. Second, you have a *very* vivid imagination."

"Hey, I majored in journalism and media. If you want to get ahead in that line of work you need an imagination," Ashley replied. "And you quickly learn to ask a lot of questions."

"Well, if you decide you care for Mark, really, really care for him, then you have the right to ask him your questions." Janie took a few steps toward the grocery. "Remember, don't judge what you don't understand. No matter what."

CHAPTER EIGHTEEN

HOURS LATER, HUDDLED in the Gregory living room, Ashley enjoyed a glass of wine after dinner. Thankfully, they had installed gas logs in the marble hearth, complete with remote control, unlike the wood-burning fireplace in the family room downstairs. The small blaze made her feel warm and cozy.

She intended to read, but her mind kept wandering to the shops sitting empty in the old part of downtown. Bits and pieces of conversations she'd had with Janie, Peabody, and the Gregorys pushed their way into her thoughts. Wasn't long before her business sense joined right along.

Dot had used the words "imminent demise" of the old buildings if Chase had his way. He'd likely tear everything down to erect plain buildings or strip malls, whatever would bring him the biggest return on his money, the fastest. One of the reasons Lloyd stayed on the Town Council was to be a vote for the old part of town. Plus, the evening she first met Peabody, he'd lamented no one could see the potential in the old buildings. He mentioned how it would be a different story if he were younger with his current finances.

She snuggled farther under the afghan and returned to her book. After reading and rereading the same two paragraphs for the fourth time, she gave up. Instead, she jotted down a to-do list for her upcoming trip to Washington, DC. For as long as she could remember, she and her mother had made an annual pre-holiday jaunt to the glorious city. This year neither her mother or Linda or Tracie were available to make the trip. Ashley had still purchased tickets for a concert at the Kennedy Center. Two, just in case someone's plans changed. She might have lost her job, but she still planned to enjoy the holidays. With or without someone by her side.

Once she'd completed the list, she aimlessly began to doodle. Upon closer inspection, the doodles were parts of the old downtown area of Nature's Crossing. How many small, connected spaces had there been? What had the old post office and grocery store looked like? What about the houses down the main side street? Churches? Why were all the churches grouped in one area? That would be a question for Lloyd. Or maybe even Peabody.

"What am I doing?" She set the pen and paper aside and turned on the television. Hungry for a snack, she pulled bread from the pantry, but that's as far as she got before pulling the pad of paper back in front of her. Randomly, she added trees and lights to the old town sketch, drawing more of the layout as she knew it to have been…or was it as it could be once again.

This was ridiculous. She was only visiting Nature's Crossing. Nothing more.

She tossed the pen down and fidgeted with the twist tie on the bread, her mind a jumble with questions and ideas. Glancing to see what time it was, she scanned the "Who To Call" list Dot had left for her on the fridge. Then dialed the number for Peabody.

"Hello," he answered.

"Hi, this is Ashley. I hope I didn't disturb you."

Peabody's congenial voice flowed through the receiver. "Not a bit. I was watching reruns before the news comes on. Is there a problem?"

"No problem." She walked to the living room. "Have you heard from Lloyd and Dot?"

"A message on the machine said they got there okay and are waiting for some test results."

"That's good."

A friendly hush permeated the space between them.

"What have you been up to?" Peabody said.

"I went by to see Janie this afternoon. Had some of the cookies you dropped off yesterday. They were delicious."

"Wait till closer to Christmas when Eloise kicks into high-gear baking. I sometimes think her motto is 'no calorie shall be left unbaked'."

"My hips will have to watch out for those." Ashley laughed. "I guess you're wondering why I called."

"You mean it wasn't for my witty conversation?"

"Yes and no. I've been thinking about the old part of town. And, well, I know you said you'd like to get out if the weather's nice. But even if it's not, would you show me the row of buildings you own down there?" She began to pace from room to room.

"I'd love to." His voice seemed to expand with energy. "Anything in particular you want to see?"

"Just show me what you think of as the town's potential."

"I'll be looking forward to that. Oh…wait a minute…oh." Peabody seemed distracted. "The Andy Griffith rerun is coming on. How about I pick you up there at the Gregorys' tomorrow morning at ten?"

"I'll be ready."

"Good night. Thanks for calling."

"Night." Ashley smiled at her placement below reruns.

She turned the radio on to a jazz station, then danced around the room to the silky beat. The melodies dug into her mind, leaving her in the arms of her imaginary partner. Maybe this time she needed to be the one to reach out to him. She dialed Janie's home number.

"Hello?" Janie sounded groggy.

"It's Ashley. Did I wake you?"

"I was watching TV. Must have fallen asleep."

They talked for over an hour. She even shared her plans for touring with Peabody tomorrow.

Ashley clicked the radio off. "Look at the time.

I'd better let you go since you've got to get up early in the morning to open the store."

"I'm glad you called. I was feeling a little down. Lonely, you might say," Janie replied.

"By the way, I almost forget the reason I called. The next time you talk to Patrick, tell him to let Mark know I have glasses. Anytime he wants, I have glasses." Ashley smiled. Maybe they could talk a little over wine. Maybe dance. Maybe continue where they left off on the patio. Maybe—

"You can count on me."

"What?" Ashley pulled her mind back to the phone call.

Janie's voice quieted. "It'll be a while before they can call again. That's why there were so many calls earlier today."

"Hey, I've got an idea. Why don't you come out for a pajama party one of these nights? Figure out when Lorna or Gus can watch the store." Ashley bubbled with excitement.

"Sounds like fun and just what I need. Me, the dog, and the cat have had the house to ourselves over a week and a half. Frankly, I think they're tired of hearing me talk." Janie laughed. "I miss my Paddy."

CHAPTER NINETEEN

MARK TOOK HIS key from the hotel's front desk clerk, then walked over to get a cup of complimentary coffee. The last couple of days had been long. One clue leading to another and another and another. The CIA putting him in positions to see if anyone recognized him. So far, so good. And his photos had been wiped from the internet, but as they always say, screenshots are a dime a dozen.

All he wanted now was a good night's sleep. He returned to the front desk just as Patrick finished his registration. The two men took the elevator to the third floor. Their rooms were on the backside of the hotel, overlooking the lot where they'd parked.

"Think I'll order a pizza in tonight. Don't know about you, but I'm worn out." Patrick slipped his key card in the lock to his room.

Something didn't feel right to Mark. Hadn't for the past hour. He glanced from one end of the hall to the other. Walked back to the elevator and peered out the window to the hotel's front parking lot. His BMW was parked in the rear, and with the location of the room he'd requested, he'd have a clear view of anything out of the ordinary in that direction, but still, he wanted one final view of the layout of the land in front.

For the past hour, the prickle on the back of his neck had increased his misgivings. Whatever was coming was close. His misgivings hinged on the doom building in his gut. More foreboding than he'd felt in a hell of a long time. He stretched his hand taut, then relaxed with a couple of loose fist movements before walking back to his room, one door past Patrick's room.

His partner still stood in the same spot, except his suitcase was on the floor, his hand shoved into his coat pocket. He raised his eyebrows in question. Mark shook his head, shoved his key in his own door's lock.

"Do you want a pizza?" Patrick opened the door to his room and stepped inside.

"Sure. Think I'll take a shower and check in with the boss. Hey, order me a salad, too."

"See you when the food gets here."

Relieved to have a chance to relax, he turned the shower on and closed the bathroom door to build up some steam. Soon enough, the warmth of the water pelted his body. At least this assignment held sanitary water and clean clothes. That hadn't always been the case in his line of work. Of course, the U. S. government had never promised him hygiene.

Shaved, showered, and dressed, he was ready for dinner. Once he called his boss, he could call it a day.

Patrick's familiar rhythmic knock on the door meant food had arrived, so Mark held the door open, motioning his partner inside, then laughed. He was loaded with two large pizza boxes, a sack on top, a liter of cola under one arm, and a full ice bucket in the other hand. Mark felt like he should tip Patrick for the delivery. The man was definitely prepared for hunger.

Mark sat down and called Brenner.

"About time you checked in." His boss answered on the first ring.

"We ran into heavy road construction. Were you worried about us?"

"Huh. Not even on a bad day. Where are you two?"

"Finishing up a once-over of the FBI's Florida setup. We'll get an early start to Washington tomorrow. Should be in your office by mid-afternoon." Mark pointed at an empty space in the pizza when his pal opened the box.

Patrick patted his stomach and grabbed another slice before dragging a chair over to the small round hotel table. He filled two glasses with ice and poured the soda.

Mark laughed at a comment from Brenner and caught his buddy's attention, pointing at the phone. "He heard the ice and wants to know if we're having a party."

Patrick leaned over the phone. "Not hardly. Now hurry up and give him the facts. Otherwise, I'll eat all the pizza and he'll starve."

Mark listened for a while to instructions coming from the other end of the line. Pizza would be stone cold by the time Brenner shut up.

"Do Patrick and I know each other this time?" Mark asked.

"No. Once you hit town, there'll be separate cars. Separate hotels. You know the drill." After a long pause, Brenner continued. "I don't need to tell you how important this mission is. Once you make it through not being recognized tomorrow, I'd say you've been spared on any computer leaks coming back on you."

"That's what I want to hear." Being reminded shoved an icicle into Mark's spine. But at least he was close to the end of the leak fiasco.

"You two be careful out there."

"Careful is our middle name." Mark ended the call, then rummaged in the sack for his salad.

Patrick set his fourth slice down, picked up his glass, and swirled the ice. He got up and walked to the window. "He doesn't say that very often. Probably joking."

Mark grabbed a wedge of pizza. "Sounded serious to me. And, before I forget, we don't know each other once we pick up the cars in D.C."

"Then maybe I'll get to eat more often." Continuing to look outside, his partner laughed, but there was uneasiness in his voice.

Mark shoved his food away and stared at the table. Maybe he wasn't so hungry after all, either. He pulled a deck of cards from his suitcase. "How about a game?"

"Maybe later." Patrick flipped the TV on and sat down.

Taking a bite of food ever so often, Mark pushed his own uneasy thoughts away with solitaire. Before he knew it, the local news had come and gone.

"Think I'll go to my room," Patrick said.

"Remember, no phone calls home."

"Yeah, I know." Patrick stood and stretched. "Oh, almost forgot. I called Janie late last night. She said she had a message for you from Ashley."

Mark's right heel tapped the floor until he willed it to stop.

Patrick tossed the last slice of pizza onto a napkin and headed to the door.

"Okay, I give up. What'd did Ashley say?" Mark asked.

"Sounded kind of silly to me. Something about her having wineglasses."

Mark's imagination kicked into overdrive. She'd actually countered his tease. Maybe she had decided to give him a second chance. He grinned at the thought of wine and glasses and her long legs tangled with his.

Patrick glanced over his shoulder. "You remind me of a buck chasing the scent during season. Done gone and got yourself snagged, haven't you?"

"I thought you were leaving."

"I am. I am. See ya in the morning." Patrick stepped out into the hallway and pulled the door closed behind him.

Mark set the hotel locks on the inside of his door, then a couple he carried with him when he traveled. He scanned the parking lot, from his window, once again. Looked like a full house at the motel tonight.

Something bothered him, though. The look of the lot. But he couldn't quite figure out why. Cold crept across his shoulders. Prickle on his scalp. He dealt himself another round of solitaire. Then another…and another. Thinking. Waiting. Waiting for what he didn't know.

Lights off about midnight, he checked the lot one last time before turning in. Two empty spaces near the end. He visualized the scene from before. What had been there earlier? What was new? Maybe he did need to get out of the agency. Stop worrying about everything.

His phone rang with Brenner's ring tone.

"Yeah," Mark answered.

"Your name has come up on the dark web."

"Okay. We already knew my alias was out there." He raked his fingers through his hair. "So, what's new?"

"I'm sorry, man." Brenner cleared his throat. "This is your actual name—Mark Garmund."

A stab of pain hit his gut. His head. His soul. He eased into the chair beside the table that had housed pizza a short time a short time ago. Bracing his elbow on the top, he rested his forehead in the palm of his hand. His world would never be the same again. Never.

Was this how his dad had felt during their last time having ice cream? Ice cream and a talk he couldn't fully remember. Had his dad caught wind of something? Something he knew could be the end. His dad had waited too long get out…too damn long.

"I quit! Effective now." Mark placed a motion device on the window and shoved one of his Glocks under his pillow. Another beneath the cushion in the chair.

All the while, his boss kept talking and talking and talking. Trying to talk him down. Trying to get him to stay. Didn't work. Mark had tuned him out while he texted the Park Service.

His boss took a deep breath, blew it out. "Now, why don't you—"

"Shut up, Brenner. Shut up and listen." He focused on the sound of the heat blowing through the room's system. Focused and calmed. "While you've been spouting your bull, I've texted the Park Service. Accepted their job offer. Bottom line, I'll train my replacement in December. But once I show him the ropes, in January, I'm gone. That's it." He ended the call and crawled into bed, fully dressed.

Already, the load seemed to rest a little lighter on his mind. Maybe he'd find a little sleep during the night. Of course, there'd be no sweet dreams. What had ever made him think he could have a normal life? Not possible. The past he carried as baggage was too heavy to risk on a life with Ashley. Too dangerous.

His phone vibrated with an incoming text from Patrick in the next room. *Got a call from Brenner. Told me everything. You okay?*

He tapped the microphone symbol to respond. "Yeah. Why wouldn't I be? I'm just a walking target."

CHAPTER TWENTY

MID-MORNING SUNSHINE GREETED Ashley as she watched for Peabody from the kitchen window. At the sight of his car, she threw on her jacket, grabbed her leather tote, and raced out the door, being sure to lock it behind her.

"Good girl. People in this area still leave their doors unlocked. But in this day and age, you've got to take precautions," Peabody said as she slid into the seat.

She slipped on her sunglasses and fastened the seatbelt. "Comes from city living. Don't think I'll ever lose that habit."

"Sad to say, but even Nature's Crossing isn't as safe as it used to be. Now, are you ready for our adventure?"

"Ready and excited. Before I forget, thank you for showing me around."

"It's me that should be thanking you. When someone shows an interest in my property it's always a pleasure. After we inspect the town, we'll go for lunch at Della's Dream over in Henton. That is, if you've got time." Peabody's expression lit with happiness.

"I'd love to. Far as time goes, I've got lots to spare." She smiled and settled in.

Ashley pulled a pen from her bag and took notes whenever Peabody pointed out a site of interest. Her sketch of the town from the previous evening was secured under the front flap of her leather notebook. Today, she began a new diagram complete with location numbers to correspond with her notes.

Peabody slowed or stopped in front of numerous buildings and vacant lots around the entire community, and a little of the close areas of the county. Most of the people who lived in the area were at work, so the narrow streets were mainly empty. The few cars parked at the curb or in short driveways wore the look of wear-and-tear for the most part. A great deal of the time, even the well-kept homes cried out for new siding or, at least, a new coat of paint. Roofs showed the signs of age along with newer asphalt shingles from a patch job.

The silver-haired man spoke proudly of his community, though. Finally, they neared the old downtown section of Nature's Crossing. "I'll give you an overview of the town before we get to my row of buildings. Since you're taking notes, you'll be able to piece together how it's changed since the past. We'll start here at the corner, where the original City Hall once stood."

For the next hour, the two toured the city, till Peabody pulled to a stop in front of his long row of adjoining shops on Lake Street.

"What happened to the City Hall?" Ashley asked.

His smile returned. "Got old like me, so the city decided to add a few government rooms to the rear of the library. City still owns the land, though, along with the old school grounds."

Gloves on and jacket hood raised, Ashley exited the car. "I noticed the new park before. That's nice for the children."

"Seems there were a number of people, named in a will, sharing interest in the property. Most of them didn't even realize they had an interest. When the city approached them with the idea of a park, they all donated their share to Nature's Crossing's Park Association."

"You have a Park Association?"

Imagining what the old part of town must have looked like in its prime made her wonder why no one had restored that vintage feel with quaint shops and restaurants. Seemed like a clear-cut way to bring more people to the town, even if they only came for a day.

"Not really, but it sounded good on paper. We had to name the project something for the legalities." Fingering a set of keys he pulled from his pocket, he searched the numbers on them to find the one he needed as they stopped in front of the first door in a long white concrete block building. "The city bought the playground equipment and had it installed. The Ladies Garden Club donates the flowers and keeps them up. Wish we could get something done with the school grounds, but we do what we can."

Peabody jiggled the key in the lock until the door creaked open, the smell of age escaping. He reached down and lifted a battery-operated lantern sitting just inside the door. "No need to keep the electricity on, so I keep one of these light things in each shop."

Unhooking one side of a cloth hanging across the front glass allowed the sunlight to pour through. "Plenty bright in here now. When we get to the smaller back room of the shop, we'll need the lantern."

Old buildings were nothing new to Ashley. She'd visited a lot of antique shops, some for enjoyment, some for the events show. For the most part, antique stores were housed in older buildings with the usual dust and cobwebs which seemed to sprout overnight. She was pleasantly surprised by this one. Of course, there were no antiques here, but the shop's feel called for something to that effect.

The newly painted pale-beige walls offset the white woodwork. The concrete floor shined in a dark green. No cobwebs hung in the corners. No brown water spots marred the white ceiling. And not a smudge on the sparkling clean front window.

The second room, maybe a few feet shorter, was a copy of the front minus the big windowpane. Here there was a double-locked back door and a kitchen-sized window. A couple of lawn chairs stood folded against the wall.

"Are the five shops all the same size in this row building?" Ashley asked.

"All except one. It used to be a café, so they

had a pass-through cut in the dividing wall." He opened the rear door and stepped out into the yard, pointing to the north. "Overall, the land runs about thirty feet back. See how it adjoins the church grounds?"

"Do you own these?" she asked.

"My sister Eloise and I inherited them from our parents. Neither of us can bring ourselves to sell."

The two of them walked the area behind the buildings, where two enormous oak trees seemed to stand guard. She imagined the shady coolness they must provide in the summer.

"I couldn't help but notice how nice the interior looked. Is someone opening a store?" Ashley asked.

He chuckled as they stepped back inside the shop. "No, that's just our way of staying in touch with our roots. Once a week, one of us cleans the rooms. You should see us when we both come. Sometimes we'll bring lunch with us and get to reminiscing till supper."

Ashley rounded the corner to the front room. Screamed and stepped back as she dropped her pen. Kneejerk reaction, she clutched the notebook to her chest. "Chase! What are you doing in here?"

He took a couple steps farther into the shop. Closer in her direction.

"What's wrong?" Peabody looked around her into the sunlit front room.

The young man leered at her. "Didn't mean to scare you, honey. Seems like every time I see you that happens."

Peabody pushed her aside and walked to the

front door. Pointing at the intruder, he gripped the doorknob with his other hand. "Get out, Chase. Now!"

"Calm down, old man. I was just trying to be neighborly." Chase loosely pumped his hands up and down. "Saw the door open. Thought the wind might have blown it in."

"My car's parked right out front. Did it ever occur to you I might be here?" Peabody said.

Chase picked up Ashley's pen from the floor and twirled it in his fingers. From his six-foot frame, he looked down at the aging yet spirited old man. "I'm still thinking about opening a real estate office here. Know of anybody who wants to rent some space? Uncle Chadwick said I should ask around."

"Can't say as I do. You'll have to excuse us, we were leaving." Peabody motioned to the open door again.

Chase turned, then stopped in front of Peabody. "How about you? You've got plenty of shops here in town. How about I rent one of your places? Maybe two."

"They're not for rent."

"I'd give you a good price."

Peabody's gaze shot arrows as he inched the door closed, little by little, behind Chase. "You could pay me a million dollars and I'd not rent to you."

Chase changed his center of attention back to Ashley, tossed the pen toward her. "I hear you'll be around town for a bit."

She grabbed it mid-air and looked him square in the face. "For a while."

"Then we'll probably run into each other again. Maybe one of these times you won't be so frightened. Don't forget, I'm still available for anything you might need." He wiped the corner of his mouth with his middle finger and grinned. "Anything at all."

"There's nothing I'll be needing from you," she said.

Chase stepped out the doorway and flung a momentary look at Peabody. "Let me know if you change your mind about renting, old man. Don't wait too long, though. I'd hate to get a condemnation order on the building."

Peabody slammed the door shut without reply.

Washington, D.C. Home of U.S. government. Flags. Laws. Rights. Memorials.

Mark's town. Felt good to be home. He loved this place.

Heading out of the garage where the government had set up a fictional car rental lot, Patrick turned right. His compact car quickly became just one of the many. His instructions were to reacquaint himself with new stats on a gun runner organization he'd dealt with years before his retirement. Let the agents currently working that never-ending case know what, and who, had changed in the organization he'd infiltrated back then. The two men wouldn't meet up again till sometime next week.

Next in line, Mark turned left in the nondescript

car he'd picked up, leaving his BMW at his house earlier today. His goal—get a feel for working with the FBI and DHS in a tourist setting. He crossed the Arlington Memorial Bridge and headed south toward Mount Vernon.

Tomorrow, he'd travel to the Blue Ridge Mountain area in North Carolina. Anything he could learn from agents already in the field in other locations would make his life easier once he had his own territory in the Mark Twain Forest, Table Rock, and Lake Ozark areas of Missouri.

All that stood between him and being able to enjoy life in the United States was one more CIA assignment. Just one.

Patrick and he would meet up again in Washington next week. Then they'd drive back to Nature's Crossing together one final time as counterintelligence agents. Only one more assignment. One more drive.

CHAPTER TWENTY-ONE

ASHLEY STOOD IN front of her mirror the next morning, combing her hair and contemplating how long she could go without a haircut and highlights. Once dressed, she darted outside to retrieve the small weekly magazine type periodical from the porch. Since the house set a-ways from the road, the carrier made a loop through the circle drive and left the paper. Just another friendly touch of the community, or a smart newspaper person trying to keep their business afloat. Either way, she approved.

Eating her breakfast, Ashley read the article on "A Smart Cook Would Begin Her Baking Now" from the Special Happenings sections. It included such hints as how to freeze the goodies and thaw them whenever needed. She giggled. A bakery was her cook when it came to pastry. Then again, she hadn't seen a bakery any place in Nature's Crossing. Or a beauty shop or barber's sign, either.

Her cell phone chimed.

"Hello," she answered.

"Are you up and about?" Janie asked.

"Yep, in fact, I'm reading the newspaper. Do you bake ahead for holidays and freeze cookies, pies, or cakes?"

"What?"

Ashley quoted the article. "Now, back to my question. Do you bake and freeze?"

"As a busy entrepreneur, I don't find time to freeze," Janie responded with a teasing Julia Child tone. "So, with that in mind, the answer would be, there is no need to bake. Problem solved."

"The weekly journal says this is serious stuff." Ashley spoke through her laugher. "I'm thinking bakery, but I haven't seen one."

"There's one over in Henton, that'll do in a pinch. Most times, folks around here hope Eloise brings them some of what she bakes during the holidays."

Ashley scrunched her hair in her hand. "What about beauty shops?"

"A lady on the far side of town has a combination beauty/barber shop in her basement. I drive over to Surryfield. It's only an hour away and lots bigger than Henton. Has a college and a regional airport. We can take a trip over sometime next week if you want."

Ashley tidied the table while put her friend on speakerphone as they talked. "I'd like that."

"In the meantime, you mentioned a pajama party. Is tonight okay?"

"Great."

"What time?"

Excited at the prospect of spending an evening

with nothing to do but have fun seemed perfect to Ashley. "I'm open. You bring snacks, and I'll order pizza. What do you like on it?"

"About anything. There is one slight problem, though." Janie's serious Julia Child impersonation returned. "In this small metropolitan area there is not a bakery. There is not a beauty shop. And, most certainly, there is *not* a pizza parlor."

Ashley stopped and stared at the counter. "Oh, good gravy grief. How do you survive?"

"I own a grocery store," Janie stated the obvious. "I'll cook up one of our special pizzas from the deli and bring it along. We can always nuke it if it gets too cold."

"Sounds good. We can binge watch old movies while we eat."

"We are really two exciting women, aren't we?" Janie laughed. "See you later."

For the rest of the morning, Ashley answered emails and searched new antique postings on the web. After lunch, she decided to make a trip to the library. At first, Ms. Lavender, the tall and slender aging librarian, was hesitant to issue her a card since she didn't "technically live" in the community. But when Eloise happened in to return an album, she vouched for her.

"I wonder if you could help me find what I'm searching for?" Ashley pulled a list from her purse, handing it off to Peabody's sister.

Eloise explained the layout of the library, until a quick beep sounded in front of the building. "Any other day, I'd be glad to stay and help, but Fred wants to go to the movies over in Surryfield. It's senior day, so our tickets will be half price." The moment the second beep sounded, she scurried out the door.

Ms. Lavender returned from her office to assist Ashley. She brought a couple of well-worn musty books out from the safe and pointed her in the direction of other topics she was interested in checking out.

After smoothing her pulled-back hair into place, the librarian cleared her throat. "As you may have noticed, the people in Nature's Crossing watch out for each other."

"Yes, I've noticed," Ashley said.

"I was watching out for you the first time I saw you, too."

"When was that?"

"That day I saw you and Chase there on the sidewalk." Ms. Lavender appeared to be a woman who knew what went on in her world but didn't pry. "Looked to me like you were a little apprehensive. After I got inside the library, I stood at the window and kept an eye on things. He's not a very nice person sometimes."

"So that was you who pulled into the parking lot that day. Made me feel better to know someone had at least seen me with him. Thank you." Ashley shuddered inside. "I must admit, there's something about him that makes my skin crawl."

Ms. Lavender pushed the return cart toward the mystery section, her serviceable shoes whisper-quiet on the floor. "We women have to look out for each other."

"Yes, we do."

Ashley read some on the community's history and enjoyed the captioned photographs. Every so often, she read a familiar name—Peabody, Andrews, Winfield, Bainbridge. Some of the neglected homes she saw yesterday stood in pristine newness on the pages. Birthdays, holiday decorations, garden parties, political gatherings, funerals…they all fluttered before her. The more she read, the more the town and people came into focus.

Nature's Crossing used to be a thriving town. But progress had taken a detour, or maybe it was a road changed direction or the effects of the economy from larger towns in the area. Without some new energy, ideas, and money, the town didn't stand much of a chance of being more than a rest stop at Red's Corner Market.

The lone town stoplight at the crossroads in front of the grocery just meant people on their way to the lake or the county seat or the airport or the National Forest had to stop for a few seconds. Did no one see the potential in the town?

She took a break from her research and wandered the library aisles, getting acquainted with the layout of the sections. Finding a mystery and biography to read, she headed to the front desk to check out. Noticing late-afternoon darkness setting in, she decided to end her day of discovery and head for home.

"I'll take these two with me," Ashley said, setting the two books on the counter. "Would you like me to help put the research books away?"

"That's kind of you, but I'm fine." Ms. Lavender clicked the info into the computer, then stamped the cards inside the books and instructed as to the return date. "I'm sure you noticed I still like to stamp the books. Comes from decades of handling looking after the books." The perfectly dressed sixtyish librarian picked up a stack of books. "It may sound foolish, but these registers are very special to me. I treat them the same way I hope someone treats me when I'm old but still full of information."

Starting out the door, Ashley turned to wave goodbye, but the librarian was already walking down the aisle, feather duster in hand.

A ringing phone greeted Ashley when she opened the front door, and a short sprint across the room got her there in time. "Hello?"

Dot's familiar voice came through. "You sound out of breath. Were you exercising?"

"No. I just walked in from the library. It's great to hear from you. How's Lloyd doing?"

"Great. Stents are in place and tests look good. We're spending some time here at his brother's house till we see if Lloyd will need a pacemaker. But everything looks good so far. He sends a big hello to you."

Ashley grabbed a bottled water from the fridge. "Fantastic. So, you'll be home in time for the holidays."

"That depends on you."

"Me?"

Dot stammered. "You know how I told you we usually go to the condo in Florida the beginning of January?"

"Yes."

"What we'd like to do this year, is go the beginning of December. Lloyd's brother, Bart, and his wife, Dilly, would drive us down and stay until after the holidays. In fact, their entire family might come there for Christmas. Maybe even my side of the family. The entire clan all together. Doesn't that sound wonderful?" Dot's tone held a world of happiness at that prospect.

"Yes. Sounds nice." Ashley smiled at the image. What did that have to do with her, though?

Dot sighed. "There's only one problem. We'd need someone there at the house until the usual house sitter returns. I spoke to her, and she's not going to be home till the middle of January at the earliest and…" Dot sighed again. "Oh, here, Lloyd wants to talk to you."

"Ashley?" His voice boomed through the phone line.

"You sound mighty chipper," she replied.

"Had a nap, so I'm good for at least another two hours." He chuckled. "Anyhow, what Dot's trying to ask is if you might consider staying at the house until the middle of January? No need to beat around the bush with the question. On the other hand, please don't feel obligated to say yes. But if money's an object, we could pay you."

She winced. Where had that come from? Sure, she liked Nature's Crossing, but what about her plans. Her Washington trip, and… Ashley ran her hand through her hair. "Well, besides the trip to Washington we talked about, I'd planned to be back in St. Louis for the holidays. You know. My friends and parties and decorating and…"

"That's fine. As I said, don't feel obligated. We'll shut the house up for a month or so. It should be okay. Of course, I always feel better if someone is there. But that's just me." Lloyd said. "Don't you worry one bit; things will be fine. So, is Nature's Crossing making an impression on you?"

"Absolutely. I can see why you all love it here. Yesterday, Peabody took me exploring through town. We lunched at Della's Dream. He sure loved his wife." Ashley's voice held excitement as she paced around the kitchen island.

"Speaking of wife, mine wants to talk to you again. We're heading out to dinner where I may even have double dessert when no one's looking. You have a great evening, and we'll chat later."

Ashley told Dot about her day around town and research at the library. "Wish you all were here to fill in the blanks."

"Sounds like you're making yourself right at home. That's always good," Dot said. "Guess I better get off the phone. Lloyd's motioning me it's time to go eat. I'll call again next week. By the way, you sound happy. So long."

Click.

Ashley leaned against the counter and downed

the remainder of her water while she thought over the Gregorys' request to extend her stay. She imagined decorating her condo. Trouncing through the snow to shop. Wearing holiday party sparkles for her friend's parties.

Then what? She'd be right back where she began. Unemployed. Divorced. And only a few years shy of forty. Nothing had come back from all the recruiters who'd called. Nothing from resumes she'd sent. Nothing positive out of so-called interviews on Zoom that lasted maybe fifteen minutes. Seemed like no one even sent rejection emails anymore.

So far, the search for herself wasn't satisfying, and the thought of holiday festivities didn't lighten her heart. Something was still missing.

She could stay in Nature's Crossing a little longer. After all, she'd made new friends, and Dot probably had lots of decorations for the house. But what about shopping for the holidays? Maybe the internet. Or Washington.

Tired from the busy day, she clicked on the fireplace and plopped on the sofa. Her head rested on the arm of the chair while she clutched the afghan up to her neck for warmth. Later, there'd be plenty of time to think about the holiday options. For now, she needed a nap.

The doorbell rang, dragging Ashley awake. Disoriented for a moment, she soaked in the comfortable surroundings. How long had she slept? The door chimed again, accompanied with loud knocking this time. She hurried to the door and peeked out. There stood Janie, tote bag in one hand and pizza balanced on the other.

"Where were you?" Janie asked as the door opened.

Ashley grabbed another bag from the porch. "I fell asleep on the sofa. What time is it?"

"Six thirty."

She locked the door and followed Janie to the kitchen. The aroma of sausage and pepperoni filled the air, and her tummy responded.

From the bag she brought, Janie unloaded dips, chips, and chocolate brownies. She'd already shoved a half-gallon each of chocolate chip and cherry vanilla ice cream into the freezer. "I wasn't sure what you liked, so I brought everything. Before you ask, no leftovers are going home with me."

Ashley hugged her friend. "I can see a lot of exercise in my future."

Together, the women decided to skip making a salad and dug right into the other food as Ashley recounted the events of the past couple of days. Any questions she had, Janie was able to answer.

"By the way, Dot and Lloyd called this afternoon. They're doing great. In fact, they plan to go directly to Florida for the winter. Wondered if I might stay a while longer. Of course, I told them I couldn't." Ashley took another piece of pizza and nibbled on the toppings.

Janie's shoulders sagged as she slightly shook her head. "Why not?"

"I need to go home."

"Why? You got a hot date waiting?"

Ashley tried to ignore the comment.

"Well?" Janie prodded.

"I'm thinking." Ashley placed her plate in the sink and snatched a handful of chips. "Hey, how about we binge one of the fashion shows tonight?"

"Sounds good to me." Janie placed the back of her hand to her forehead and fake-swooned. "Of course, I figured you'd want to watch a movie with Paul Newman or Chris Pine."

Scrunching her eyebrows inward, Ashley couldn't think of what would have made Janie say that. "Huh?"

"They both have blue eyes." Her friend giggled. "Just like Mark. But, oh, that's right. You're not interested in him."

"I'll have you know, I'm trying to ignore blue-eyed men right at the moment." Ashley felt the heat of her blush. "Now I'm going to get a refill on snacks before I get myself in trouble."

They took munchies to the living room, and each of them settled under an afghan. They commented about the styles and contestants. The first time they'd each visited New York. Europe. L.A. They both agreed they'd each look sexy in big sunglasses, four-inch heels and a plunging neckline dress.

"I loved those earring-thingies on that one model. The ones from Tiffany's." Ashley made a mental note to check the price on those. Maybe get a pair for Janie and her…maybe one pair that they could share.

Janie shuttled dishes to the kitchen sink. "Ah, Tiffany's. By the way, we don't have one of those stores in Nature's Crossing, either."

"Very funny." Ashley followed her friend. "I'm going to have ice cream. Want some?"

"First, I'm going to change into my jammies. Then look out ice cream and hips." Tote bag in hand, Janie went into one of the guest bedrooms and closed the door.

The phone on the counter rang, startling Ashley as she passed. The clock read ten thirty. Her heart jerked anytime someone called after nine o'clock. Always had, always would. "Hello?"

"This is Mark. If Janie's there, don't say who it is yet. Okay?"

"Okay." Ashley tried to focus. He sounded serious. More than serious.

"Is she there?"

"Yes. We're having a girl's night, and she's staying over. Do you need to talk to her?"

"I will in a minute. First, you need to know Patrick has been in a car wreck. He's in the hospital. Critical."

The words cleared her head in an instant. Ashley steadied herself against the counter. "How are you?" she whispered.

"Good."

Her sigh of relief was intense. "I'm glad. Really, really glad."

He paused—a long pause. Had he heard the catch in her voice? Could he possibly realize her insides were trembling? Ashley waited for him to go on at his own pace.

"We were in different cars. Different places."

Voice hoarse and subdued, he continued. "A drunk driver went through the light and hit him broadside. They cut Patrick out. Airlifted him to the medical center. I got there as they dropped him off."

"What can I do?" Ashley asked.

"I'll explain this all to Janie, but what I need you to do is get her to the small private airport halfway between Nature's Crossing and Henton. "There's a pilot ready and waiting by a private plane I chartered. The sooner you get her there, the sooner she gets to Patrick. I'm texting you the directions."

"I can do that. What else?"

"Stay with her. Make sure she gets on the airplane. I'll pick her up here in D.C."

Ashley's mind questioned why they were in different cars. Different locations. And what were they doing all the way in Washington, D.C., but this was not the time to ask.

"Mark?" she whispered.

"Yeah?"

"I'm sorry about that night at the hospital." She had to apologize...now. This call could have been about him, could still be, and she had to say what she felt.

Again, he paused. "We both...overreacted. I'm kind of...a tough man to read sometimes. Maybe you should find—"

"Shhhhh. I don't think I like where that sentence is headed. Do you?" Ashley's heart froze while she waited for his answer. Another long pause shook her to her core. What if he closed the door between them?

"No, I don't. I'll call you in a couple of days. We'll talk about why a beautiful woman like you keeps popping up in my life."

"I'd like that."

Their moment was shattered when Janie walked into the room dressed in her penguin-patterned pajamas, brushing her hair. A happy smile spread across her fresh-scrubbed face.

"Where's my ice cream? Oops, I'm sorry. You're on the phone." She slapped her fingers to her lips.

"Is that her?" Mark sighed.

"Yes. Are you ready?" Ashley asked.

"As I'll ever be."

Ashley turned to Janie and held out the phone. "The call's for you."

"Patrick?" she mouthed.

"No, it's Mark," Ashley said.

Eyes twinkling, Janie took the phone. "I don't want to talk to you. I want to talk to my Paddy."

Ashley didn't move from her friend's side. Thirty seconds in, she watched Janie's face dissolve from happiness to concern to panic—the hairbrush dropped to the floor.

CHAPTER TWENTY-TWO

STILL DARK, STILL the middle of the night, still in crisis mode, Ashley waited in the hangar office at the small private airport until Janie's plane took off. Between the both of them, in less than an hour, they'd made arrangements with Lorna and Gus to tend the store. And Ashley had quickly packed a bag for Janie.

Back in the car, Ashley dialed the number Mark had given her and reached a recording. When it beeped, she spoke. "This is Ashley. Janie's plane just took off. Be sure you let me know how Patrick is doing. Take care of yourself."

Her hand gripped to turn the key in the ignition but stopped. From nowhere, tears erupted, flooding her eyes and rolling down her cheeks. She grabbed a tissue from the box and dabbed at her face. What was wrong with her? She only met these people last month. How could they mean so much? "No. I won't let this happen."

After the divorce, she'd shut out all unnecessary emotions. Caring had caused her enough pain, and life could be lived in her own confines quite easily.

She'd worked hard to keep it that way.

For the past couple of years, she smiled when appropriate, laughed with the flow, been serious and helpful if needed. But she'd always worn that mask like a coat to be taken off and hung in the closet when no longer required. Shut off and viewing the world, she'd survived.

Now, Mark flooded her mind. What if he'd been hurt? What if he'd never heard her apology? What if…

Finally, her wave of thoughts and tears subsided, and she dried her face. After a deep breath, she started the car and started back to Nature's Crossing. On the horizon, the sun made its morning appearance. How long had she been sitting there? Too long, way too long.

She loved the sunrise.

Ashley stopped briefly at the house to shower and change before she headed out again. Decided she'd do whatever was needed until Janie and Patrick were back in town. Called the Gregorys to let them know she'd be glad to stay till the usual house sitter returned. And felt a shift in the tension that had been following her ever since she'd accepted the severance from the news station. Life wasn't just about her. Life was about helping others, also. She'd forgotten that somewhere during the past few years.

It was barely eight o'clock, but Red's Corner Market was in full swing by the time she arrived. Customers stopped for gas on their way to work and to grab a breakfast roll, coffee, pre-made lunch.

Lorna and Gus had everything under control, probably because they had owned the store for twelve years prior.

Hanging her coat on a hook in the stockroom behind the counter, Ashley shoved her hat and gloves in the pockets. A cold front was inching its way through, snatching the warmth of fall as it went. "What can I do to help?"

Lorna moved around behind the deli counter, comfortable in her surroundings. She sliced meat and made requested sandwiches for people's lunch boxes. Preordered cakes and donuts for businesspeople occupied her other time. "Nothing right now. Soon as the morning rush dies down, we'll reorganize."

Gus worked the register and kept an eye on the pumps. "Who is that pulling away without paying?"

Lorna glanced out the front window. "Mrs. Pruitt. Probably late for work. Write down the amount, and we'll get it the next time she stops in."

The husband and wife informed the townsfolk of Patrick's accident on his camping trip and how Janie had gone to be with him. Some joked that he probably got on one of the interstates and drove so slow, he got run over. Others were seriously concerned and asked numerous questions, some a bit personal, some offering advice. Didn't take long to realize customers passed the information on, because by eight thirty, people asked if there was anything new on Patrick.

Mid-morning, a woman walked in holding a little boy in one arm and clutching a little girl's hand.

The children wore warm coats, but the mother had nothing but a flimsy sweater to cover her drooping shoulders. Emptiness filled her gaze except when she spoke with the children. Then she smiled and came to life in a way that led the children to think everything was fine. Yet she seemed old compared to the youth of her body, which looked tired.

"May I help you with something?" Ashley asked.

The woman shifted the maybe two-year-old boy to her other hip, then took the girl's hand again. She furtively glanced around the store. "Is Janie here?"

"No. She's out of town for a few days, but I'll be happy to help you, though." The little girl was a real doll. Had her mother's blue eyes, only happier.

"I see." A look of panic filled the woman's twenty-something face, and she headed toward the door.

"Sheila, why don't you warm up in the back room before you start back home?" Lorna called out and the little troop turned around. "I'll be there in a minute."

"Okay, Mama?" the girl asked.

"Thank you." The woman looked at Lorna and nodded. "Okay, sugar. Let's rest a minute."

Ashley led the way into the storeroom, moving anything that the children might get hurt on.

Once in the back, the children scrambled out of their coats and headed to a box full of toys in the corner. She got the feeling they'd been there before. Lorna stepped into the room long enough to leave three small bottles of milk and three donuts on the table, then went back to the front of the store. Seeing the food, the children put the toys back in the box and came running to the table.

"By the way, I'm Ashley Lanovan."

The young woman pulled the boy onto her lap. "I'm Sheila. This here is Benjamin, and this is—"

"Natalie. I'm Natalie. And I'm four years old." She held up five fingers…then pushed her thumb down. "Can I have—"

"May I have," the mother corrected as she sat in one of the chairs.

"*May* I have a straw?" The girl clambered onto the other one and sat on her knees.

Her mother slightly lifted the lid from the tall soda-fountain style container on the table and gave it a spin. Giggling, Natalie's tiny fingers carefully pulled a green one from the rainbow swirl of colors.

"Thank you, Mommy." The little girl angled the straw in the carton and took a sip. A bite of chocolate donut next. "This is good. I was gettin' hungry."

Ashley evaded the statement and stroked Natalie's soft, shiny hair. "I wish my hair was as soft as yours."

"My mama's is soft, too."

"I can tell." She figured Sheila wouldn't eat while she was in the room, so she headed back through the curtain. "Excuse me, I'd better get back in the store."

"Thank you," Sheila murmured.

"You're welcome."

Ashley waited for the rush to be over before she approached Lorna to inquire about the family. The older lady took a break from lunch preparations and walked to the cooler behind the milk display, motioning her to follow.

"I knew you'd have some questions," Lorna said.

"Please don't think I'm prying. But is there anything I can do to help them?"

"We've got some families in the area who fall on hard times every so often. Sheila and her children are one of them. She's a good mom, but sometimes her husband has one of his…spells, for lack of a better word."

Lorna's face hardened, along with her tone. "He'll take off and leave them without any money. There's probably not a bit of food in the house. Lucky if the heat's even on yet."

"Where does he go?"

Lorna started to back stock the milks. "Can't say for sure. One place and then another. He loves to gamble. Says it's his way of getting free drinks. Seems to lose mostly. May hit a run once a year."

The woman's knees popped when she knelt to get to the lower shelf. "In between times, he works odd jobs in the community. Mind you, people wouldn't hire him if it weren't for those little ones in there. And Sheila."

To help, plus keep warm, Ashley back stocked the drinks in the other cooler. "Can't she go to a shelter?"

"Nearest one's in Surryfield. Not possible when he's took the car with him."

"What about her family?"

Lorna shook her head. "None close. Anyhow,

just so you know. There's a few more that show up sometimes." She held onto the middle, resting for bit. "Janie and Patrick say if someone comes in hungry, feed them. When they leave, send them on their way with more than they came in with— groceries, a meal, gas. Those two are good folks."

Ashley offered Lorna a hand getting up. "Just like you and Gus did when you owned the place?"

Lorna shrugged. "That's how we all get through life. I started a bag behind the counter for them to take home. Bread, peanut butter, jelly, cereal, mac-and-cheese." Lorna opened the cooler door and stepped out. "Almost forgot. They'll need milk."

"I'll grab the milk. You add some lunch meat to the order." Ashley realized just how lucky she was to be able to take some time off before finding another job. "Let me know the total, and I'll pay for everything before I leave today."

Lorna nodded as she returned to her deli duties.

Ashley sat on the stool, out of the way behind the front counter, watching Gus ring up customers and flip the pump switches. "Janie said you'd let me know what I could do to help. I had some experience with a cash register during a charity event once. Maybe you could train me on this one."

The curtain on the doorway to the stockroom slid back, and Sheila, Natalie, and little Benjamin emerged. The children were bundled snug in their coats, hats, and mittens. Sheila had buttoned her cardigan to her neck and looked like a child herself.

Lorna glanced at the young mother. "Have you got a coat for the winter yet? You went all last year without one."

"I don't get cold. My sweater does fine." The family walked slowly to the door.

"Wait a minute." Ashley walked into the storeroom, pulled her hat, and gloves from her coat pockets, then returned to the store. She held them out to Sheila. "These were left in the back. Someone should get some use out of them."

Sheila looked at Lorna, who nodded. She took the offered warmth and pulled them on.

"Mommy. You look pretty in that hat," Natalie said.

"You look pretty in yours, too," the mother replied.

Lorna handed a small bag holding bread to the girl and a larger bag to the mother. Sheila hooked it over her left arm, lifted her son onto her hip, and took her daughter's hand. Gus held the door open.

"Thank you," Sheila said, looking first at Lorna, then at Ashley. "For everything." She tipped her head at Gus, then the tiny group walked out the door to begin their trek home.

"That was mighty nice of you," Lorna said, looking at Ashley.

"Surely, the local churches must have donated coats." Ashley stood at the glass and watched the family disappear down the road. A trio of love and determination.

"They gave her one last year, but she sent it to her mama, who didn't have one, either." Lorna meandered back to the deli, shaking her head.

Gus motioned Ashley over. "The second lunch

rush'll start soon. I should have just enough time to teach you this register."

Before the day was out, Ashley learned the cash register, how to check deliveries, and which customers were given discounts—veterans and people in need—or carried a pay-once-a-month bill—veterans and people in need. The next couple of weeks, Ashley stayed busy at Red's. The store had part-time help for the evenings, so she worked a few day hours to give Lorna and Gus time off in the afternoons. It didn't take her long to be on a first-name basis with most of the community. She felt needed. Felt good.

For days on end, Janie called the store at least once every afternoon. Evenings, she called Ashley at home. Patrick was doing better. Rehab was tough, and they might not be home till the middle of January. The one time Ashley spoke with Patrick, he'd been emphatic about being home before the beginning of the year.

Mark had called when Janie got to Washington. Called Ashley again the next day, and the next and on and on. Nothing special, just to talk. Music, art, antiques. Hunting, fishing, hiking. Nothing personal except on her part. Of course, the calls usually lasted at least an hour, sometimes two. They'd end with "So long," and "See you later."

Tonight, their conversation was filled with silence. A lot of silence. If they'd been together, they'd have danced or cuddled or kissed. Taken that first kiss to a whole different level.

"What are we doing, Mark? Our calls, our talks.

I probably shouldn't ask, but I need to know." Ashley fidgeted with the afghan on her lap. "Are we headed somewhere? Or just…"

His deep exhale filled the phone. "You're the best thing that's ever happened to me."

"But?"

"Can't we leave things like they are?" Another sigh from him. "Why do you need to know where we're headed?"

"Because I feel vulnerable. I know technically we've only had one date, but I feel as if our phone calls, FaceTime and Zoom meets are like long-distance dating." She felt the wind of change falter. "If we're headed nowhere, then that scares me. After my divorce, I thought I'd never feel anything for a man ever again. But with you, I feel everything. Everything. Maybe even forever."

The quiet was long. The silence longer still. In that moment, she realized they were different—two different winds. She shouldn't have asked. Could she take the question back? No. The question hadn't been a quest for commitment, only a question of what if. She could exist with the two of them being friends, but if that were all there was, then she needed to pull her emotions back. Lock them behind her barrier.

"I don't want to hurt you. Please believe that." His tone held a lock on emotion. "I hoped talking, being together sometimes, would be enough. Now I realize that's not fair to you. You deserve more than what I can give."

"You're wrong. Please don't turn me away. Not

without trying, at least."

"I have a job, Ashley. A job more important than you or me or anything else. And even when I quit, even when I take a new job at a different agency, the past will always be waiting to raise its ugly head."

Job? A good guy job...a bad guy job? Sure, there were lots of questions she still hadn't asked, but she knew deep inside that he wasn't a bad guy. And what if he was? She pondered. She'd face that when and if the time came.

"Trust me when I say you have more of me than anyone ever has." He cleared his throat. "More than anyone ever will. But..."

She cringed with the word *but*. He hadn't finished the sentence, and the silence was long. "But what, Mark?"

"The past few weeks have been great. But there's not a forever in my life. There's not commitment... at least not any I can give you right now."

"Are you married?" She blurted the question before she could stop herself.

He laughed...slightly. "No, Ashley. I'm not married. Never have been. Never will be."

"Don't you want marriage? Family? Children?"

"No. I will never put a child through what I went through when my father died. Or bring a child into a family legacy that dictates what I do every day."

His words and honesty jarred her soul. Who was this man? So secretive yet so direct. So emotionless. This man who was committed to something...

what? What could be more important than a
person's hopes and dreams and future? Her mind
skittered through possible scenarios but didn't find
the answer.

Yet Mark knew the answer. His life was based on
the answer. And that answer was worth everything
to him. Her insides convulsed with another
shattered dream. She bit her lip to stop the tremble,
but her tiny whimpers fused into the receiver.
"We'll talk another time."

"Don't you understand, I'm trying to tell you
there can never be a 'we.'" Mark's voice cracked.
"Do you want children, Ashley? Is that important
to you? Truly important?"

How could she answer that? The only thing she
knew for sure was that being thirty-eight made her
choice even more pressing. Yes, she'd always wanted
children. Two or three. But she wanted Mark, too.
Wanted him in her life…forever.

"You know, I'm really tired tonight. Had a long
day helping at the grocery. Can we talk tomorrow?"

"Sure. You get some rest."

"You, too. Good night."

Mark eyed the phone once the call with Ashley
ended. They might not be face to face, but he'd
picked up on her tone and the sniffles and pauses
in conversation that she'd been quietly crying. The
type of cry where tears flood your eyes, bubble
over, and cover your cheeks. Crying for him. For
them. She'd answered his question about children

when she didn't answer.

Their relationship had reached another step. He squeezed the bridge of his nose. One he couldn't take. She'd asked if he were married. Hell, yes, he was married. For half his life, he'd been married to the U.S. government, the CIA, and family obligation. Even leaving the CIA for the Park Service wouldn't get rid of the past. That would always follow him.

He didn't want to put Ashley in harm's way because of his job. Already, he cared more for her than he wanted to admit. Letting her go hurt, but that was best. She'd find someone else.

No more talks, no more laughter. No more time to dance. No more scent of magnolia.

In the past, he'd made love to women for the job. Even for a few weeks of personal passion at times. But he'd never loved a woman. This was new. Beyond comprehension, yet real and all-encompassing. Terrifying.

He loved this one so much his insides fought to rip him apart with emotions. He loved this one so much he couldn't imagine not hearing her voice again. He loved this one so much he'd let her go to protect her from his life, his job, his enemies. From him.

Who was he kidding? His past career would always be there. Lurking like a lizard waiting patiently for a fly.

Swiping his palm across his eyes, he focused on the contact list on his phone. Pulled up Ashley Lanovan. There was no other way to save her than to let her go. No other way. He pushed the delete button.

"Delete contact? Yes. No," flashed on his screen.

He stretched his hand taut to stop the quiver, but still it trembled. His fingers hovered over the question. There was no other way. None. Jaws clenched, he pushed the button.

Yes. Delete.

CHAPTER TWENTY-THREE

ASHLEY STRETCHED AS part of her wanted to stay in bed all day, yet another part shouted to get moving. She was looking forward to spending the day with Peabody's sister, Eloise. Over a week had passed since her last phone conversation with Mark. So had a lot of long, restless nights of sleep, non-sleep, half-sleep.

Eager to get on the road, she showered and grabbed a protein drink before bundling into her coat, plus an old pair of Dot's gloves she'd found in the mud room. She'd even found last winter's headband ear warmer in the glove box of her Jeep. The SUV was barely warm by the time she stopped in front of Eloise's house. Agreeing to help her clean the little shops in the block building had seemed like a great idea yesterday. Maybe staying busy would help keep her mind off the what-ifs that seemed to have disappeared.

Eloise met her at the door with a hug. "I almost called you back to remind you to dress warm. Looks like I didn't need to after all. Seems like the insides of those buildings are always colder than outside."

The elderly lady stepped on the front porch, then locked the door to her house. With only a couple blocks to old town Nature's Crossing, they'd already agreed to walk since the cleaning supplies were already in the building. Along the way, their chit-chat revolved around the need for a local food pantry and used-clothing for the community. Didn't take long to reach the first shop, and Eloise smoothly unlocked the door.

Following her inside, Ashley locked the door behind her and unhooked the material across the front for light. Getting right to work, she navigated the long-handled brush with ease as she dusted the walls, corners, sills, and ceiling.

Meanwhile, Eloise swept from the front to the rear, opening the back door to push the dirt outside. "Where does it come from? The shops are closed up tight from cleaning to cleaning, but there's always dust."

The two women moved from store to store down the row with Eloise chattering about the history. Occasionally, Ashley noticed a slight difference in the details from what Peabody, Dot, or Lloyd had told her.

"Have you been back to the library?" Eloise asked as they finished up the last shop.

"No. I keep meaning to stop by, but I've been helping at the store while Janie's away. In fact, this is my first day off since she left." Ashley hooked the last shop's curtain back in place, but the glow of sunshine still found its way around the edges, giving the room almost a candlelight atmosphere.

Eloise wrapped her woolen scarf around her head and tossed the ends over her shoulders. "Well, I sure do appreciate your help. Now we can go enjoy lunch at my house. You'll need to save room for dessert because I made applesauce fried pies."

"Those sound delicious. I've worked up an appetite."

The sound of car tires trickled through the window. They crunched on the gravel in front of the building before coming to a stop. Doors slammed, and the sound of two men's voices rang through the cracks around the door.

"This is it. The center of old downtown." Easy to recognize, Chase's voice filled the air with sarcasm. "Aren't these buildings a hoot? Now you know what I mean when I say this place needs a shake-up."

Eloise reached for the doorknob, but Ashley stopped her with a gentle touch while placing a finger to her own lips.

"Did you ever think of turning the area into a tourist attraction? Might do well with quaint little shops and restaurants. Some local cuisine. Maybe fine dining." A deep voice with a slight East Coast brogue tumbled out when the other man spoke. "Lots of older towns bring in a lot of foot traffic and money that way."

"Nope. Tear it all down and start new is my plan," Chase sharply rebutted. "Besides, some of the old-timers need to learn there are other people in charge now."

Eloise pressed her clenched hand to her mouth and leaned against the wall. Ashley quietly opened one of the lawn chairs stacked against the wall and steadied the woman to the seat. Then she returned to the front of the room to hear better.

"One of the rules for good business is let the past go," the deep voice declared.

"What?" Chase asked.

"Don't let your feelings interfere with a deal. I've seen lots of people fail because they couldn't let go of a grudge. To make money in development, you've got to evaluate what's best in the overall plan."

"Taylor, Taylor, Taylor." Chase snickered. "You can't tell me you've never blown a deal to dig at somebody. Just to let them know they can't mess with you."

"That's exactly what I'm telling you. I'll never let personal feelings mix with business. My company's reputation is on the line every time I sign a contract. More importantly, *my* reputation is on the line. That's something I value more than any deal," the deep voice exclaimed. "Who owns these buildings anyway?"

"Name's Peabody."

"Does he want to sell?"

Malicious laughter mixed with the howl of the wind when Chase spoke. "Not hardly. Him and my uncle have been enemies for decades. But if the buildings were condemned, they'd have to be torn down. No reason for him to hang onto the land then."

Ashley paid close attention to the particulars of the conversation. Who was the other man? Not from around here, for sure. From her travels, he sounded more like New York. Very business-minded, unlike Chase. Even seemed to be of a much better cut, maybe unaware of Chase's devious nature.

"How do you plan to accomplish that? I mean the condemnation part," Taylor said.

"When I'm on the Town Council, I'll have more leverage. Get all these old buildings declared eyesores and tear them down. Hell, I'll tear them down myself if I have to."

"You might have a fight on your hands. These buildings look in good shape to me."

"Don't worry about that. I've got ways," Chase bragged. "Then you can build a hotel. Or a whole convention center. Now wouldn't that make this town come alive?"

"I'm only interested in the Haney property you told me about. Nothing else. I'm not into anything illegal."

"Good man," Eloise whispered and sharply nodded, then gripped her hands together in her lap. The purse of her lips showed her fortitude.

Chase stammered, "Your loss. You do agree there's potential. Right?"

"I'll put some figures together and see how they lay out." Taylor's voice held authority. "Anyhow, I didn't think you lived in Nature's Crossing, so how are you going to get on the Town Council? Your uncle?"

"It was his idea, but I'll do all the leg work. I

came up with the plan for a real estate office here also."

Eloise gasped.

"Ran it by him. He agreed with my ideas."

"You know, I'd like to meet your uncle," Taylor said. "He sounds like a smart businessman. What say we take a drive over to his office?"

"Uhhhh, maybe next time. He's real busy, and I haven't had a chance to fill him in yet. He'd want to know all the ins and outs before he held any discussions," Chase sputtered. "If you're like me, I like to keep my details kind of close to the vest. Know what I mean?"

"You insinuated he *was* part of the deal all along."

Ashley had already picked up on Chase's evasiveness regarding his uncle. Evidently, so had the other man.

"Could be I'll bankroll everything myself," Chase replied.

From what she'd heard around town, Chase owed too much to bookies to think of bankrolling anything more than a corned-beef sandwich on St. Patrick's Day.

"Don't plan too far ahead. Just owning a business in town won't get you on the Town Council." The East Coast brogue came through more emphatic this time.

Eloise pushed to rise from the chair, and Ashley braced beneath her arm. The two women inched quietly to the front of the building again.

Chase laughed. Louder and louder. "No problem. I'm gonna buy a nice piece of property at the edge of town. 'Course, I plan to chop down a lot of trees." Chase snickered. "You should see the place. Pine trees all over. Gonna sell them to the lumber mill before I subdivide the ten acres."

Ashley's shot a look at Eloise, who seemed to have resigned herself to listen.

"Let's take a look at the place," the man said. "Ten acres might be worth looking into for a small development."

"Can't today. It's not for sale yet. But don't worry, it will be," Chase said.

"What makes you so sure?"

"The old guy that owns it has come down with heart trouble. Ain't that convenient? Probably won't have to wait long." Chase's eagerness mingled with sarcasm. "In fact, Lloyd and his wife are in St. Louis for tests right now. You know how it is when people get old and sick. They downsize."

"If nobody's there, we can at least look around," Taylor said.

Now Ashley understood why the Gregorys always made sure someone was house sitting their property. In most ways, Nature's Crossing was safer than some places she'd visited, but people who owned acreage around here were prime for trespassers or just noisy passersby...or neighbors.

"Can't." Chase sounded scared. "I mean...some newscaster lady from St. Louis's staying there, and I get the feeling she's smarter than the average broad. And, like I always say, getting a woman to thinking can only spell trouble. Here's the best part, though. The owner's also on the Town Council. When I buy the house, the town will have to replace him."

"Appears to me you've got yourself a maze to work through before your plans fall together."

Chase continued. "Maybe a few hoops to get through. But don't you worry, I'll get it done. Follow my lead, and we'll both get our share of the action."

"Like I said before, I'm not into pieces of action as you call them." The other man's voice sounded dubious of what was happening. "I'm purely business. Above-board business. Nothing else. Understand?"

"Yeah, yeah. Whatever you say. You're the man with the money." Chase's tone eased into condescending. "I wouldn't think of involving you in my personal dealings. Let's go take a look at the Haney river property next."

Outside the plate glass window, car doors slammed, and an engine turned over. Tires spewed pebbles against the front window in their wake. Ashley realized she'd been holding her breath, hands fisted. Chase was dangerous to this town.

Eloise folded the chair and placed it against the wall, then the two women stepped out the front door. Under a cloudy sky, Ashley supported Eloise's elbow while they walked down the crumbling sidewalk toward her house. Neither of them spoke till they got to her front porch, which, after what they'd just heard, beckoned like a welcome port in a storm.

"Are you okay?" Ashley asked.

"No, I'm…I'm…I'm mad as a spiky porcupine,"

Eloise muttered. "Peabody. We've got to call Peabody."

Shadows were long by the time Ashley trudged into the Gregorys' house hours later. After tossing her coat and purse in the nearest chair, she dropped to the sofa, clicked the fireplace remote, and kicked off her shoes. The golden glow and soothing warmth relieved the day's stress. She turned on the jazz station before curling up under what had become her favorite afghan. Her mind needed to rest along with her body. Cleaning was a tough job, and the turmoil from Chase's conversation had sapped the remainder of her energy.

An hour later, she woke to mellow tones, and for a moment, her mind drifted in and out of the dream she'd been having. Had the dream been of Mark, or was it only a feeling? She tried to revive the sensations and stay within the fantasy. The smell of leather and the taste of wine. Dancing in moonlight and feather-soft kisses. Her emotions soared through the clouds one minute and floated on air the next.

Finally, she opened her eyes and stretched. "Ummm. Ashley, old girl, you need to get up and…food. Oh my gosh."

She jumped to her feet, grabbed the keys from her purse, and headed for her car. Good thing it was cold outside because the containers of food Eloise had sent home with Ashley were still there. Returning with the bundle, she warmed the food while checking her cell phone for messages. In her hurry-up state that morning, she'd left the phone on the table, so she'd missed a few calls. On the good side, everyone had left voice messages.

Lorna's message said everything was okay at the store. They'd see her tomorrow. Janie's message said Patrick was improving, and she was sorry to hear Ashley's mother couldn't make the holiday outing in Washington. But she was more than excited to take her place and have a girl's weekend. Said she needed that. Ashley smiled; she needed that, too. And the idea of putzing around D.C. with Janie sounded perfect.

Ashley thought back over the day, and her mind raced through Chase and the other man's exchange, spoken and unspoken. There was no doubt about Chase's feelings for the town and some of its people. She wished there'd been a way to follow them. See the other places they went today, but Eloise needed her attention more.

Finished eating and stuffed already, she started to pass on the two fried pies. Figured she'd only take a nibble and save them for tomorrow. Before she knew what happened, she'd eaten one of them. "After the way this day turned out, I deserved that."

She returned Janie's phone call, and the two made a tentative schedule of what they'd like to do in Washington. What clothes she'd need for the weather.

"By the way, have you talked to your blue-eyed guy lately?" Janie asked.

"No." Ashley wouldn't share her fear that Mark

had vanished from her life. Shut her out. Her emotions refused to be locked away again, and one of those emotions was hope. "Have you seen him around?"

"Not really. Patrick talked to him a couple days ago. I said a quick hello is all."

"How's he doing?" That sounded like she cared.

"Busy. Almost like he's not giving himself time to think. Thought he might have called you." Janie yawned. "Sorry, guess more tired than I thought. What with all this going back and forth from my short-term rental apartment and the hospital to visit Patrick, I'm running on empty. But that's okay…at least I'm here with my Paddy."

"You get some rest," Ashley said.

"Okay. I'll see you soon. Can hardly wait." Janie clicked off the phone.

Mark hadn't called her. He'd called Patrick. Even talked to Janie, but he hadn't called her. Of course, that was probably just two buddies staying in touch. So why didn't he want to stay in touch with her? Even if they were only friends.

She'd scared Mark away with her need. Why else would he stop calling? She'd wrecked everything when she asked where they were headed. Or maybe he'd met someone else? Maybe he…he… Maybe what?

The pain of missing someone she barely knew, couldn't care less about, and didn't need in her life, was worse than…what? As the response settled into her soul, Ashley fought to ignore the answer. Fought to ignore the pull of Mark. Fought to ignore the gaping hole in her heart.

What was worse than this emptiness she felt since Mark quit calling? Nothing.

Not the day she discovered Bradford and his mistress on the yacht. Not the day she realized her husband hadn't loved her for years. Not the day she signed the divorce papers and walked out of the courtroom alone.

Absolutely nothing felt worse than the cavern Mark had dug into her being and then left empty. Emptiness wasn't an option she chose any more. Her trip to Washington might give her a chance to see him if he was there. If not, maybe Janie could cajole Patrick into saying where Mark had gone. No matter what, Ashley planned to see him again, and when she did, she'd…she'd…

Ashley smiled. If one ounce of womanhood still oozed within her, she planned for more than finishing their dance. Status quo was not an option. Just because he might not be her forever man didn't mean they couldn't enjoy each other. In fact, it was time to break some of her self-imposed standards—like thinking everything had to be forever. Life was passing her by as she waited for forever, and enough was enough. Life was short. Too short.

From now on, she'd take what she could get. Ashley walked straight to the counter, opened the container, and ate the last fried pie. And right now, she'd sure like to get him naked.

All she had to do was track him down. Of course, Washington, D.C. was a big place.

CHAPTER TWENTY-FOUR

THE DAYS FLEW by, and Ashley's trip to D.C. snuck up on her, but as she boarded the plane, she felt nothing but excitement. Used to going on assignments, she was fine with traveling on her own. Besides, she and Janie planned to make the most of their time together.

There'd still been no call from Mark. Worse still, there'd been no return call the night she broke down and called him.

Thanksgiving dinner with Eloise, Fred, and Peabody had turned out wonderful, even though they had discussed the Chase incident. A few of Peabody's friends in the county and state government had made general inquiries in their departments, but no one seemed to know anything about a big project headed for Nature's Crossing.

She righted her seat as the plane zeroed in on Washington. Looking down at the patchwork of Washington gave her a thrill. Monuments brought back how much she loved D.C. and everything about the city. Surrounding areas might change with time, but the heart of the town stayed the same. This was the backbone of the nation.

A limo service carried her to the hotel near the Convention Center, a place with easy access to the DC Circulator bus, which would take her close to wherever she wanted to go. Taxi service at the front door would supply the rest. She spent the entire limo ride watching for Mark. Most any other place in the States, his SUV would be easy to spot, but in D.C. the BMW seemed to be in abundance.

The suite itself provided a sitting area in the front room and a luxurious king-size bed in the adjoining room with plenty of covers to keep her warm and comfy. Pillows stood at attention across the headboard. Inviting. Too bad she had no one to share the luxurious invitation. Not that she wanted to share. Not that she wanted to think about what filled her thoughts every night, either. Or, for that fact, who.

The next couple of days she planned to be a tourist, complete with sightseeing and shopping and ogling all the holiday decorations. She had two tickets for an evening at the Kennedy Center. She'd even bought a new dress for that night. And Janie was over the moon at the idea of dressing up. Museums would round out her itinerary.

Back in her room after an hour of exercise in the fitness center, she ordered dinner from room service, took a quick shower and donned a pair of sweats, then sat down to eat. Her phone rang.

"Are you finally here?" Janie asked. "I figured you'd be in sooner."

Ashley crinkled her toes and rolled her neck. "I

got settled in the room but needed to go to the gym to work off some tension. And calories. My body's already saying I did one machine too many."

"What kind of tension?"

"Never you mind."

Janie giggled. "Has he called?"

"What say we change the subject for now?" There'd be plenty of time to talk about Mark tomorrow. Today, she was looking forward to just spending time with her friend wandering around D.C.

"Okey-dokey then."

"How's Patrick today?"

"Grumpy." Janie exhaled noisily.

Ashley smiled at the opening. "He doesn't look like one of the seven dwarfs."

"Very funny. PT increased the resistance today, and Patrick didn't want to follow the routine. Guess him and the tech got into it. For the rest of the day, that's all Patrick could talk about. That and how no one was going to make him do anything." Janie sneezed. "I finally left."

"Don't worry. The next few days you're going to enjoy yourself. Are you ready for some marathon shopping?" Ashley coaxed.

"Yes, yes, yes. Marathon eating, too," Janie replied eagerly. "I'll take a taxi to your hotel in the morning."

"We can start with breakfast in the restaurant downstairs if you'd like."

Janie sneezed again. "I'll be there about eight. Look out Washington, here we come."

Too excited to stay in her room the next morning, Ashley waited in the hotel lobby until Janie arrived. On time and complete with sniffles. The two women wandered from shop to shop in Georgetown and other specialty shops in the Wharf area of downtown Washington. They spent the better part of the day buying as much for themselves as they did for gifts. And she made sure to buy a variety of winter hats, ear muffs and a few pair of gloves, even some fuzzy white ones that teased of winter fun.

"My Paddy seems kind of down lately." Janie purchased a few items for her husband.

"I thought you said the therapy was going great. Only tougher."

"It is, but he'll most likely walk with a limp for a while. Maybe forever. Might even need a cane." Janie rolled her eyes. "You can imagine how that idea's going over with him."

Ashley laughed, imagining the patience Patrick was extracting from his wife. "I'd like to see him while I'm in town. What do you think?"

Janie bit her lip, looked down then up again. "Well, let me put it this way. I asked him about you visiting him at Walter Reed. He said to tell you he appreciates the thought, but he'll be home soon. In fact, his words insinuated you're a hazard to his health."

"Hazard?"

"He said he can't chance a visit that might land him flat on his back like Mark did that day at the Gregory place."

"Okay, okay, I get the picture. Give him a hug from me, though." Ashley laughed, while her hope of coaxing Mark's whereabouts out of Patrick, floated away. "In fact, if I see a can of food today, I'll buy it and you can tell him I sent a gift. One that hasn't been dropped on the floor…or in the mud."

Janie giggled, sneezed, and coughed in conjunction. She wiped her eyes. "That I can do. I'll even wrap it up with a bow."

Ashley rummaged through her purse. "Before I forget. Here's your ticket for the Kennedy Center this evening. I'll meet you at the seats."

"Thanks. I'm looking forward to the music. Paddy and I used to go all the time, but since we moved to Nature's Crossing…" Janie sighed. "Oh well, life is full of give and take. And I do love our life there."

"This evening should be fun."

Tissue in hand, Janie sneezed again. "Patrick even had me get a new dress."

"And shoes."

"Of course. I better be careful with the tissues, or I'll look like Rudolph tonight." Janie sniffled and blew her nose again.

Ashley held the door to a neighborhood bistro. "Maybe we should feed your cold before it becomes a fever."

"I'm all for that," Janie snuffled. She looped her arm around Ashley's. "You never answered my question earlier. Has Mark called lately?"

Ashley straightened her shoulders, trying to act nonchalant. "No. He hasn't. I just have to accept the fact he's not interested. Guess we really didn't click, after all."

"You two looked perfect to me. Even Paddy laughed about Mark being tied up in a knot just thinking about you."

"I'm all tangled up, too." Time to admit she needed help. "To be honest, Janie. I really miss Mark. I was hoping you'd seen him."

Janie shook her head. "Sorry. Last I heard, he was out of town on business."

Might be time she finally faced the truth. Her blue-eyed man was gone from her life. In the past, that's exactly what she'd have done. Given up. She'd always given up on her dreams. Not this time.

"Patrick might know where he is. Maybe he'd help me find him." She realized how needy she sounded, but this was important. "Can you at least ask him to get a message to Mark?"

Sneezes overtook Janie as she nodded. "Let me see what I can do."

Ashley breathed a little easier. At least this was worth a try. Because, so far, she wasn't very good at tracking him down by herself. There had to be some way to connect with Mark again. She had no idea how, but she had a few more days in D.C. to try.

CHAPTER TWENTY-FIVE

A FEELING OF GRANDEUR washed over Ashley as she entered the Kennedy Center and the crystal chandeliers and mirrors greeted her with reflective beauty. She left her wrap at the coat check, then returned to the Grand Foyer. Attending a function here was her treat to herself every time she was in town. She deserved this. Always.

Her royal-blue dress swirled inches above the floor as she walked down the aisle of the Concert Hall. Her diamond earrings with matching necklace accented her slender neck. She didn't allow herself to really dress up very often, but her once-a-year visit to Washington offered a perfect time for luxury. At least as much as she could afford.

The earrings and necklace were left over from the divorce, but they didn't make her unhappy. On the contrary. These were among a few things she planned to keep forever. Things she planned to hand down…sometime in the distant future…to children she might…might not…ever have.

Eyes turned to watch her pass, and she returned the smiles of unknown people. For a moment, she felt like Dolly from her favorite musical. *Hello, Dolly!* Hello, Ashley! When had she begun to feel so wonderful about herself again? About life?

She settled in her seat, savoring the auditorium and the hubbub of voices. The excitement of promised entertainment. She glanced at her bangle watch. Only a few minutes to curtain and still no Janie. Ashley hoped Patrick hadn't taken a turn for the worse.

The lights flickered, and she watched the stage in anticipation of the first note.

Next to the empty seat beside her, a man cleared his throat. "Excuse me. Is this seat taken?"

"Mark?" She quickly turned in his direction. Could it be? Her heart, her breathing, her imagination kicked into overdrive. Butterflies tweaked her insides. Her mind fuzzed as the lights dimmed and he slipped into the aisle seat beside her. "What are you doing here?"

In the shadows, she struggled to see his face. His bearing was strong. Strong. Polished. Classy. And the little she'd seen of his tuxedo, it fit him perfectly. The clean-shaven profile and trim dark hair ricocheted through her mind, waiting for an answer.

Leaning against the armrest, he turned and gave her his two-finger salute. "Janie's sick. She thought I might do for the evening. Okay?"

Ashley's pulse tripped over itself when she tried to respond, plus his cologne converging with his scent affected everything from her brain to her core. Speechless, she stared at him as people around them applauded the orchestra taking the stage.

"If it's not okay, I'll leave," he said.

Afraid he would go, she slid her hand over his, then back to her lap. He stayed.

"Shhhh." The lady behind them tapped him on the shoulder with her program. "I'm sure it's okay, or she'd have already told you otherwise."

Ashley smiled weakly at the elderly woman, turned back around, and concentrated on the music. She struggled to keep her mind off the man next to her. From the corner of her eye, she glanced at Mark. Even caught him looking a couple of times.

Before long, the melodies mixed with the moment to carry her away. She applauded when appropriate. He tapped his fingers to the beat, gripped his program to the building of a crescendo. She longed to lean into him, but he sat straight. The proper gentleman. Nothing at all like the man who tripped over the woodpile.

At intermission, the two of them mingled with others in the aisle on their way to the foyer. His hand rested lightly against the small of her back, keeping contact, steering her through the crowd. His touch fell away once in the open.

"Would you like something to drink?" Mark asked.

"I don't think so. Excuse me for a moment. I'll be right back." Not even sure she could walk straight, she made her way to the powder room to freshen her makeup.

When she returned to the Grand Foyer, Mark was speaking with someone she'd seen walking with the president on television the night before. The man patted Mark on the shoulder as the two of them shared a laugh. The moment he saw her, he excused himself from their conversation and joined her by the windows.

"Don't let me interrupt," Ashley said.

"We were finished."

She glanced upward at the high ceilings. "I love standing here, don't you?"

"If it weren't so cold, we could go on the terrace. Catch sight of the lights reflecting in the river." Lightly, his arm brushed hers, and in with only a smooth movement of his hand, his fingers tangled with hers for a moment. "Maybe another time."

"Yes. Uh, no." She inhaled, blinked. What was he talking about? Rivers? Lights? What? She wasn't sure. "Maybe."

He grinned. "Relax, pretty lady. We're okay. Tonight, we're okay. And you look beautiful."

"Thank you. And thank you for coming tonight." He hadn't left her after all.

The lights dimmed, and the pair returned to their seats moments before the music flourished. He, again, took her hand as they settled in, making sure she didn't stray to the far side of her seat. When he leaned back, his upper arm rested gently in front of hers, against hers. She tried to remember the last time she felt so cared about, so content—nothing came to mind.

Way too soon, the final note echoed away. The crowd stood. Applauded. Once again, they blended with the crowd moving toward the exit. And once again, she felt his guiding hand. Nothing suggestive. Rather, a feeling of being protected. He piloted her to a spot by the Kennedy bust. Would this be where they parted way? The end of the evening?

"Did you wear a wrap?" Mark asked.

"Yes, I almost forgot." Ashley retrieved the stub from her bag.

He took the coat check, placing it with his own. "When the crowd thins, I'll get them."

They stood awkwardly silent. *Don't let this end* whispered through her mind.

"Did you enjoy the selections this evening?" Ashley asked.

"Yes, I did." Mark eased in his stance. "The conductor did a great job. You might say music is one of my hobbies. I bought a trumpet about a year ago. Told myself I'd learn to play it in record time."

"And?"

"It's in the closet with the violin, the clarinet, and the others."

She felt herself relax, soften. "So…do you play anything?"

"The drums." His hands bounced as if tapping the sticks in rhythm to an unheard song. He ended with a pounding thrash of his hands. "Ba dahhhhh!"

For a moment, she saw in him the flicker of a teenage boy banging on the skins, probably driving his parents deaf.

His expression changed. "I also play racquetball. How about you?"

"The piano. In fact, I used to sing. Seems like

years ago."

"How about I get our coats and we find a place to listen to some more music? Maybe some jazz? Unless you prefer a different style." His gaze questioned. Or did it offer? Or did it ask?

"Jazz is fine."

"Great."

After a short cab ride to a local cabaret, they spent hours listening to music while they tested the waters of their relationship. They danced. They danced again. Closer. The night moved on. They eased against each other. Leaned. Molded to each other. Whispered their thoughts. Their breaths close and personal. They danced till the music ended.

Later, when the taxi pulled to a stop in front of her hotel, Mark paid the driver with a fifty for a twenty-dollar fare and waved him on his way. This was clearly not a man you offered to pay your share on anything. Their escape to the warmth of the lobby signaled the end of her dream evening.

"Some time I'll have to hear you play the drums." Ashley stopped walking down the corridor to the elevator bank. Good grief, she'd invited herself to be with him again. Maybe this was only about tonight.

He shook his head. "I warn you, you'll need earplugs."

The two of them stood lost in an awkward good night. She didn't want this night to end. One of them needed to nudge this relationship forward. what-ifs, appearing fearful to keep talking, fearful of saying goodbye.

"May I walk you to your door?" he asked.

"Uh…"

He held up his hand. "That didn't come out right, did it? I'd just like to make sure you make it to your room safely. Nothing else."

"In that case, sure." She leaned toward him just a bit. "Truth be told. There's always something a little thriller-esque when I'm alone in a long hotel hallway this late at night." A tiny shiver shook her shoulders. "There's even been a few times doing news assignments in unfamiliar places that heading to my room during the day felt off, too."

They stepped onto the elevator, and she pushed the floor button.

"Don't ever doubt your instincts. Not ever." Nervously, his fingers fiddled with hers as they faced the soon-to-open door. "What are you doing tomorrow since Janie's sick?"

"We planned to be tourists. There's even a pair of tickets on hold for a trolley. I think I'll still go." They stepped off the elevator, and all she could think was— Ask to go, ask to go… Please, please, please ask to go.

"Would you like some company? I'm in town for a few days."

Smiling, she tilted her head and looked at him. "Sure. Since you happen to be in town for a few days."

His lips parted in a bashful smile. "With nothing to do."

"With nothing to do." Thank goodness.

As they stopped in front of her room, he tucked

his scarf into his buttoned black cashmere coat. "I had a nice time, Ashley."

"Me, too."

Mark inched closer, his fingers caressing up her arm. He tilted her face up to him, leaned forward, sliding his cheek next to hers as his breath tickled against her hair. He cupped her face in his hands and kissed her. Not gentle and warm. But sure and inviting. She responded. Not long. Not short. An open window. Her insides quivered with the awakening.

"I'll see you in the morning," he whispered, then turned up the collar on his coat and pulled on his sleek black leather gloves as she opened her door and stepped inside her suite.

She swallowed the catch in her throat. How would she ever sleep after this? "Right. In the morning."

They turned their separate ways. She in her suite. Him headed to the elevator. Her insides ached for more, but even deeper inside, her fear of betrayal roared its warning.

"What time?" he asked in a loud whisper a few doors away.

"Nine?"

He gave his casual-salute and disappeared out the door.

Her fingers brushed her lips. What could possibly be better than this evening?

CHAPTER TWENTY-SIX

ASHLEY MADE A quick call to Janie the next morning and was met by a hoarse hello she could barely hear. Then three sneezes in a row.

"You sound terrible," Ashley said.

"I feel terrible. I've got a fever. A headache. Think I'll stay wrapped up in a blanket all day and read. I sure won't be seeing Patrick for a few days," Janie lamented. "I hope I didn't get you sick. I thought this was just allergies."

"Don't worry about me. Do you need anything?"

"No. Mark stopped by this morning and brought me some food. Said he was on his way over there to go sightseeing with you."

The two women were quiet.

"Ummmm?" Janie said.

"Ummmm," Ashley replied.

Janie's laughter ended in a coughing fit.

"You take care. I'll talk to you tomorrow," Ashley said.

"Okay. Have fun."

After showering, she dried off and wrapped the oversized towel around her. Took time to get her makeup exactly right. Not too little. Not too much. Just enough to hide some of the tiny wrinkles intent on letting themselves be known. Then blew her hair dry. After years of being groomed into place by the hair and makeup people at the station, her hair had learned to fall into a free and loose version of the same style.

Dropping her towel, she turned to reach for her bra and panties and was blindsided by the full-length mirror on the back of the bathroom door. Facing the reality of what was in front of her, she stared straight on, taking in her body from the top of her head to her toes and back up. From the neck up, she looked great. From the neck down, life had started a slow run of age.

She turned from one side to the other. Boobs a little droopy. Tummy no longer flat. Butt curve teeny-tiny sag. Waist? Blah. Her waist had always been a problem even when she was a teenager. And there it was, staring her in the face. She wasn't eighteen anymore, not even twenty-five. She was thirty-eight and thankful for every day. Loudly sighing, she blew out through her lips.

Finally, she angled the hand mirror over her shoulder so she could see her back. First one side and then the other. She looked at the full mirror and smiled. "Booty? Not bad. Not bad at all."

And she still had the best set of legs of anyone she knew.

Time to get dressed and head down to the restaurant. She'd already finished her omelet moments before Mark joined her.

"Sorry I couldn't make breakfast. Got tied up in a meeting."

She didn't ask what kind of meeting. Didn't ask where he worked. Didn't ask anything. And she was proud of herself. Taking Janie's advice, she'd let him tell her about himself when he was ready.

Pouring himself a cup of coffee from the urn on the table, the two of them settled into a comfortable chat. Finally, they decided to walk to one of the sightseeing trolley stops only a few blocks away. Partway there, the idea seemed ludicrous. Faces reddened from the cold wind, their breaths billowed foggy in front of them. Ready for warmth, they ran the last block and burst through the store's entrance.

Once onboard the step-on trolley, the driver provided humor intermixed with facts, and the tour moved ahead. Ashley had a mental list of places she always tried to visit while in town—Vietnam Veterans Memorial and Korean War Veterans Memorial, Arlington National Cemetery, and the vigil of The Old Guard at the Tomb of the Unknown Soldier. Mark agreed.

The day warmed, and Ashley discovered how nice it was to have someone beside her to talk with about the places. She quickly learned that Mark was an avid history buff. With him sharing seldom-known facts, she saw places in a different light than ever before.

At the Tomb of the Unknown Soldier, Mark straightened to attention, gloved hands held beside him. His eyes focused on the slow cadence of the soldiers for the Changing of the Guard. She straightened beside him.

Instincts told her there was a lot more to him than she might ever know. She was still a coward, though. Too afraid to ask him any more questions. She couldn't risk shattering what they might be building. Yet, she knew there'd come a time she needed to ask some questions. Not about them this time. About him. She'd already shared about herself, so turnabout was only fair.

The two exited the trolley again near the Korean War Veterans Memorial. They walked by the life-size stainless-steel soldiers and the sandblasted images on the stone wall. Mark stopped near the Pool of Remembrance and stared at the words inscribed on the black granite— "Freedom Is Not Free." Before long, he reached out and touched the letters.

"These words mean a great deal to me, Ashley. They're the words I live by," he said.

Unprepared for the commitment in his voice or the brief vulnerability he displayed, she was speechless. A quiet calm engulfed her thoughts before an echo of Janie's answer to her question about Mark's job flooded through her. The need she felt for this remarkable man was deep, and she caught herself holding her breath. Her heart ached with feelings for him, and she realized there were choices to be made. Soon.

What if she couldn't accept what he told her about his career? Worse still, what if he never trusted her enough to tell her?

"Where next?" he asked.

"The Vietnam Veterans Memorial." She walked a half step in front of him, and at the monument, she didn't need to count the panel to the one she knew. She simply walked, stopped, and placed her hand on a name. No need to count, she knew the place by heart.

"This was my dad's brother. My cousin Kenny's father. When I was growing up, Kenny lived with us, and every time our family came to Washington, we'd come here. My dad would tell a couple of stories about him and his brother from childhood. Then my cousin would lay a Clark bar, his dad's favorite candy, on the ground." She brushed her hair back.

Mark stood straight and still and solemn. He nodded.

She kissed her fingertips then pressed them against the name and gave a gentle pat. "Kenny was killed serving in Afghanistan. I always feel closer to him here than when I'm at his grave." She turned toward Mark. "You see, I know how much freedom costs."

Mark brushed a tear from her cheek. "I'm sorry your family has paid a price for freedom."

"We weren't the first. And we won't be the last." Ashley pulled a Clark bar from her purse, and an Almond Joy. She tapped them lightly against the name and knelt to place them on the ground at the foot of the wall. "Almond Joy was Kenny's favorite. I figure his dad will see that he gets it."

When she stood again, Mark was braced against

the black granite. Face serious as if making a vow, his hand rested on her uncle's name. Her gaze met his, and for a moment, silence enveloped the two. They started back to the trolley, side-by-side yet separate. He reached over and took her hand. She stopped. Too much was happening. Too fast.

He paused in his steps but didn't look back at her. Didn't let go of her hand. His solid grip felt safe. Felt right. "What are you afraid of, Ashley?"

She shook her head. Honestly, even to herself, she wasn't sure. All she knew for sure was here and now, and she wasn't too sure about that. What if she took the wrong step? Everything Mark had told her so far had been only superficial life stuff. Things even a friend would learn in time. What if he never shared the rest with her?

"We'll work through whatever's bothering you." He stepped in front of her. Still didn't let go. "Like you said on the phone that night. Give us a chance. You know you want to."

"What if you leave?" She bit her lip. "What if you decide not to give us a chance?"

His brow wrinkled. "You need to think in the moment. Let the future stay where it is."

"Is that what you do?"

He stepped back beside her. Arm across her shoulder, he pulled her close and kissed the top of her hair. "I learned a long time ago that all we really have is the exact moment we stand in."

Something in that statement made sense to her. She wasn't sure she could fully accept the full concept, but she could try. Still, she needed their pasts to mingle. And how could she expect him to share when she hadn't shared herself.

"Do you mind if we cut our day short and go back to the hotel?" she asked.

"Yeah. Whatever you want."

She sighed deeply and folded her fingers over his. "I'd like to tell you about my ex-husband. I need you to understand why my trust doesn't come easy."

"Tell me anything you want." He brushed the windblown strands of hair from her cheek, then they began to walk again.

Thirty minutes later, sitting across from each other at the small table in the front room of her suite at the hotel, she poured them each a cup of coffee. Unsure of where to start, unsure of even what to say, she delayed by finishing her cup with a creamer and sugar packet. Then stirred and stared at the tabletop and stirred some more. He took his black.

Finally, he placed his hand on hers and stopped the stir. "You don't have to worry, Ashley. I'll always understand."

She nodded and lifted her head to face him. "I met Bradford the first day of my junior year at college. I was twenty-one. And we stuck like glue from the beginning. Shared the same music. The same taste in books. Same sports. Before I even grasp what was happening, we became known as a couple on campus." She took a sip of coffee. "Years later, I realized he'd just been an upperclassman, a senior, looking for an inexperienced undergrad that day. Music, sports, and books were simply his way of ingraining himself into my world. When really all he'd needed—wanted—was someone who'd be there when he needed a date. Someone to help with his homework. Someone planning their own career, so they wouldn't take too much of his time. We married four years later.

"I won't bore you with particulars except to say all of our friends, family, and business acquaintances thought we had the perfect marriage. And I convinced myself that even though everything wasn't what I'd dreamed of, it was perfect for our careers." Taking her cup, she moved to one end of the sofa. "There was only one thing that bothered me. I wanted children. He didn't. Always talked about how children would take away from our careers, tie us down, cost money that could be invested. I finally gave up and shoved myself deeper into work, thinking once we had the house and the boat and the bank account he wanted, he'd agree to having children."

She sat down her cup and shivered. Fought back a tear. The one thing she'd adamantly refused to do throughout everything had been to cry. She would not begin now. "It came out in the divorce that he'd secretly had a vasectomy years before."

Tears flooded her face. Memories and hopes and dreams bombarded her with emotions, and she fought to regain control. This couldn't happen. She wouldn't allow it. Wouldn't. The tears didn't stop.

Instantly, Mark was beside her, sliding his arm across her shoulder, gently offering her his own.

She leaned into him, letting it fully sink in just how cruel Bradford had been in that regard.

"Why? Why would he do that to me? Keep me thinking there was a chance. He knew how much I wanted children. How hard I worked to achieve our goals." Jerky, long-held sobs took hold, and she let herself grieve after all those years. "Year…after year. Why…why…?"

"I don't know, honey. I really don't know what would make a person do something like that." He held her tighter and tighter, letting her cry.

When she finally looked up, she saw the pain in his eyes. A touch of tears on his cheek. And he kissed her lightly on the forehead.

"Trust me. I'll never hurt you like that. Never." He said, kissing her lightly on the forehead. "You've got my promise."

Her insides believed him. And she gradually composed herself as he refilled their cups of coffee. His black. Hers with sugar and creamer.

"You know, I thought the worst day of my life was the afternoon I found Bradford and his assistant on the boat. Evidently, that wasn't the first clothes-optional meeting they'd had. And she hadn't been the first to be there. The divorce got even worse."

She leaned back in the corner of the sofa and sipped the warm liquid. "My attorney and I had to fight for everything. But at the end of this year, I'll finally be able to sell the condo free and clear. And the money from selling the boat is already invested. He got the house in the settlement, but he's already sold it, and I have yet to see my share of the money from the furnishings."

"How long have you been divorced?"

"Three years. Three long years of finding myself. Strict budgeting. And working my tail off for first one news station and then another." She slightly smiled. "Which brings us to me losing my job. But I'm a fighter, and I will survive."

He grinned then kissed her deeply. "I would expect nothing less."

When they parted a short time later, she walked him to the door. Once again, they kissed. Once again, she didn't invite him to stay. Not because she hadn't wanted to and not because she hadn't worked up her courage…maybe. But afternoon delight was not the way she wanted their first time to happen. She'd been okay with how she looked in the mirror this morning. Besides which, vanity didn't fit in her personality. But the idea of dimming the lights for the first time they made love, well…somehow that made her feel better.

He wouldn't have been able to stay anyhow. He'd already told her the phone call from his boss this morning had led to a couple of meetings he needed to attend this evening. Only time would tell if he phoned to cancel their plans for tomorrow. But that would at least be better than if he just didn't show up in the morning.

CHAPTER TWENTY-SEVEN

ASHLEY AND MARK walked the long block to catch the DC Circulator bus for the short trip to the Smithsonian area of the National Mall. The morning briskness in the air was chilly but refreshing. Once there, they trekked to the National Museum of Natural History.

Somewhere along the way, he took her hand. It felt so easy to be with him. The wind picked up, and their breaths fogged a bit, their steps quickened.

"Are you cold?" he asked.

"Some."

"Come on, I'll race you."

His long strides were hard to keep up with, but he dragged her along. Never letting loose of her hand, he took the museum steps two at a time, while she climbed one by one. Almost to the door, she purposely dropped her handbag. When he bent to pick the purse up, she darted into the lobby, laughing.

"I won. I won," she said, flapping her arms against her body when he appeared. She took her gloves off and rubbed her hands together for warmth.

"You cheated. Maybe I'll throw your bag outside again." He stepped toward the door.

She grabbed his arm with two hands and gave a pouty expression. "No, no. You wouldn't do that, would you?"

"Maybe we can negotiate." Biting the side of his lower lip, he glanced at the ceiling as if thinking. Then slowly back at her. "Maybe I could be persuaded if you showed me a few of your salsa moves."

"Here? Now?" She glanced at the crowds meandering past them. Dare she? "What do I get in return?"

"Only your purse." He held up her purse with a tiny shake, then leaned close to her ear. "How about I sweeten the deal with an IOU for later?"

Now that was a deal she couldn't turn down.

Humming a quick-paced salsa song and trailing her hand across his chest, his shoulders, and his neck, she danced around him one time. Stopped in front of him. Gave a quick hip wiggle. And winked.

"I'm going to hold you to that IOU," she said as she lifted her purse from his fingers.

He cleared his throat and bowed slightly. "I would certainly hope so."

After removing his gloves, he took her hands in his, rubbing them quickly. Warmth tiptoed into her body, not only from her hands, but also her heart. Again, she asked herself the question. Besides the obvious, what is it about him that attracts me? I don't even know what he does. What's his background? Who is he? What do I really know about him?

He let her hands fall and unzipped his leather bomber jacket. "Where do you want to start?"

She smiled. "I'll get a brochure."

They wandered for the next couple of hours from level to level, investigating the world. Dinosaurs to mammals. Reptiles to gems and minerals. They tugged each other to different exhibits, pointed out specifics, and read the placards. They laughed and smiled and mulled over the universe.

"When I was a boy, I loved to play in the dirt. Had all kinds of trucks and moving equipment. I sure liked digging. Maybe I should have been an archeologist. Liked being outside in the sun. The wind."

She visualized him sitting on the ground, moving dirt from one spot to another. "Ever find anything important?"

"Once. How about you?" he asked. "What did you want to be?"

"First, I planned to be an opera singer. Figured I'd get to wear the big beautiful gowns. Then I changed to wanting to be a dancer. Took ballet for a while." She demi-pliéd. "At night, I'd lie in bed and imagine myself twirling in a white tutu."

"Why didn't you?"

"Schools didn't exactly emphasize dancing for an occupation. So, I studied, made good grades, and went off to college like a proper young lady." The day she'd thrown the ballet shoes away flicked through her. She had cried. A lot.

Mark's phone beeped, and he read the text

message. "I think there's a café here someplace. Why don't we get some lunch?"

"Okay." She thought his phone was shut off since it hadn't rung anytime in the past couple of days.

"You go ahead, and I'll meet you there soon as I make a call?"

"Sure. Take your time." After a stop at the gift shop for postcards, she proceeded to the Atrium Café. For some reason, him taking a phone call didn't seem to bother her as much this time.

A short time later, Mark joined her at the table, pulling his chair close to hers. "Sorry, but I'm not going to be able to stay for lunch. Some business has come up. If I leave now, I'll be on time for dinner."

The air slipped out of her sails. "If something happens and you can't make it for dinner, just give me a call. I'll be fine."

"Don't worry, I'll be at your hotel by six o'clock." His hand briefly covered hers resting on the table. "You can count on me."

"Where are we dining?" She couldn't stand to think this would be their last evening together. Tomorrow, she'd be back in Nature's Crossing, and he'd be… Where?

He stood to leave. "It's a surprise."

"What should I wear? I need a clue at least."

"A clue?" His fingers brushed her cheek. "Okay. The restaurant is top of the line, with a premium wine list. And a great view."

His fingers continued to her lips, and she reacted with a barely-there kiss as they brushed across.

"I'll be ready," she murmured. No man had ever made her feel so beautiful, so sexy, so special.

He gave a brief nod, then she watched him and his muscle-filled jacket disappear out the door. Was it the clothes or the man that made her feel fuzzy? Either way, she could imagine life with him. Almost. A home together. Almost. Trust and tenderness. Almost.

Nothing in life was perfect, she'd learned, and the thought of surrender, only to be broadsided by betrayal again was more than she was willing to risk. They'd talked about her a lot, but him not so much.

"Postcards," she said to herself, reaching for her coat.

Out of the blue, Mark was back. He picked up her coat and held it for her as if he had all the time in the world.

She slipped her arms into the sleeves. "I thought you were gone."

He turned her around and zipped her trim-fitting ivory jacket. Then rested his fingers beneath her chin. Silent, she etched this moment in her memory. Don't let this end. No, beware. Stay on guard. Caring causes pain. Trust causes pain. Pain causes sadness. No, no, no… Yes, yes, yes. Don't let this end. Don't let this end.

He leaned in and kissed her lips lightly. Leaned in again, pulled her close, and kissed her solidly, letting his tongue tease her lips. She responded in turn, slipping her arms around his neck.

Resistance crumbled within her, piece by piece

by piece. Freed of herself, she yearned for whatever the future might bring. But she'd follow his mantra…one moment at a time. She couldn't live without him, even if it meant only stolen moments of time. Moments were better than growing old without him.

"I will be there tonight," he stated in a firm whisper against her cheek.

"I believe you," she whispered in return.

CHAPTER TWENTY-EIGHT

ASHLEY DASHED ACROSS the hotel suite to the ringing phone. "Hello?"

"Are you ready? I'm in the lobby, if you are," Mark said.

"I'm not finished dressing."

"Are you kidding me? What did you do all afternoon?"

"I went shopping and came back to the room."

"And?"

"Alright, I fell asleep. Okay?" She clicked the phone to speaker mode and deftly applied mascara while she talked. Makeup done. "Come upstairs and watch television while I finish. I'll hurry."

She hung up before he could answer. That's when a small voice shouted through her brain… "Why not stay here for the evening?" Even the piece of blue sea glass she'd bought today, and laid on the bedside table, seemed to coax her to stay in for the night. Just her and Mark and dinner and see what happens next.

That was not the plan. And, truth be told, she was excited to see what he'd arranged for their last evening in Washington.

She grabbed her short black dress from the hanger, tossed it over her head, and let it shimmy down her body before zipping. After sliding on her heels, she rushed to retrieve her silver earrings, bracelet, and necklace from her travel case. A knock at the door jiggled her composure. What composure? She was a basket case.

"Just a moment," she called out.

Ashley slid the necklace through the loop of an oval emerald pendant and tried to fasten the clasp, but her fingers wouldn't cooperate. Before long, he knocked again. She smoothed her dress, crunched the auburn tresses framing her face, and did a final look in the mirror. After checking to make sure who was on the other side, she took a deep breath, smiled, and opened the door.

Mark braced against the doorframe with one hand, the other on his hip, and appeared to be deep in thought as he stared down at the hall carpet. Looking up slowly, he took his time surveying the scenery along the way—her legs, hips, waist, breasts, and on and on—till he met her gaze. She blushed.

He angled his head and raised his eyebrows slightly. "You look dressed to me."

"Well, I'm not. Can you help me with this necklace?"

He stepped inside and tossed his overcoat on the sofa as she closed the door. She handed him the necklace, turned around, and lifted the back of her hair. Slow and deliberate, he brushed her neck with the sides of his fingers before smoothly hooking the clasp. Easing his hand to the neckline of her dress, he pressed it slightly toward the side, kissed the nape of her neck. Caught unaware, she arched into his touch, letting herself enjoy the moment, she tilted her head slightly backward.

Leaning his cheek next to hers, his mouth brushed her ear as his breath lightly caressed the tender spot on the side of her neck. Then, as if they'd done this a million times before, he slipped his arm around her waist and pulled her back against him. Even through their clothes, his erection pressed hard against her back.

"Is that everything you need me to do?" He said as he began to inch his lips and kisses along her jawline. Turning her slowly to give his mouth access.

"Uhhhhh...I thought you had dinner reservations for us." Kissing him had become as easy as breathing, and she wrapped her arms around his neck. Pressing against him in return.

"Reservations can always be canceled."

His breath gentle in her hair, the feel of his hands sliding down her back, palms rounding over her bottom, brought her core to life. His fingers gently inched one side of her dress upward, and she bent her knee, angling her thigh into his hand. Sexy as sin in his suit and tie and long-sleeved white shirt, buttons to the top, her mind wandered to what he'd look like lying beside her with none of that between them.

She was lost. So, so lost. Pushing back from him

as she straightened and turned to her bedroom doorway, she realized she was lost. So, so lost. "Excuse me while I get my bag and wrap for the evening."

"Don't forget your hat and gloves, either." Sighing, he let her fingers trail away. "It's cold out there. Looks like it may snow."

Once in the bedroom, she closed the door and blew out a trembling breath. Pacing in front of the dresser till she finally caught her breath, she knew dinner was out of the question. Maybe later, but not right now. Now was about her and him and courage.

Opening the closet door, her eyes lit on the perfect first-time outfit. A zip-front jacket. The white fuzzy gloves she'd bought. And a white snowball hat. That's all she needed. Oh, except for the silver heels she planned to wear to dinner… later. Quick as she could, she slipped out of all the clothes she'd worked so meticulously to make perfect. Everything but the necklace.

She checked herself in the mirror, making sure the jacket skimmed her upper thighs at the appropriate length. Adjusted the hat to the appropriate angle. Then, quietly, she opened the bedroom door and slipped into the doorway.

Bracing her right forearm against the doorframe, she cocked her knee toward the other, being sure to hold her gloved hand on her hip. "Sorry I took so long. I had a little trouble finding my hat and gloves."

"No problem." Mark stood up from the sofa as he tossed aside the magazine he'd been reading while waiting for her to finish dressing. "I was just reading—"

He looked up and stopped stone cold still. A shot of lust zeroed in on his mind. His chest. His dick. Shucking his jacket in one swift move, he loosened his tie as he walked toward her. Quick and to the point, she slid the tie from his collar.

Matching her speed, he untucked and unbuttoned his shirt and tossed it to the floor. A second later, his pants and underwear were on top of his shoes and socks. This was moving too fast. Not at all what he'd planned for the first time. He should slow this down, but— His gut twisted in a million knots.

Damn, she was hot. He was hot. And—

She lightly kissed the hollow in his throat. Brushed the fuzzy white gloves against his chest then let them slide down the front of him as she slipped her hands free and looped them around his neck. "Just so you know. I'm keeping the tie."

Sliding the zipper of her jacket downward, all he could think about was her and him and this. "Honey, you can keep *anything* you want."

He swooped her up in his arms and headed to the bed. His world could end tomorrow, and today would have been worth it. This. Now. Ashley.

CHAPTER TWENTY-NINE

A SHORT TIME LATER, in the elevator, Ashley snuggled against the crook in Mark's arm as he pulled her close and gave her a resounding kiss. He pressed a button on his phone and alerted the valet they were on the way down. Anxious to see what he'd planned for the rest of the evening. A tiny bit hungry. And completely sated. Life had her safe within its arms, and she was happy.

As they stepped out of the hotel into the night air, he led her to a waiting limo. He instructed the driver to show them the holiday sights of Washington. The bright lights. The carolers. The wreaths and garland and holiday hubbub. The National Christmas Tree, Georgetown GLOW DC, the National Cathedral, and even a bit of the National Zoo Christmas Lights.

"You really went all out on this evening," she said, clinking her glass of champagne against his.

"I tried. But this afternoon surpassed anything I could have planned for today." Giving his head a slight jerk, he bit the side of his lower lip. "You are really something, Ashley Lanovan."

"Glad you liked the spontaneity."

"Oh, I liked everything." He eased her legs over his, brushing his hand up the side of her thigh, then kissed her lightly. "Simply… Everything."

Their future hummed just below the surface, and she wondered if his heart was pounding as hard as hers. Finally, he buzzed the driver and instructed him to take them to the Reflecting Pool by the Lincoln Memorial.

"I want to show you something." His fingers intertwined with hers as he leaned against the door and tugged her closer.

The chauffeur nodded, and after returning to Washington and the Mall area, the limo eased to the curb. The driver handed Mark a stadium blanket from the front seat.

Ashley stepped out into the cold, took his arm, and they walked some of the same paths they'd walked yesterday in daylight. There was a chill, but she'd dressed warmly. As they neared the base of the steps leading up to Abraham Lincoln, a light snow began to fall. Standing there quietly, side by side, she once again wondered at the strength and peace, yet tiredness, which seemed to fill Lincoln's face. This was the first time she'd ever come to the Mall at night in winter. Seemed even more majestic in the falling snow.

Mark turned her toward the glass-like water of the Reflecting Pool, where the Lincoln Memorial was reflected. The shimmer of the Washington Memorial reflected in the still waters at the far end of the Pool encapsulated her with awe. She held tighter to Mark's arm, then laid her head against his shoulder. Neither spoke.

After guiding her down a few steps, he brushed away the snow from a step behind them. He spread the blanket in the cleared space before he held her hands to lower her to the seat. A second later, she felt the warmth of his body as he sat beside her and folded her arm around his.

"Are you too cold?" he asked.

"I'm okay."

He stared at Reflecting Pool for a good while, caressing her gloved hands ever so often, then finally turned to face her. She smiled and started to speak but stopped when he shook his head. Slowly, he lifted her fingers to his lips, kissed them lightly, then placed them back on her lap before letting go.

"I was about twelve the last time I came here with my dad." Mark took a deep breath and blew it out through his mouth. "Usually, he was gone with his job, so most times it was me and my mother going places. I missed him not being around. Never seemed to bother her. Later, I learned how much she'd given up. How strong she really was. How much she loved him."

Ashley wanted to reach out to him, but she didn't. This was his story to tell, not hers to interrupt.

"Anyhow, that day, it was just me and him. Spent the whole day here on the Mall. From one end to the other." Mark's voice was hoarse. Steady, but hoarse. "It was a great day. A *really* great day. Kind of like yesterday and today with you."

His chin quivered for an instant, but Mark

fisted one hand inside the other and steadied his emotions.

"That day, I got up the courage to ask him the question that kept me awake at night. Why couldn't he always be at home like other kids' dads?" He swiped his sleeve across his eyes. "We sat right here in front of the Lincoln Memorial, right here in the blazing June sun, and he gave me his answer. He told me about his job with the CIA. The importance of right and wrong. How much me and my mom meant to him.

"And, finally, he told me about the obligation he felt to help keep the nation strong for the future. He talked about being a soldier, but not in the real sense. About wanting to help others in the world. I didn't understand all of what he said, but he sounded sure. Truthful."

She noticed wetness filled his eyes.

He wiped his face again and straightened. "He died a few years later on a CIA mission in another war-ravaged developing country. His name's not on any of the memorials here on the Mall." His voice was sure and strong again. "You see, sometimes there are people who give their lives, and no one ever knows."

The cold crept in, and she gave an involuntary shiver.

"We'd better go before you freeze to death." He got up and reached back for her hand.

Ashley shook her head as she motioned him to come back beside her on the step. Their gazes met and held. He finally unbuttoned his overcoat and sat back down, wrapping his arm and coat around her shoulder. She huddled against him. Closer than she'd ever been.

"You asked about my job, do you still want to know?"

"Yes, Mark. I want to know you." She felt the rise of his shoulders as he drew another deep breath.

"Like my dad and my granddad, and even further back, I work for the CIA. I've been part of the clandestine operations for over ten years. Sometimes assignments take me away for weeks, sometimes months. Years." Mark's cheek rested against her hair, and the muscles in his arm tightened. "I've lived in places you may or may not have heard of. Dangerous places. I've been captured. I've been hurt. I've hurt others. And I will again. Even though I'm in the process of taking a job with the Parks Service, there's always that possibility.

"But the one thing you have to understand, is that everything I've done has been for the right reasons." He paused as if waiting for her to run away. "Are you sure you want to hear more?"

Solemn in her thoughts, she nodded.

"I have a few close friends, like Patrick and Janie. And that's only because he and I worked a lot of missions together." He took her hand and held on tight. "For the most part, though, I've never made commitments to anyone besides the U.S. government. I don't get involved because it's not fair to the other person. Sure, my assignments are dangerous, but I'm trained to handle the danger. The people closest to me aren't, and I wouldn't want them to live in fear all the time."

He paused, kissed her forehead, then turned up the collar on his coat as they wrapped the blanket across their legs. "That's why I never called you after the Gregorys introduced us."

"And that's why you stopped calling me a while back?" She covered his grip on her hand with her own and pulled it to her. His words were like tiny bulbs lighting the way, illuminating why he did what he did sometimes.

"Yes. I don't want anything to ever happen to you because"—he smiled, slightly—"as I'm sure you've noticed, we click just fine."

She scrunched against him. "I think so, too."

His body relaxed slightly. "Fact is, you're the first one I've ever told any of this. But there's more, and you need to hear this now."

She nodded. "Okay. Tell me whatever you want."

"I'm good at my job, Ashley. And I'm proud to be who I am. I do whatever the government tells me to do. Even if I don't know why at the time, I trust there's a bigger reason than me. Do I question sometimes? Do I ignore sometimes? Hell yes. I've even had some mighty powerful people in a lot of different governments see my way instead of theirs. But, in the end, I stay alive." He faced her, looked into her eyes. "Any. Way. I. Can. I stay alive. Do you understand what I'm saying?"

Her mind struggled to block the implications of what he said. On the other hand, her heart understood that if she wanted the love of this man, if she was to give him her love, then she needed to accept the implications. Could she? Was she strong enough? Was she able to accept his staying alive might mean someone else didn't?

A haunting steel–blue color had settled in his eyes, masking his emotions. She knew he wouldn't ask her to stay. The decision had to be hers, and hers alone. The muscle in his jaw quivered for an instant, and she realized that although he wouldn't ask, he hoped. She wasn't the only one vulnerable in their relationship.

His expression was noncommittal, his shields in place. Yet, she saw beneath the screen, beneath his armor. No one else in the world knew this man like she did, and no one else ever would.

She didn't lower her eyes from his gaze. "There are lots of people in this world who fight to defend others. And none of them want to die. I would expect nothing less from you."

For a while, they sat in silence before he kissed her hair softly and then tilted her face up. "What I told you isn't specific, but that's all I can do right now. Even this much may ultimately drive you away. I hope it doesn't, but I'll understand if you get up and leave. In fact, you should run to the limo and lock the doors right now. I've already instructed my driver to take you wherever you want to go if you show up back at the car alone."

"I know what you're saying. I understand what you're saying." Squeezing his hand against her, she made her choice. "And I'm okay, Mark. I'm okay with who you are and what you've done."

Mark's expression steeled even further, eyes

narrowed. "Being around me is dangerous, Ashley. More dangerous than I hope you ever know. And there's nothing I can do about that if you decide to stay. Nothing except protect you with my life." He swallowed. "Sometimes even that's not enough. Anyone in my line of work, whether it be CIA, FBI, DHS, any type of law enforcement, know what they're getting into. And even with the Park Services, there'll be times I'm assigned to criminal cases. Life happens...and so does death. Not only to an agent, but sometimes to the ones he loves."

The magnitude of their conversation crept through Ashley's mind and heart and soul. He seemed to have practiced what he was going to say and needed to get the words out all at one time. Honest and to the point. She'd never anticipated his strength and conviction for what he did, or what he planned to do in the future.

What more magnificent place for them to be than here when she ultimately met and understood the man beside her. Here, where she accepted him for who he was and what he did, had done, and would do again if the need arose. Yes, she was strong enough. That realization brought her peace and pride and conviction. She was strong, too. Strong enough for this man and his life.

"I love you so much, I don't have the strength to push you away anymore." He released his hold. "So, you have to make the choice. To live in peril. Or to run far, far away from me."

She leaned into him, knowing she'd never witnessed such honesty. Such selflessness. Her warmth mingled with the cold and she saw her breath float in the winter air. "Don't you know? I don't run anymore. Never. Unless I run to you."

He stood and held out his hands to help her up. After removing his gloves, he cupped her face and softly kissed her. There was no cold, only warmth and honesty. When they parted, she slid herself inside his woolen overcoat, hands resting against his chest as his arms encircled her.

"I promise I won't ever lie to you," Mark said.

"Good," she whispered.

His mouth found hers, and one powerful kiss after another propelled her to another world. Their bodies melded together as his hands on her back pressed her closer against him.

She responded and returned the sensations racing through her as she circled his waist with her arms. Her fingers gripped his shirt in finality while she strained to breathe when they parted.

The gentle snow falling around them had gradually changed to big pure-white fluffy flakes, landing on their eyelids, their faces, and still they clung to each other. Smiling people passed in the nighttime. Some nodded. A few took their partners' hands.

"I guess we should go to dinner now." He kissed her cheek once again.

"Guess so. But I thought you canceled the reservations."

She didn't move.

He slightly raised his eyebrows then kissed her forehead. "I made new ones. The view may not be as good, but it's still a nice place with a great Christmas tree."

CHAPTER THIRTY

ASHLEY SLID INTO the back seat of the limo and snuggled into Mark's warmth, reflecting on what had just transpired on the steps of the Lincoln Memorial. And as the driver drove them to dinner, she didn't even pay attention to where they were going.

A while later, the driver turned into a circle driveway in front of a welcoming house that dreams are made of. Mark exited the limo and spoke briefly with the driver, then walked around and opened the passenger door for her. Stepping out of the car, she felt his arm slide around her pulling her close as the limo drove away.

She couldn't help but admire the scene in front of her. One like a holiday movie or Christmas card. Greenery entwined with sparkling lights festooned the porch entryway, a balsam wreath with silver balls and red bows adorned the door, lights flickered in every window on both floors. The two-story home, decades old and stately, appeared comfortable with the dressings of the season.

"Where are we?" she asked as he looped her arm

through his and they walked side by side to the front door.

Mark lifted her hand to his lips. "Welcome to my home, Ashley. I hope you like it."

"This is beautiful. Magnificent. Must have cost a small fortune."

"Probably would nowadays. Probably did back when my mother's family first had this built well over a century ago, also." He lightly laughed. "No way my salary would ever buy something like this. But her family was wealthy, and I inherited everything as the last one in the line."

Without so much as a pause, the front entry door opened, and a tall balding man, dressed impeccably in a black suit, red tie, and black shoes buffed to a gleaming shine, greeted them. The man's face showed no expression as he nodded and motioned for her coat. "Good evening, Mr. Garmund."

Mark removed his overcoat, which was promptly taken. "Ashley, this is Mr. Sawyer. He's my house manager, butler, valet. Fact is, we've never hit on exactly the right job title for him. All I know is he keeps everything running around here while I'm out of town. Does a mighty fine job of it, too."

The butler reddened, shook his head, and glanced down momentarily. "Reallllly, sir."

"Mr. Sawyer, this is Ms. Lanovan."

"Hello." Ashley smiled. The unspoken goodwill between the two men spoke volumes.

The valet nodded then disappeared through a door across the foyer, coats in hand.

Mark showed her from room to room on the

first floor, and she absorbed the ambiance along with the impeccable decorating. The den was masculine, but the remainder of the rooms were slightly traditional yet also modern. Her favorite was the living room, complete with a reading nook nestled in a bay window. Her gaze was caught by French doors on one end of the room, leading to a walled patio. The other end of the room held a spectacular Christmas tree.

Maybe this was all a dream, and she would wake up. Alone again. When his arms slipped around her and she leaned her head against him to watch the tree-topper sparkle above, she knew it was real. He felt too good for it to be otherwise.

"I told you there was a beautiful tree," Mark said. "Almost as beautiful as you."

"Ummmm. Did you decorate this yourself?"

"When I'm not away on assignment, I always place the star on top and a few ornaments here and there. For the most part, though, the staff takes care of it. This is their home, too."

He excused himself for a moment, giving her time to enjoy the view of the courtyard rimmed with pruned holly bushes covered in tiny white lights. The brick pavers were laid in a circular pattern surrounding a beautiful fountain, shut down for the winter but still beautifully decorated with pale-blue lights. Small benches beneath the trees, and a round patio table completed the atmosphere.

Ashley saw Mark's reflection in the windowpane as he returned to the room. She noticed his tie was gone and the top buttons of his shirt undone. He watched her for a moment, then made eye contact with her reflection in the glass and moved to stand beside her.

"Your home is wonderful. Thank you for bringing me here," she said.

"You'll love the patio in the spring and summer. Lots of flowers. Last summer, Nina added a swing beside the cherry tree over to the side of yard. Sometimes we sit there and talk about old times."

"Who's Nina?"

He pressed one of the buttons next to the French doors. Then, enfolding her in his arms, his lips brushed her ear with a whispered, "You might say she's my upstairs maid. Feather dusters are her specialty. Of course, she's extremely good in the kitchen, too. Did you know feather dusters can be used in every room in the house?"

She tensed. Pushed out of his arms. Was there someone else in his life even now, and he'd slipped with the name? Her mind tensed with the thought she might have mistakenly let her emotions be melted by him. She felt the momentary twitch of her right eye as she strove to keep her doubts in check.

"Yes, sir." The softness of the woman's voice caught Ashley off guard even before she looked into the face of a short, silver-haired lady. A crisp white bib-apron, with a holiday wreath applique on the top covered a simple navy dress. A smile lit the corners of her eyes.

"This is Nina. Nina Reynolds. The woman who actually keeps things running around here." He smiled. "Just don't tell Sawyer I said that."

Ashley needed to learn his style of joking. Because he'd clearly teased her to see her reaction. Good to know he had a little sense of humor behind that serious, sexy, and stressed exterior.

"Hello, I'm Ashley Lanovan. It's a pleasure to meet you." She shot him a sideways look, then extended her hand to Nina. "I was a little unsure why I was here once he told me he had an upstairs maid that was really good in the kitchen, too."

Nina looked perplexed as to why that would be a problem.

"Oh…then he said something about…" Ashley cupped her hand in front of her mouth and leaned toward the gray-haired lady as if to share a secret. Placed her other hand against her chest in mock embarrassment. "*Feather dusters.*"

Nina straightened. Ashley nodded. Mark burst out laughing, covering his face with both hands, then glanced at her. He quickly offered a two-finger salute, insinuating she'd got him.

"Mr. Garmund!" Mrs. Reynolds crossed her arms in front of the apron bib while she rapidly tapped her foot on the polished floor. "What am I going to do with you?"

The housekeeper turned to Ashley. "He's really a nice man. But sometimes he's a real pain in the bazoo. Worse than when he was young. Back then, I couldn't keep the cookie jar filled. He'd eat the fresh-baked cookies right off the cooking rack."

"Ummmmm." Ashley tilted her head at Mark.

He winked at her. "I still like cookies."

"It's a pleasure to meet you, too, Ms. Lanovan. Will you be needing anything else now?" Nina asked.

"No. Thank you. But please call me Ashley."

"Certainly." Nina headed out of the room, calling over her shoulder. "Dinner will be ready in about an hour."

Ashley's wait-till-I-get-you smile flashed a second before she teasingly lunged at Mark, aiming a punch on his bicep. He took refuge behind the sofa, and she charged around the barrier but slipped on the hardwood floor. As if in slow motion, her heel flew out from under her. Too late, Mark grabbed for her, and the two of them ended up on the floor. Their thud mixed with laughter echoed through the comfortable house.

He propped himself on his elbow, inches away from her. "Are you okay?"

"I think so. At least there's no woodpile this time."

Gently, his fingers tweaked her nose. "You know, you're pretty feisty when you get angry. Or was that a touch of jealousy?"

She ignored the question. "Do you try that feather duster joke on every woman you bring home?"

Mark nuzzled her neck with his lips. His body eased closer alongside. "You're the only woman I've ever brought to my house."

Ashley's neck arched into his kisses. She lost her line of defense when a moan found its way to the surface from somewhere deep inside. She sighed with pleasure. Breathless and floating, she whispered, "Ever?"

He turned her face to his and traced the outline before capturing her chin between his thumb and fingers. Leaning halfway in, his index finger caressed the outline of her lips.

"Ever," he answered.

His arm slid around her, pulling her to him. She didn't resist. His hand slid down, eased around her backside, pressing them even closer. With a mind of its own, her leg slid up his pant leg, leaving a clear pathway for his hand to continue the trail to her thigh, her calf. Smooth and slow, his palm traced down and up again, each time higher.

When it dawned on her the direction this was taking, she pushed on his shoulders. "Don't you think dinner should be ready soon?"

"Dinner?"

"You know. Food, wine, plates, glasses. Dinner."

He rolled to his back. Hands clasped behind his head, he stared at the ceiling. "Sure, if that's what you want."

"No, no, no. That line is not going to help you this time." This time it was Ashley who leaned on her elbow to face him. Her fingers tickled a trace on his ear lobe. "Dinner is why you brought me here. Right? And I'm hungry."

For a few seconds, the want in his gaze reeled her in, and she thought he'd pull her to him again. She'd go willingly—the heck with dinner. To her chagrin, he clenched his jaw and looked to the ceiling again. When his hand moved to cover her touch, she shivered. The next moment, he sat up.

She joined him as they leaned back against the sofa where he drew her into the curve of his arm, and she eased her head against his shoulder, her hand against his chest. The splendid Christmas tree, decorated in old-fashioned ornaments and bubble lights, held her attention. What-if?

"It's lovely," she whispered.

Her ear caught his breath along with his voice. "So are you."

Dinner, from appetizers to dessert, proved to be better than most Ashley had ever been served anywhere in the world. Even delicious chocolate mousse with real whipped cream. Afterward, she and Mark took their coffee to the chairs by the French doors and talked.

He explained further how his mother's family had been well off. And the history of his home. Nina had been part of the family since he was a young boy—reprimands included. Nothing ever harsh, but lectures on good and bad and why had made frequent visits. He had to admit most of the reproaches had been well deserved.

Sawyer, a retired ATF agent, had been hired the first time Mark had gone on an assignment years ago. He hadn't wanted to leave his mother alone for long periods of time without someone to protect her if need be. A white Lincoln, updated every year, had been bought for Sawyer to chauffeur his mother around.

Eight years ago, Mark had added a mint-condition early Corvette. That, and a few others, were in the five-car garage behind the house.

"One of the few toys I have for myself," Mark said.

"What about all those musical instruments you told me about?" Ashley teased.

"Maybe. But I bet you indulge yourself in something every so often."

"Maybe."

"Like what?"

"Art is my passion. I have a few paintings in my condo that I spent way too much money on. Couldn't resist. When I'm feeling down, they transport me to another world."

Ashley's turn to expound on her world, she spoke of her upbringing in a moderately sized Midwest town, her travels for the events show, and how she loved shopping for a special antique or a one-of-a-kind trinket. Like the piece of blue sea glass she'd bought that afternoon.

The grandfather clock chimed eleven.

"It's getting late." She set her cup and saucer on the silver coffee service tray Mrs. Reynolds had placed on the side table.

"I guess I should take you to the hotel…"

Question or statement? She wasn't sure.

Arms looped around each other, they strolled to the entry hall and stood by the stairs. He ran his fingers through her hair, holding firm, while his kisses found their way from her forehead to her neck to her mouth. Her lips parted, gave him entry, and a feeling of magic she'd never experienced tickled her inside. His tongue danced with hers then pulled away, nipping her lips with his teeth before the dance began again.

When they parted, he kept the hold on her hand, stepped onto the first stairstep leading up to the second floor. He paused, looked at her as she glanced upward. Sure of the question this time, she wasn't sure of her answer.

He released her hand, took another step up and held out his hand. Palm up in invitation. "Stay with me, Ashley. Let go of the past and come upstairs with me."

Heaven help her, she wanted him with every bit of her body. She wanted to climb those stairs. She wanted to stay.

At this point, she couldn't speak. Could barely stand, but she took his hand and started up the stairs, one step at a time. Earlier this afternoon had felt different. Tonight? Tonight was about trust. About their future.

CHAPTER THIRTY-ONE

ASHLEY HEARD MARK close the bedroom door behind them then set the lock.

"I should have never met you." He kissed the curve of her neck, and she leaned to give him more. His breath fanning her desire. "Should have never let you touch my soul." Another kiss, a nibble of her ear. "Now I can't get away. Don't want to get away."

He toed off his shoes and socks. And she stepped from her strappy heels as he wrapped her in his arms and pressed her closer. Those two actions were like an unspoken agreement they were both headed in the same direction.

"Good." She gasped for air. "I don't ever want you to go."

"Are you sure? Real sure?" He skimmed his hands down her arms, her hands, her fingers.

With the hint of a wiggle, she leaned back against him, the only reply she had the strength to give.

"Say it out loud, Ashley. Make this real. Are you sure?"

She quivered, "Yes. Very sure."

His hands caressed back up her arms…up…up…
up… "What do you want, pretty lady?"

"You. I want you." Heaven help her, she was
more vulnerable than she'd ever been in her life.
But she trusted him with her life. The life she'd
finally discovered after all these years.

As if sculpting clay, he lightly slid his palms over
her shoulders, across her breasts, ending at her hips
with slow circles, then slow and easy he caressed
upward once again. Past her tummy. Past her waist.
Until, slower and slower, he stopped at her bra line.

Her soft voice combined with a moan as her arch
escaped its restraint. Eyes closed, arms raised and
reaching for him, she gave all of herself. Shameless,
she curved her body to his, caressed his in a side-
to-side glide.

He cupped her breasts, stroking his fingers across
her as she pressed into his hands.

Yes, yes. She never wanted this to stop.
"Ummmmmm, more. More…"

"I'll give you everything you want, Ashley. Any
way you want." Hoarse with desire, he lured her
with his words, his movements.

She spun to face him. Pushed her body against
him, closer than before, as she slipped her fingertips
into this hair. Gripping, tighter and tighter, she
matched his show of passion with her own. The
scratch of his beard's regrowth against her cheek
shot straight to her core. Powerful. Sensual. Their
mouths consumed each other while he eased the
zipper down the back of her dress. All the way.

She fumbled with the buttons on his shirt until

his hands covered hers, steady and supportive. When the last one came undone, he eased the shirt off and flung it aside.

Resting her cheek against the warmth of his chest, she heard the strong pounding of his heart as his fingers skimmed to her collarbone, dipped beneath the neckline, and gently eased the material from her shoulders. The dress swished to the floor and puddled at her feet.

He kissed first one shoulder, then the other before he outlined the lace of her bra with his eyes and fingertips. On and on and on, until finally, his thumbs eased the straps from her shoulders a moment before he released the lace-covered hook, allowing the bra to join the dress.

Slipping his palms down her spine to the edge of the black silk panties she'd bought only yesterday, he rimmed the edge with his fingers. Slowly, he slipped his hand beneath the silk and eased them from her body as he slightly bent. Gradually standing, he traced his hands beneath the arch of her foot to her ankles, her calves, her thighs, then rested one hand at her waist. Staring into her eyes, he watched for her reaction as the other found her core. A second later, he kissed her slow and easy, again and again, rhythm and rhythm, till she melted against him, her fingers splayed across his chest.

"If you'll have me, I promise there'll be only you, Ashley." The space between their lips narrowed with his whisper. "Yours till you kick me out the door. Or as long as I live."

Listening to the words she'd longed to hear, she

caressed his cheek and kissed him gently. "Then you'll be mine forever."

She loosened his belt, and he boosted her upward until her legs bent to his command, wrapping around him as he walked to the king-size bed. Laying her down, he stepped out of his pants and briefs.

Her lady parts rocketed to attention at the sight of him. Nothing shy about him. Nothing to be shy about. At the same time, she *was* suddenly shy, and reached for the sheet. He pushed the cover aside as he stretched out beside her.

"I've waited my whole life for you. Don't ever think I won't find you beautiful." He smoothed his fingers across her body, drawing a path to her trigger spots and hidden places. His kisses followed the path, and she arched against his touch, aching and alive.

Breathing on short intakes of air, she let herself fall into a haze of oblivion. "Mark?"

There was no answer except the love he continued to caress into her soul. Into her body. Into the intimacy of her life. His hands, his fingers, his lips all giving her what she'd longed for forever. He paused, breathing raggedly as he reached for the condom.

"Don't stop, Mark." Her voice, softer than soft, filled the room. "Don't ever stop."

"Never. I'll never stop." He winked, then rolled toward her, bracing on his elbows as he covered her. And she relaxed into his rhythm.

CHAPTER THIRTY-TWO

SEATED ON THE plane to Surryfield, Ashley pulled out her notebook and began a list of things to do once she got to Nature's Crossing. Call her parents about her change of plans for Christmas and make plans with them to spend the holidays with her in Nature's Crossing. Call Linda and Tracie to see if they could pop in for a couple of days between Christmas and New Year's Eve. And call Janie to let her know she made it home okay.

She watched the clouds outside her window, but all she saw were images of falling snow, sparkling lights, and welcoming candles. A glistening tree surrounded by hardwood floors. She and Mark curled against the sofa. His kiss… His touch…

No sleep for her on this flight; she had too much on her mind. By mid-afternoon, her plane had landed, and she was driving into the circle drive of the Gregory house. Peabody, who'd volunteered to housesit while she was gone, hurried out to the car. "Need any help?"

She gave him a hug. "Thanks. If you carry my

tote bag, I can get the other."

After bringing both big suitcases in and depositing them in her bedroom, she moved the car around to the garage. Gratefully, she took the hot cup of coffee he offered once she got inside and had a moment to sit with him at the table.

Peabody moved a plate of cookies and lemon bars in front of her. "Eloise sent these over. You'll also find a casserole in the refrigerator for your dinner."

She loved how the people in town had taken her into the fold. "I'll call and thank her later. By the way, thank you for staying here. How'd everything go?" She nibbled on one of the walnut sugar cookies.

"Felt like I was on vacation myself. You did have an interesting visitor one day."

"I thought everyone knew I was in Washington."

"Evidently, not everyone." He laid out the day Chadwick Andrews stopped by. "As much as it pains me to say this. I got the distinct impression he didn't know anything about tearing down the buildings or gambling. Just like you figured."

She frowned a bit, trying to make sense of the happenings. "Do you think it's all Chase's doing?"

"Don't know. I'll lay you odds, though, if it is all Chase, he's about to be confronted by his uncle." Peabody deposited his cup in the sink.

Ashley walked to the picture window. "By the way, did I tell you I've decided to stay here until Dot and Lloyd return?"

"Wonderful. You look refreshed. Did you enjoy

your trip to Washington?"

"Very much."

"I detect a smile," Peabody teased.

Standing at one of the back windows, she saw the buck wander out of the pines and into the clearing near the back of the property. The stag stopped and looked at the house for a moment, then continued across to the other trees. Her contentment was complete.

Peabody donned his coat and hat. "I'd better be gettin' on down the road. Supposed to stop by Fred and Eloise's for dinner. May decide to beat them in a game of Rook."

Ashley carried his bag to his car and thanked him again. Once she locked up for the evening, she decided her suitcases could wait until tomorrow to be unpacked. All except for the small tote bag she'd tossed on the bed. She deposited her notebook and reading materials on the coffee table, then unzipped the side pocket and retrieved Mark's tie.

She held it against her cheek, then slid the tie into the nightstand by her bed. Thoroughly exhausted, she stretched across the bed, wrapped the bedspread over herself, and fell into a quiet sleep.

Darkness had settled in by the time she woke. The casserole in the refrigerator looked tempting, but the slice of pie tempted even more. Sitting at the table to enjoy the sugar jolt, she jotted down a quick list of her financial assets and liabilities. She wanted to make sure she had the money to spend on a project before she wasted time drawing out a plan. Reviewed the to-do list she'd written on the plane. And started a new page of notes.

About nine, she dialed Janie's number, and even then, she wasn't sure what she wanted to say. Or ask.

Janie cleared her throat on answering. "Hey there."

"Did I wake you?"

"Not really. I figured you'd call tonight."

"I know it's late, but I wanted to see how you were feeling."

"Better. No fever today. May get to see Paddy tomorrow."

The conversation shifted to shopping and Christmas. Ashley told Janie about Chadwick's visit and Peabody's suspicions.

"Hey, I really miss you around here." Ashley yawned. "When will you two be home?".

Janie gave a light chuckle. "The therapist said not till the end of January. Patrick says we'll be home for the holidays."

"My money's on Patrick."

"So's mine."

The two women filled the air with silence.

"Guess I should let you get some rest," Ashley sighed.

"Patrick said Mark left on an assignment today," Janie said.

Just the words were soul-wrenching. Pain like she'd never experienced crept into her heart. "How do you do this?"

"Do what?"

"How do you stand there and let Patrick leave

each time?"

"It's part of the deal," Janie replied.

Ashley sniffled. "If it hadn't been for your darn cold, I wouldn't have seen Mark. Now look at me."

"As soon as he heard about our plans for the evening, he asked if he could use the ticket. What was I supposed to say?"

"I'm glad you didn't say no."

"Did you two get a chance to talk honestly?"

Ashley's face and heart lit with joy at memories. "Yes, and before you ask, I didn't run away. He even took me to his house for dinner. I got the impression that doesn't happen often."

"We've been there a few times. His home is gorgeous, but not many people ever see inside. Few even know where he lives." Janie coughed lightly. "I'm thinking he's never taken anyone like you there before."

"I felt like a princess being given the empire."

"And?"

Finally, Ashley continued. "When we left the house this morning, my insides felt like part of me had been yanked out. Funny thing, though, I don't feel empty. I feel like something else has filled the void."

They chatted another five minutes before deciding they were both tired and ended their call. She curled up under the afghan, trying to figure out exactly what the past few days and nights had meant.

Mark certainly wasn't a nine-to-five man like she'd planned. As long as he worked for the CIA, they'd never be able to share his workday. Work trips could happen in an instant. And half the time she'd have no idea where he was headed. Once he left the CIA and joined the Park Service, life would be easier. Or would it? He'd said his past would always be there. A possible danger to them both. She could live with all of that. Trusting him would be easy.

There was still one discussion they hadn't broached. Children. He'd shared his feelings about that topic during his phone call a few weeks. In fact, he'd stopped calling. That's why she'd been surprised when he walked into the Kennedy Center and took the seat beside her.

But there'd been no further conversation about children. Not even after he'd held her as she cried on the sofa in her hotel room. That meant he hadn't changed his mind.

She understood how each person had to make their own decision about raising a family. From their talks during her time in Washington, she knew how much his dad's death had affected him growing up. And, whether spoken or not, she realized he'd made his decision on children long before he ever met her.

Now, she needed to decide if she could live with that decision, also.

CHAPTER THIRTY-THREE

EARLY THE NEXT day, Ashley opened her notebook and started work on her phone calls. First one was to the Gregorys.

"Happy holidays," Dot answered.

For the next few minutes, they talked about Washington, Nature's Crossing, and how things were going in Florida.

"By the way, since I'm going to be here through the holidays, do you mind if I use your decorations?" Ashley asked.

"Wonderful idea. Everything you'll need is in the closet beneath the stairs leading downstairs. There's even an artificial tree for upstairs and downstairs. Boxes of ornaments. And lots of other decorations." Dot's voice was filled with excitement. "Check with Peabody on who to call to install the outside decorations and lights. Those are stored down in the red barn at the back of the property. Here, I'll put this call on speakerphone so Lloyd can join in."

The tone and clarity of the phone call changed just a bit.

"Hey, you two ladies better not be conspiring

behind my back." He chuckled.

Ashley laughed. "Of course not. Dot and I are mere amateurs at plotting. You're the head schemer in this bunch."

The conversation quickly turned to the encounter between Peabody and Chadwick. Nature's Crossing goings-on. And the talk of a development company trying to get permits to turn the Haney property into a housing development at the edge of town.

"Like I've said before, life has to change to move forward with the times." Lloyd's tone held no sadness, just a matter-of-fact excitement.

Finally, Ashley came to the last thing on her to-do list. The one that could decide the next chapter of her own life.

"There's one more thing I wanted to talk about." She took an extra deep breath and charged ahead. "I know you and Dot are going to be in this house for a long time to come. But when you decide to sell, would you please call me first?"

He laughed. "I've always heard of a seller's market, but never knew what that meant until now. You're the fourth person in the last week to contact us about buying the place."

Ashley's shoulders drooped as she sighed. "Then I'm way down the list."

"Nope. Two of them aren't even in the running," Dot said, forcefully and the point. "Right, Lloyd?"

"Ditto. First, Chase called and asked us not to tell his uncle he was inquiring. Said he was planning a surprise gift for Chadwick. Next day,

Chadwick calls to see how we're doing. Wondered if the Florida weather might be better for my health. Wanted us to know he'd be honored to list our property when the time came. Would even negotiate his commission." Lloyd mumbled something else under his breath.

Ashley thought it best not to ask him to repeat the last part. "Sounds like you've been popular these past few days. May I ask who was the third one to call?"

"Some real estate agent from Surryfield called to say she had a buyer willing to offer top dollar. Said the buyer was looking for a country home and about ten acres. Wanted to build a heliport in his backyard. Then she let it slip, the buyer's out of New York."

"I'd say that's all too coincidental. I'm not sure what all they're up to, but sounds to me like they're all going behind each other's back." Ashley tried to evaluate the information.

"Our thinking exactly. Thing is, once me and Dot got to Florida, we discussed selling the property there in Nature's Crossing and making The Villages our permanent home. Quite frankly, this might be better for my health."

Ashley didn't know what to say.

"Then all these phone calls made us wonder who's up to what. So, we decided to hold onto the place a bit longer." Lloyd took a deep breath, cleared his throat. "But since it's you asking, that makes a whole big difference. We do need to talk to one more person who had expressed interest last year. But give us a couple days to get our thoughts organized and we'll fax you a proposal. If it's agreeable, you've bought yourself a house and ten acres."

The rest of the conversation, Ashley was in pure shock. Shocked that she'd asked to buy the property. Even more shocked that the Gregorys might sell to her…now. The call had ended on an upbeat note for everyone.

After unpacking her suitcases, Ashley searched for the holiday decorations. Stored exactly the way Dot described, boxes were labeled upstairs or downstairs, memory tree or big tree, maybe and for sure. Ashley unpacked the lower level items, laying them carefully around the family room, and then toted the other boxes upstairs. The decorations were beautiful, some from around the world. Not all of them were her style, but they would be a nice change for the season.

As she passed the patio door, she caught sight of someone near the rear of the property. Using the land telescope, she watched as he walked around the open ground. He carried a pad of paper and made notes every so often after using a walking tape measure. When he reached the far end of the property, he turned and stared at the house. Even checked to see if he could get in the red barn's door. Thankfully, that was locked.

She went on the deck and waited for him to walk back to his car. The one he'd conveniently parked in the back drive. From this angle, she couldn't see the license plate but made note of the make and color. Also, she drew a mental picture of what the man looked like; mid-to-late thirties, slender but fit, a little over six feet tall, and completely bald.

Halfway back to the house, he glanced up from his notes. She saw the exact moment he noticed her standing on the deck, then quickly tucked the note pad under his arm. Waved. She didn't wave back. Approaching the house, he appeared friendly. As if he had every right to be her the property.

"Mrs. McGee?" he asked, stopping on the patio below.

"No." Ashley fixed him with her stare.

His tanned complexion accented the whitish shine on top of his head. Well-dressed, he carried himself as a man usually in charge.

"Are Mr. or Mrs. McGee at home?"

"There's no one here by that name."

He force-smiled, but his brow wrinkled as his eyebrows pinched together. "This is the McGee property, right?"

"Sorry, but it's not." Something about the voice seemed familiar. Where? Where had she heard him before?

"Guess I must have made the wrong turn. I'd been told the McGees asked me to take a look at their land. Might be wanting to sell." The tone of his voice had changed from friendly to distant with a touch of anger. Not at her. "I'll be getting out of your way. I'm sorry about the mix-up. Unless you're looking to sell."

"No." Still, she held her stare. "May I ask your name?"

"T. Randolph of T-Randolph Environmental Development." He nodded. "I assure you I was told the McGee family had invited me to view their property. I'm sorry for the intrusion."

"Seems your source misled you."

He cleaned his jaw. Nodded. "So it seems. Won't happen again. Have a good day."

Pulling his phone from his pocket, he headed to his car. His steps long, firm, and purposeful. Rounding the back bumper, he dialed someone.

"Next time, get your facts right before you send me someplace." Obviously, he didn't realize he was close enough for his voice to carry on the wind. And the tone was not happy. "Don't give me any excuses. I don't do business on a lie, Mr. Andrews."

He ended the call before getting into his car then pulled the white Lexus forward to turn around, giving her a view of the license plate—New York. And the call he'd just made had been to a Mr. Andrews. Chase? Chadwick? Who?

Suddenly, his voice clicked. He was the man who had been with Chase the day she and Eloise heard them talk about leveling part of Nature's Crossing and buying the Gregory property. She quickly read the license plate and car description, even the man's description, into her phone's Notes.

She waited for the man to exit the driveway before heading back inside and locking the door. Her insides tensed with fear, and she double checked all the door and window locks in the house. Main floor and lower level. Then made sure the garage door was locked, also. She was surprised that the Gregorys didn't have a security system, but, then again, this was the first time she'd felt any insecurity here at the house.

After calming, she called Peabody. No answer, so she left a brief message of what had transpired. "By the way, do you know of anyone who might have a nice dog for adoption? One with a loud bark… and lots of love."

An hour later, she answered the phone on the first ring, and Lloyd's voice came through the receiver. He verified her suspicion. No one in Nature's Crossing or the surrounding area went by the name of McGee. That's what she'd figured. Yet part of her believed that Mr. Randolph had been truthful in believing he had permission to be there.

"Question is, which Mr. Andrews did he call?" Peabody said.

"My money's on Chase." Ashley sipped on the cup of tea she'd just made. "And there's no need to ask, either. They'd both say they never heard of the man."

"You got that right. Now, what's this about wanting a dog?" Peabody asked.

She referenced the backyard story again. "Ultimately, I think a dog might be what I need. Besides, I may get lonely otherwise."

"Just so happens, last week, Mrs. Beacon went to live with her children in California. They own a small house and already had a poodle, so Mrs. Beacon left her chocolate Lab with me. Cocoa's a nice dog. Maybe three years old. Housebroke. Shots up-to-date."

"Sounds good, but isn't she pretty big?" Ashley's idea of a dog had been something small. Something to sit on her lap and yip whenever anyone came to the door.

As if ignoring her question, Peabody cleared his throat and went on. "She loves to go outside for walks, but you need to know upfront she's used to being inside most of the time. Little spoiled, but a real sweetie. Like you. Why don't you let me bring her over for a day or so? Try each other out."

She figured there was nothing to lose in giving the dog a chance. "Okay. You know you're pretty sneaky at getting your way."

"Comes from years of practice. I'll see you tomorrow morning."

The rest of the day, Ashley spent getting back into the swing of life without Mark at her side. She unpacked. Washed clothes. Made a sandwich for lunch. Stood staring out the back window, thinking about the past few days in Washington, until she lost track of time. Tired, she took a nap. Then woke to make dinner and watch a little television.

About eight, her phone rang, and caller ID showed Lloyd Gregory. She hadn't expected them to call back so soon. That could only mean one thing. The interested buyer from last year had jumped at the offer. She finally answered on the sixth ring.

Lloyd started with friendly conversation then paused. "Well, I guess I should get right to the point."

He hadn't even given their polite refusal yet, but already she hated the idea of leaving Nature's Crossing. Leaving all the friends she'd made. Leaving all the endless possibilities she'd scribbled on Post-It notes.

She reached over and grabbed a tissue. "Uh… Okay."

"Well, it didn't take me and Dot long to decide to sell. Could have told you that five minutes after we hung up this morning. But, of course, then I had to talk to our accountant about some things. Then took some time to type up the proposal. And then we took a nap, so we could say we slept on it." Lloyd chuckled. "We've never made a major decision in our life without first sleeping on it. But we're ready now."

"Uh… Okay." She didn't want to be rude, and she'd loved hearing that anecdote, but the longer he talked, the more she was dying. "Were you able to reach the other person who'd been interested in the property last year?"

"We did. That took some time, too." Lloyd paused. "Well, once he heard how much you love the house and Nature's Crossing, he decided you should be the owner."

She blew out a sigh. Half the battle was over. Yes, yes, yes. Now for the price.

"I'll send you an email with the proposal attached, including the price. Now, this is a big decision for you. Take as long as you want to decide." He sounded like her father had when she told him she planned to get married in her junior year of college. "Dot and I are in no hurry. Take as long as you want to decide."

"Uh… Okay." She really needed to stop saying that, but until she read the price, her brain couldn't come up with anything else. "Thank you. I'll talk to you all tomorrow."

True to his word, within a minute, their email came through, and she printed out the attachment. A whole two pages. She made a cup of tea and carried them to the sofa to review.

The proposal held a closing date. How they'd like the payments spread out for their tax purposes. And a price so low she reread it five times to make sure of the figures.

"That can't be right." She dialed the Gregorys right back. They'd made a mistake.

"I think you may have mistyped the price. Or maybe some of the paperwork didn't come through," Ashley said.

"What makes you say that?" Lloyd asked.

"Because this is a more than reasonable price for the house and land. I'm sure the other people who offered to buy would pay at least twice this amount." Ashley stared at the figure. Truth be told, Chase or Chadwick would have probably paid five times that much.

There was the click of another phone being picked up, and Dot joined the conversation. "We knew you'd be surprised."

"Do you want the deal at that price?" Lloyd said.

Ashley stammered, "Well, yes."

They decided Lloyd would contact the necessary people to have the paperwork drawn up and processed. She would have her attorney look it over. And when the couple came home in mid-January, everything could be signed. Now, if anyone asked about the house being for sale, they could say Ashley had bought the property.

Once the call ended, she floated from room to room, saying hello to her new home. She felt like a child with a new toy and wanted to share the news with someone. There was no way to contact Mark. She wanted to tell her parents and friends in person when they came for Christmas. Janie? She dialed her friend's number.

"I bought this house," Ashley blurted out.

"You what?

"I bought the Gregory house and property."

"Don't tease me like that."

"I'm serious. Absolutely serious!"

"What about your condo?" Janie had seemed groggy with sleep when she first answered. Now the news seemed to have woke her up completely.

"For now, I'll keep that, too. I'm so excited."

Janie squealed. "We're going to be neighbors."

Ashley told her all her ideas, including a dog and why.

"It won't take long for this news spreads around the area. Watch out for yourself. Chase won't be happy," Janie said.

"What do you mean?" Ashley's forehead wrinkled in a frown.

"Chadwick will be mad because he didn't get

what he wanted. Give him a week and he'll be over it." Janie paused. "Chase is another story. He's going to be livid that he didn't get his way."

She hadn't thought of the transaction like that. Yeah, he'd lost the Gregory property, but Lloyd would still be gone from the Town Council. Chase could find something else to buy in town, so he could run for the vacant position. Surely, he understood that people never get their way all the time. From the little she knew of him, he was creepy and callous, but she couldn't imagine him letting a business loss fuel his anger. Everybody lost things in life.

"Patrick and I met him the very first day we looked at buying the store. He wasn't happy. And we've had a few problems with him." Janie sighed. "All I'm saying is, don't take any chances where he's concerned."

CHAPTER THIRTY-FOUR

EARLY THE NEXT morning, Ashley greeted Peabody at the front door as he dropped off a beautiful chocolate Lab. The moment Ashley looked into Cocoa's dark-brown eyes, she lost a piece of her heart. Peabody carried the dog food and dishes into the kitchen and laid a soft blanket in the entry hall, then high-fived her. "Welcome to Nature's Crossing. Guess you'll need to have a housewarming after the holidays."

"The grapevine has been busy, I see."

"More reliable than the evening news." Peabody splayed his hands in a full circle. "Think I'm gonna make a video of how to have a reliable grapevine in a small town. What made you decide to stay?"

"Like you said before, this community kind of reaches out and grabs you."

He headed back out the door. "Sorry, but I gotta run. Eloise, Fred, and I are going Christmas shopping over at the lake's outlet mall. See you later."

She waved him on his way. The holidays were in full swing all around.

Filling Cocoa's dog dish and water bowl, she made a note to get some doggie treats and toys. Throughout the day, the two gave each other space to adjust. Cocoa snooped through the house while Ashley did more holiday decorating. After a while, she found her new companion curled on the blanket in the foyer and made a mental note to get a big doggie pillow. Maybe two or three for different spots in the house.

Hours later, Ashley retreated to the living room for the evening news, curling up with a magazine for some light reading also. From the corner of her eye, she saw Cocoa peek around the end of the sofa.

"Well, how are you, cutie? Are you finally awake?" Ashley said.

The dog glanced around the room, stretched, and wandered to the front door.

"You want to go out? Okay." She fastened the leash, and the pair ventured into the cold. Until Cocoa got used to her surroundings, she'd walk her on a leash. Although it shouldn't take long for her to know the pine tree boundary and be able to run free on the land.

During their brief walk in the front yard, Ashley's cell phone rang. Caller ID showed Bradford Lanovan. He seldom called. Usually when he wanted something. The last time had been the beginning of summer when he'd wanted to use the boat—she'd said no.

She contemplated letting it go to voicemail but figured she might as well get it over with.

Otherwise, he'd probably just keep calling back. "Hello."

"Ashley? Bradford."

"I know the voice. Why have you called?"

"Do I need a reason?"

"Yes. Why. Did. You. Call?"

Clearing his throat in one of his patronizing gestures, he prolonged the answer. "I stopped by the condo the other day. Imagine my surprise to find out you no longer live there."

Ever since she'd moved into the condo permanently after the divorce, she'd tried to figure out who in the multi-story complex kept track of her comings and goings. Any time something out of the ordinary had happened in her life, he'd called. Always asking to stop by. She'd always said no. For a while, she'd been paranoid about the whole thing, but gradually she'd learned to ignore it. Besides, she had a good idea of which neighbor was doing Bradford's spying.

"Is this going to be a long call, Bradford?"

"Yes. If you've sold that condo, then you owe me my percentage of the profit." He paused. "Or did you forget our divorce agreement?"

She counted to ten. Counted again. If she didn't answer, how long would it take before he finally hung up? Part of her wanted to give it a try. She didn't. Because everything came back to the fact that he'd just call again.

"Listen closely. First, the divorce papers say nothing about me having to live in the condo. I only have to not sell it within three years. Which, by the way, happens to be this upcoming February. Second, I will be putting the condo up for sale in March." She smiled to herself. Sounded good to hear. "So be sure you let your snitch in condo three-ten know. She keeps a close eye on my place and might want to make an offer on the property."

"Where are you moving?"

Staring at his photo on her phone, she felt as if she were truly seeing him for the first time. Why had she ever said yes to his marriage proposal? Why had she said yes the first time he asked her on a date? Why had she said yes the first day of college when he walked up and asked if she was lost? Why?

"That is none of your business. I don't owe you any explanation about anything ever again." She might have been lost back then. Even the past few years. But she wasn't lost anymore. Not even close. "Don't ever call me again, Bradford. And don't ever just happen to drop by. We. Are. Done."

She pushed the red button, and the line went silent. Like clockwork, he called back ten seconds later. She didn't answer. He called again. She didn't answer. He called and left a message. She deleted the unread voice mail. Deleted his picture from her phone list. Blocked his number. She meant what she'd said. They. Were. Done.

"Come on, Cocoa. That's a good girl." Ashley held the front door open. "Let's get back inside where it's warm."

After hanging her coat on the hall tree, she unsnapped the leash, and the two of them headed to the sofa. Ashley at one end, Cocoa at the other.

Pulling her legs up on the seat, she cradled her forehead in her hand on the armrest, contemplating all that had happened since she left St. Louis a little over a month ago. Life was full of surprises. All she would have needed was Bradford stopping by. She sat up and did a neck roll. Resting her head against the cushion, she closed her eyes and exhaled a deep sigh.

Something wet nudged her hand and brought her back to the moment. She glanced down. There was Cocoa, chin resting on Ashley's knee and tail slightly wagging. She scratched behind the ears of her gentle pal with the soulful gaze.

"Don't you worry, cutie. No matter what happens, we'll be fine. Won't we?"

CHAPTER THIRTY-FIVE

ASHLEY FILLED THE next couple of weeks with shopping, online and locally, wrapping gifts, and final garnishes outside. The last card and package were mailed a week before her company was to begin arriving.

Eloise called to say she would be sending over cookies, cakes, and pies from her and Fred, their holiday present. Peabody sent a card saying a fresh smoked turkey would arrive on Christmas Eve, compliments of himself, Lorna, and Gus. Friends made her life full. She still missed having Janie around, but most of all, she missed Mark. Lots.

On her way to pick up her parents at the Surryfield Airport, she realized how at home she felt even if the paperwork on the Gregory property hadn't been signed yet. Luckily, the plane was on time, and the drive to the house was catch-up time for the three of them. Ashley pulled into the front circle drive and eagerly watch their reactions.

"This is beautiful," her mother said.

"Wait till you see inside." Ashley laid her hand on her mother's. "You'll love the fireplaces."

Dad, the more reserved of the two, didn't offer an opinion.

She got her parents settled in their room before pressing them to accompany her on a walk around the grounds before dinner. They agreed, and she presented each of them with a mug of hot cider to ward off the chill in the air.

Cocoa frolicked ahead of the group, completely at ease with her domain. Eventually, the dog returned to Ashley's side. "I'm sure sometime while you're here, the deer will make an appearance."

Dad picked up a stick and threw it for the Lab to gleefully retrieve, and the two of them played the game while he seemed to survey the surroundings. Nearing the back door after the tour, he turned to look out over the property as Cocoa slid her head under his hand. Handing off his empty mug to Ashley, he picked up an armload of firewood and deposited it in the wood bin by the downstairs fireplace. Then the three of them unbundled, and the women headed for the kitchen, chattering constantly, while Dad took his attention to the telescope.

"Hey, you two, the deer are out," Dad yelled.

Her mother actually squealed as she ran to see them. Ashley tagged along behind, glad to simply hear the excitement in their voices as dad explained how to use the land telescope.

Finally, he glanced over at her. Smiled. "Okay, you've convinced me. This is a really nice place and I like it. But you know what I like even more?"

"What?" Ashley asked.

"Your smile. You're the happiest I've seen you look since… Well, let's just say, in a long time." He reached out and gave her a hug.

"It's nice to see the sparkle in your eyes again." Mother twirled her fingers and pointed at her. "Been longer than you realize."

Ashley needed to tell them about Mark. Of the man she couldn't get out of her thoughts, day or night. But, for today, she'd hold onto him for herself awhile longer. Just the simple gesture of her dad bringing in wood had stirred up memories of her and Mark and the woodpile. She missed him more than she'd ever imagined possible.

"From things you've been saying, it sounds like you plan to live here," Dad said.

"That's my other news. I'm in the process of buying the house and acreage from the Gregorys. I've made wonderful friends here in Nature's Crossing. And, like you said, I'm happy here."

"I know, but are you sure you'll want to live here forever?" Mom asked.

"All I know is that right now, this is where I belong." Ashley felt pride in herself. Pride that she'd made a major decision and stood up for that decision to two of the most important people in her life.

Dad strolled to the sofa. "Are you keeping the condo in St. Louis?"

"Need to until February. That's when the stipulations in the divorce decree run out. Otherwise, I'd have to share the proceeds with Bradford. And I'm not letting that happen." She'd done her research the last couple of weeks, and had a plan for the condo. "I plan to list the condo in March. The realtor I've been speaking with thinks I should get a good price fairly quick."

The next few days flew by with carols and laughter and games. Food and love and family. Neighbors stopped by to wish happy holidays and meet Ashley's family.

Christmas Eve morning, FedEx delivered a large package. Her parents shoved it to the living room, and Ashley slit the tape. Bubble wrap and Styrofoam peanuts surrounded a large rectangular package inside. Lavishly wrapped in gold foil paper and entwined with wide red velvet ribbon, even a packet hung from the multi-loop bow addressed to Ashley. Writing on the envelope said to open it and read immediately. A red sticker on the gold package read, "DO NOT OPEN UNTIL CHRISTMAS."

"Look, the sticker has a fluffy white frame around the edge. Isn't that cute. Who's it from?" Mother asked.

Ashley removed the card and read the handwritten note silently.

Hold on to your gloves. I'll be back for them—and you!

Love, Mark

She smiled and touched the sticker, then slid the card in the envelope.

"Who's it from?" Mother reiterated.

Ashley brushed at her hair and enjoyed the pitter-pat of her thumping heart. "Someone very special. Anyone need anything?"

Her mother glanced at her dad and smiled. "No, I'm fine."

For the rest of the day, the gold foil package sat under the tree along with all other presents. The three of them went to Midnight Mass and returned full of sleepiness. Her parents headed right to bed, vowing to wake bright and early to open presents.

Ashley changed into her gown and pink satin robe, then quietly stole to the tree and pulled the velvet-ribbon package to the middle of the floor. Cocoa ambled in from the bedroom and lay beside her, and she stroked the half-sleeping dog, receiving a soft groan of sleepy contentment in return.

"You know, girl, the tag doesn't say what time to open. Only not until Christmas. It's after midnight, so technically, it's Christmas. What do you think?"

Cocoa barely opened her eyes and plopped to her side. Clearly out of the conversation.

Carefully, Ashley removed the bow and undid the ribbon. The fluffy sticker radiated all kinds of happy memories. Carefully, she slid her hands under the tape, loosened the paper, and slipped it from the box. She removed the lid easily and pushed aside the tissue paper to reveal her gift—a framed oil painting of the Washington Monument shimmering in the Reflecting Pool. At night, complete with snowflakes.

A slight whimper escaped her lips as she clutched the note to her heart. She missed Mark. Missed him more than she thought possible. Her fingers stroked the frame, the painting, the spot where she and Mark found each other on the steps in front of the Lincoln Memorial. After a while, she pulled a pillow from the sofa and draped an afghan over herself. Her hand still clutched the bow as she fell asleep on the floor next to his perfect gift.

Christmas morning, Ashley told her parents about Mark, how they met, and how much he meant to her. They listened, told her to be careful, but more important—follow her heart. Of course, she hadn't shared the line of work he was in. When she had asked him what she could tell people he did for a living, he said tell them he had a nice job with the government in a quiet little office.

She hated lying, but she would for Mark. He'd told her once he joined the Park Service, she'd be free to say what he did. But his past would always remain a secret.

Her mother had easily accepted the explanation. But when her eye twitched, her dad shot her one of his famous raised eyebrows looks.

But when he walked to the fireplace and removed the oil painting of Dot and Lloyd from over the mantel, then replaced it with Mark's gift, Ashley knew Dad had made his decision. He liked the man from just what she'd told them. Plus, she was happy again. Ashley smiled and nodded appreciation. Mark would like them, too.

Her parents flew out of Surryfield the next morning. Tracie and Linda arrived the next day.

The college-days friends filled hours with catch-up on family, ideas for interior decorating, and sketches of possible building layouts in case Ashley decided to open a gift shop or antique shop or whatever type of shop took hold in her mind. Tracie kept track of snowfalls for her upcoming ski trip, while Linda text messaged her husband and kids repeatedly.

Of course, her friends wanted to know everything there was to know about Mark. She gave the quiet government job answer once again, but Tracie, always in police mode, eyed her with suspicion. They shared a bit of the fun and games and sightseeing they'd done in Washington.

The night before they were to leave, Linda and Tracie stood, in support, right beside Ashley as she phoned Peabody regarding the two corner lots downtown. The ones she wanted to build a store on. His favorable response met with high-fives he couldn't see from his end. He and Ashley agreed to talk specifics after the first of the year.

"I'm going to miss you two when you leave tomorrow." After dinner, Ashley sandwiched between her friends for a group hug. Each of them had their own lives to get on with, but at least they'd had a few days together.

Linda headed to her bedroom to change for the night and phone home one more time. Heading downstairs, Tracie had mentioned she had some phone calls to make.

Cocoa barked. Loud. Ran to the entry foyer. Ears alert. Eyes watchful. Barking. Barking. Hair on her back bristling. A moment later, the doorbell rang. Again and again and again.

Ashley turned on the porch light and peered through the side panes. At first, she didn't see anyone, then jumped when Chase popped into view and banged on the storm door. She remembered being the last one in through the front and pushing the lock. Confident of this, she eased the front door open, leaving the security chain in place. Cocoa stood next to her, a low growl rumbling in the dog's throat.

"About time you opened the door, Mssssssss. Lanovan. No, I think I'll call you Ashleeeey." Chase's glazed eyes and wobbly stance spoke of too much partying. Too much booze. Too much who-knew-what.

She grasped the door firmly, ready to shove it closed at a moment's notice. "Can I help you?"

His face pressed near the storm door pane, eyes narrowed and harsh. "I guess you think you're pretty smart, don't you, Ashleeeey? Guess you think buying this place'll stop my plans. It won't. You'll never be able to outsmart me."

"It's late. Go home, Chase." The pit of Ashley's stomach clenched, and Janie's words of warning came flooding back.

"I've come to visit you at your precious home. Why don't you be friendly and invite me in, Ashleeeey? We'll get to know each other better." Chase slammed his fist against the doorframe. "I think you need a little man company around the old place."

He jerked the storm door handle repeatedly. Cocoa growled, flashed her teeth as she lunged at the entry. Chase jumped back, stumbled, and plummeted against the siding with a bang. Ashley pulled the dog back, slammed the door, and flipped the locks as Linda came running into the foyer.

Instantly, fear inched into her as she pushed 911 on her cell phone.

"911, may I help you?"

"This is Ashley Lanovan. I'm staying at the Gregorys' place in Nature's Crossing. Chase Andrews is outside my house and won't leave. He's drunk and trying to get inside."

He yanked on the storm door once again, and Ashley heard the sound of scraping metal ripping from the wooden doorframe. The next second, Chase banged on the front door.

"Are you hearing this?" Ashley asked, unable to stop the quiver in her voice.

"Help is on the way, Ms. Lanovan. Lock your door and stay inside till the police get there," the dispatcher said.

"What's going on?" Tracie shouted, running up from downstairs, followed close behind by Linda.

Ashley's breath was rapid. Adrenaline pounded through her body. "It's that Chase guy I told you about. Don't worry, I've called the police."

The doorbell rang over and over again.

"Come on, open the door, honey. I'm not leavin', so you might as well invite me in," Chase bellowed. "We'll have a little party."

Tracie ran to the foyer, her police weapon in hand.

Ashley grabbed her arm. "No, don't go out there."

Chase's slimy, threatening words continued to spew forth while Ashley taped him on her phone.

Within minutes, Trooper Wheat McIntosh arrived, followed by two police cars. By then, Chase had yanked her screen door from its lock. She didn't go outside until the police had him under control. Followed by Linda and Tracie, with her badge and holstered gun now clearly displayed, the trio explained the altercation.

"Do you want to press charges?" one of the policemen asked.

"You should," Tracie said. "Talking to you as your friend and a police officer, you really should."

"No. Not this time. Just get him off my property. And keep him off." Ashley eyed Chase, slouched against the squad car.

"It's not your property yet, Ashleeeey." Chase labored to push himself away from the police car. Cocky to the end.

"Get him in the patrol car and call a tow truck to pick up his Jag." The cop talking to her added a notation to his notes. "We'll hold him overnight. He should be okay in the morning."

Watching the two police cars drive away, Ashley hoped they were right.

Wheat continued to stand at the edge of the porch. "It's been a long time since we got a call on him this wound up. Like you said, you buying the house must have set him off. That and the liquor. After his uncle gets done with him, he shouldn't give you any more trouble." He stepped off the porch. "If he does, just call."

"Thanks for getting here so fast."

He tipped his hat, then headed toward his SUV.

After a few steps, he turned around and looked at Tracie. "Where was that you're from?"

"Kansas City. You can check me out if you want to." Tracie leaned against the side of the house. Arms crossed in front of her sweater.

"If I'm ever over that way, I'll let you show me around."

Tracie stood up and smiled. A tiny toss of her dark-brown hair, long and layered, set the tone. The one leg straight, hip slightly tipped, other leg just to the side stance, set the image. Hands slid into her back jeans pockets, set the sass. Little nuances only long-time friends would notice.

"Sure. You've got my badge number from the report," Tracie said.

"Yes, ma'am. I sure do."

After the squad car pulled away, Tracie turned to her friends. "What?"

"What was *that* all about?" Linda asked as Ashley and her each tossed their hair and took her straight-leg stance.

Ashley laughed till her stomach hurt. "Who'd have thought? After all these years wearing that badge and hoisting thugs into the back seat of a patrol car, Tracie could still be a flirt?"

"Me? I'm a flirt? You've got a lot of room to talk." Tracie tossed her hair again, then nudged Ashley's shoulder. "From what you said about afternoon delight in your hotel room, you could give lessons on flirting."

Cocoa nosed in next to Ashley, who bent down and gave the dog a hug. Things would have turned out different if Mark had been the one answering the door. Good? Bad? Worse? She hoped to never be in a position that she found out. Tonight had been bad enough. Next week, she needed to get estimates on a security setup.

CHAPTER THIRTY-SIX

TIME HAD GONE too fast for the women, but at least they'd decided to wait until right after lunch to leave. Ashley cleared away the dishes from the table so her friends could get the SUV packed and on the road. Tracie had already tossed her suitcase and tote bag in the back seat, but Linda always took longer.

Tracie walked into the kitchen after making her final walk-through of her guest bedroom, then grabbed a cookie from the platter still on the kitchen table. Crumbs left a trail as she went to the front window. "Looks like you've got company."

"Who?" Ashley asked.

"I don't know. Some guy getting out of a shiny black BMW." Her friend grinned.

For a moment, Ashley's breath caught. She froze. Mark? Yes, yes, yes. It had to be Mark. Instinctively, her hands combed through her hair as she glanced at her reflection in the microwave.

"Mm, mm, mm. Mighty fine." Tracie grabbed another cookie. "Are you gonna let him in? If not, he looks like someone I'd like to know."

Ashley flew down the hall, snatched open the door, and sped on to the porch. "What are you doing here?"

"I came to see you, pretty lady."

"I've missed you."

Ashley tilted her face upward as he grabbed her in his arms, pulling her closer before their mouths devoured each other's. When they parted, she leaned into his chest, her core pleading to pull him close again.

"You're driving me crazy, Mark."

He trailed his hands down her arms. "What say we spend a couple days driving each other crazy?"

"Oh, yes, I'd like that." She tugged the front of his jacket. "I'd like that very much."

He didn't speak, only stepped into her body, her heat once more. His hands tangled through her hair and held as his mouth brushed against her neck, and she arched into him. Mark's whisper filled her ear, "You feel good. Really good."

"You do, too."

"Maybe we could stay like this forever."

"I have company." She reluctantly pried herself back, pulled him toward the front door, and tugged on his hand. "Come on. You have to meet Linda and Tracie, the friends I told you about."

"Now?"

"Don't worry. They're leaving soon. I told them about you."

He groaned, his look questioning. "Everything?"

"Not everything. They think you work in a nice little office with lots of cubicles."

"That wasn't what I meant by everything." He grinned.

Ashley stroked his cheek. "Maybe a little. The rest is for only me."

"You got that right." Mark rubbed his hand over the broken storm door latch as he passed. "Who?"

"I'll explain later." He wouldn't be happy when she told him about Chase. In fact, she figured Chase should consider himself lucky Mark hadn't been there last night.

Warmed with happiness, Ashley couldn't stop smiling. "These are my friends, Linda and Tracie. This is Mark."

The genial handshakes made the rounds. Linda beamed, and Tracie appeared to be evaluating. Ashley explained about the ski trip her friends were taking. Mark told them how he'd brought Patrick and Janie home because Patrick insisted. They'd arrived in Nature's Crossing about thirty minutes ago.

Her insides lit with joy. "I'll have to call them to come over. I'm having a few friends to celebrate this evening. Do you think they'll feel like it?"

"I know Janie will. We'll see what we can do about Patrick."

Ashley eased toward the living room. "Why don't we all sit down?"

"You go right ahead. You'll have to excuse me, though. One of my daughters is having a meltdown because she can't find her favorite blouse, so I need to calm her down." Linda continued to run up and down the stairs to finish packing.

"Hey, Linda. Are you ever going to be ready to go?" Tracie shouted.

The bump of suitcase wheels on the stairs announced her readiness. Final packing of Linda's SUV complete, suddenly it was time for goodbyes. Linda shook Mark's hand, hugged Ashley like she didn't want to let go, wiped the corners of her eyes, and hopped in the driver's seat.

Tracie hung back then turned toward Mark. "We didn't get much of a chance to talk today. I figure my friend here's a good judge of character, and if she says you're okay, then you're okay with me. Maybe I'm speaking out of turn, but I get the feeling you care about her."

He nodded and hooked his thumbs into his jean pockets. Ashley couldn't tell where this conversation was going, but it appeared some type of bonding was happening. Maybe there was some type of undercurrent connection between the different branches of law and protection forces. A trust they didn't even realize existed.

Tracie shoved her hands into her ski jacket and continued. "Ashley's a tough cookie and can pretty well take care of herself, but—"

Linda issued a long blast of the car horn.

"Just a minute. Anyhow, the bottom line is this. First, I'd appreciate it if you didn't break her heart. She's been hurt enough."

He smiled. "No problem. I don't plan for me or anyone else to ever hurt her again."

"Second, make her tell you about the storm door. I'm not saying this because I'm a cop, but she needs a security system."

His jaw clenched with his nod, and it seemed to satisfy Tracie.

She embraced Ashley in a giant hug and whispered in her ear, "Quiet little office, my rear. You did good, girl. Now find one for me."

As her two friends drove away, she turned to Mark and hooked her arms around his neck. "I'll tell you about the door later. Right now, how about I show you my bedroom?"

"I thought you'd never ask." He swooped her up in his arms.

Brushing her fingers against the back of his neck, she nibbled his ear. "I thought they'd never leave."

CHAPTER THIRTY-SEVEN

A FEW HOURS LATER, Ashley glanced around the kitchen and sighed. "I'm done. Everything's ready for the party."

Staying on schedule hadn't been easy. Neither one of them had wanted to leave the bedroom, but Mark had spent the rest of the afternoon only a few feet away. Helpful and teasing, yet very distracting. She'd succumbed a couple of times when his hands found their way to places not at all concerned with cooking or cleaning. Hopefully, there'd be time in the next few days for them to concentrate entirely on themselves.

"What time will the guests arrive?" Mark asked.

"Seven or later. I doubt if anyone's still here at midnight."

"I'll be here."

She walked across and leaned against the strong arm. "You better be. How long can you stay?"

"Let's not think about it right now." He draped his arm around her shoulder and gave her a squeeze.

"It's easier for me if I know." His look drew her to him, and she went willingly. "Promise you'll always answer me honestly when I ask how long you can stay. How long you'll be gone. Even when you're with the Park Service. Please."

"I promise."

"So, when do you have to leave this time? I thought you were on assignment already."

"Told my boss I wanted a break before I head out on assignment." He turned to face her. "Tomorrow afternoon I need to head out. I go dark not long after."

"Dark?'

"Undercover. No contact. Might be a long time before I see you again." He searched her face for a reaction.

She felt her eye twitch as panic flew straight from her brain to her heart to her face. Gone? Dark? What if he got hurt? Didn't make it back? As if in slow motion, she saw him reach out for her and pull her into his arms. Why couldn't she focus? Air whooshed through her ears, making her dizzy. Why? She couldn't breathe. How? How could she keep him from going?

Then it registered. There was no way to keep him with her all the time. The price for loving him would be paid with unknown reality and spur-of-the-moment departures. She had to get a handle on herself. Right now. This first time.

Mark sat down in the closest chair, pulled her on his lap, and laid his cheek against the top of her head. Slowly, he rocked them both back-and-forth. "Shhhh. Take a deep breath. Deep, Ashley. You're okay. We're okay."

She couldn't tell him not to go. Couldn't ask him to stay. This was his job. This was the man she cared about. In control again, she breathed normally. She straightened and pulled her strength from deep inside, pushing the fear aside.

He leaned back, and his eyes watched her again. "I know it's hard, but this is who I am. At least for a while longer. Can you do this? Can you live this way?"

"Yes. I can do this. I *will* do this." She snuggled closer to his chest and hoped he didn't notice the catch in her voice. "Now see that wasn't so hard, was it?"

His shoulders relaxed, and from the look on his face, she realized how difficult the conversation had been for him, too. What if she had said no? Would he have turned and walked away? Yes, that's who he was. Broken and hurt, he would have shoved her and him to the recesses of his mind and walked away. She would never say no to him. Never.

"Yeah. Like walking over a bed of hot coals." He quirked the side of his mouth. "Come on."

"Where?"

He tugged her to the coat closet. "Bundle up warm. There's something I want to show you."

"What about the party?"

"You've got four hours till then." He grabbed a couple of throw pillows and an afghan from the sofa, two mugs and the thermos he'd filled with coffee as she finished readying for the party. Nudging her forward with his elbow, they locked up the house and piled into his BMW.

At the end of the driveway, he turned right, and within thirty feet, he turned right again, heading straight at the pines.

"What are you doing?"

Maneuvering between the towering pines, he eased along a gravel path barely wide enough for the limbs not to scrape his SUV. Suddenly, the trees cleared, and they emerged in what appeared to be a man-made glade. Once he parked, he pointed through a tiny break in the pine needles.

She followed the line of sight. Gasped. "That's my house."

"Sure is. Lloyd made this area for me. A great place I could camp, so to say, with some privacy. The night I left you and Dot after Lloyd's heart attack, I came here to sleep."

"You must have been cold. I'm sure Dot would have offered you one of the guest rooms for the night."

Mark removed her snowball hat and fingered her hair, caressing her neck with his palm. Soft sighs crept from deep inside Ashley. He leaned across the console and pulled her toward him, his lips sweeping across her own, slow and teasing. "As I recall, you're the one who kicked me out the door that night. Emphatically. Never wanted to see me again. Thought I was a—"

"I remember." She'd never do that again.

Motioning her to stay where she was, he opened the driver's side door and headed to the back of the BMW. Once there, he climbed inside, lowered the seats, scattered the afghan and pillows he'd brought from the house, then stretched out his arm and hand in a waving welcome gesture. "Your chalet awaits."

She eagerly went to him. "I always envisioned chalets being much bigger."

"Just wait." Jumping inside, he closed the door behind him. "I think you'll see that this chalet has a lot of perks that make the intimate interior come to life."

Intrigued by what he might have planned, she fluffed the pillows, then leaned against the side panel. Stretching out beside her, he clicked on the custom-designed heater. Filled their cups with of hot coffee from the thermos. And to complete the setting, he tossed the afghan over their laps.

"See?" He grinned. "What more could you want?"

"Only you, darling. Only you." She lightly kissed his lips, then sipped her cocoa.

"It may take a while, but if we're lucky, the deer will come into the clearing to bed down. Sometimes they're so close you feel like you could reach out and touch them," he said.

"Won't they see us?" she asked.

"Not through the tinted glass. At least not enough to scare them away. Now, tell me about the screen door."

Ashley relayed the incident with Chase. "Don't worry. If I need to, I can get a restraining order. From what I hear, though, his uncle Chadwick will straighten him out."

Mark's jaw clenched. "I've seen this guy around

town before, and he's a— Never mind. Just stay away from him. Spunk you've got, but I'm not so sure about power behind those muscles. You need to be realistic. Know your limitations."

"Let's not talk about him right now."

"Okay, but we will later." He pulled her closer, and she nestled in like a newly born bear cub searching for warmth. "So, pretty lady, what would you like to talk about now?"

Time passed while they discussed her ideas for the house. How she had an appointment with one of the local radio stations to discuss her ideas for a twice-a-week show. And that she planned to build a couple of shops on the vacant lots Peabody had agreed to sell her.

"Of course, the new buildings probably won't be done till early summer. So, I'm going to see about leasing a couple of the white storefronts from Eloise and Peabody. That way, I can get a foothold on the spring season. Kind of ease into the business. See exactly what I want my store to be about. Antiques. Gifts. Coffee—"

"Hold it right there." He stop-signed her with his hand. "You've got so many ideas"—he tapped her forehead—"running around in there, there's not going to be time for me."

She tweaked his nose. "You've got lots going on, too. What's this I hear about all the antiques you have in storage?"

Sharing his passion for historic items took front stage for a while. "I've never thought much about why I bought those pieces. And on closer inspection, some of the pieces are a little strange. But they were there, and I liked them. To me, the search was always part of the enjoyment."

"You could sell them in my shop. I'd only take ninety percent commission." Leaning into him, she stroked his forearms.

"I'd gladly pay the price." He enclosed her in his arms as his knee slid over hers. "I think that's enough talk. How about you?"

"Maybe."

His lips lightly tickled a path along her neck while his fingers deftly unzipped her coat. "I guess we should go."

"Ummmmm."

"After all, you've got your party to think about."

"I know," she whispered, sliding out of her coat. Out of her sweater. Out of her bra that he'd quickly unhooked.

A moment later, they slipped farther beneath the afghan. Later, it dawned on them that if the deer showed up, they'd been too busy warming up the back of the BMW to ever notice.

Later that evening, the party came alive with a large part of Nature's Crossing coming and going at different hours, and Ashley, along with Mark, made sure everyone enjoyed themselves. Peabody brought Eloise and her husband. She came loaded with assorted appetizers and desserts.

Even Miss Minnie flounced in wearing a sparkly red dress with a couple of gold feathers tucked strategically in her freshly styled hair. She made sure everyone knew she was on her way to Chadwick's house for a New Year's celebration. And even though Minnie was twice her age, she noticed a touch of seduction to the lady when she said his name. Ashley's insides warmed as she realized there were still plenty of sparks left in her own life.

By ten thirty, most everyone was ready to call it an evening. Lorna, Gus, and Ms. Lavender lingered another half-hour until the only ones left were Janie and Patrick, who'd arrived around eight. Janie drove their car to the front door, making it easier for her husband to navigate into the passenger seat.

Patrick grimaced as he shuffled to the door. "Stop by the store on your way out of town tomorrow."

"Sure." Mark leaned close to his friend. "In case I forget to tell you in the morning, be sure to keep an eye on Ashley while I'm gone. See if she needs anything. Okay?"

"You can count on me."

"I heard that." Ashley pinched her love's side. "What? You think I can't take care of myself?"

"I think you can most of the time." He glanced at the lock on the screen door. "Sometimes, not so much."

"Okay, okay. I get the point."

Mark helped Patrick into the car, then stood in the driveway with his arm draped around Ashley's shoulder as the last of the partiers departed. She knew they were exactly where they belonged. Did he?

When they passed through the front door, he

reached out and hit the broken doorframe with the side of his fist. A tiny smile filled her heart and mind. Even though she felt she could take care of herself, it was nice to know he cared about her. A backup safety shield was a knight in a shiny black BMW.

"Now don't get yourself all riled and don't think I'm telling you what to do." Mark locked the door behind them "But I'd like to make a phone call tomorrow and have someone install a security system for you later this week. Okay?"

Ashley felt a reactive stubbornness rush her mind for a moment before she allowed it to ebb. "Okay. Tomorrow's New Year's, though, so places won't be open."

"Where I'm calling, they're always open. I'll make arrangements with Patrick to bring the guy over next week."

Mark dimmed the lights, turned on some soft music, and poured them each a glass of wine. He leaned against the comfort of the sofa, and Ashley curled against him. Cocoa stayed on her oversized doggie bed near the window.

Ashley nodded toward the picture over the fireplace. "Your Christmas gift is beautiful."

"Looks like it belongs right there and no place else."

"Your gift is on the way to Washington since you weren't supposed to be here. By the way, I've noticed you always seem to turn up unexpectedly."

"Is that a problem?" He lightly sucked her earlobe.

She arched her neck to the feel of his lips. Mmm, that felt good. Really good. "No. But this is our first New Year's together. I want to give you something special."

"How about a nice soapy shower?"

The collectible fisherman Santa figurine she'd found for him, complete with fishing vest, hooks and lures, flashed through her mind. It paled in comparison to Mark's suggestion.

She giggled. "I think I might be able to manage that."

A little before midnight, they swayed to the slow rhythm of "Strangers in the Night," and at the stroke of twelve, his mouth found hers. The breathtaking kiss washed over her as he lifted her in his arms. She buried her face on his shoulder and tightened her hold as he carried her down the hallway.

"I love you, Ashley." Mark's blue eyes searched her face. Open and honest, he'd shared his life with her. He'd shared his past. Now he gave his love. "I love you more than life itself."

CHAPTER THIRTY-EIGHT

LATE IN THE afternoon on New Year's Day, Mark and Ashley walked out the downstairs back-patio door, then over to the BMW parked near the rear of the house. Overcast with wind out of the north, winter seemed to have blown in during the day, and their breath fought the cold air.

"I wish you didn't have to go so soon." She bundled her coat around her.

"Me, too." He should have been on the road early this morning. But it wouldn't be easy to drive away. Now or another five hours from now.

"Look. Someone taped a note on your windshield."

Mark deactivated the security system, opened the door, and tossed his bag into the back before he reached an arm-length across to pull a small envelope free from the glass. They'd used two-sided tape, but at least it hadn't left any adhesive when he pulled it loose.

"Here you go. It's addressed to Ashley. Probably someone thanking you for a great party."

Looping her hands around his middle, she smiled.

"You didn't write me a thank-you note."

He took her face in his hands and kissed her gently, deep and sound. "I thought I thanked you pretty well last night."

She blushed and hid her face against his chest as his arms held her close. He loved her vulnerability when he embarrassed her. How she felt so tiny and trusting in his arms yet could stand her ground when she wanted to. Her reactions were so real, they only made him love her more.

"I forgot my coffee," he said.

"I'll get it."

"Nope. You read your note, and I'll go grab the thermos from the kitchen." Once inside the house, Mark pushed himself and took the stairs two steps at a time.

Why hadn't the alarm sounded on the BMW when the note was attached? Surely, they had to lean against the side of the SUV to reach so far across the windshield. Should have only taken a light touch to set it off. Very light. He made a mental note to contact the dealership and have the flaw taken care of while he was on assignment.

Not many people knew the trick to working around a security-enhanced vehicle. Even now, there were times his touch could be off and he'd end up with a blaring siren. The back of his neck prickled. But when he was successful, the mission was accomplished. The target was blindsided.

The back of his neck prickled again. And again. *The target was—*

Ashley?

His arm swept the thermos from the counter a second before he charged out the door leading to the deck. He vaulted the rail and halfway to the ground, he saw the look of fear grip Ashley's face as she stared at the red dot of death, zooming from her to him and back to her.

The dot zeroed in on her forehead and stopped.

"Noooooo!" he roared.

Realization flashed in her eyes. She crumpled to the ground. The crack of a high-powered rifle ricocheted through the pines at the same moment. Had she made it? Had there been time? His legs caught him, and he stormed around the BMW.

Three seconds at most had passed since he rushed outside. Another crack rang out, and the concrete patio took the bullet. Ashley lay motionless on the ground behind the vehicle. Dead? Alive? Mark flew through the air and covered her body with his. Another shot bounced off the hood.

She trembled beneath him. Alive. He gripped her around the middle, opened the back door of the BMW, and shoved her inside ahead of him. With the push of a button, the security-enabled light on the dash steadied on. He retrieved the Glock from the console while he speed-dialed Patrick. "Get in the back seat, Ashley, and stay down. Are you hurt?"

"No. I'm not hit." She jumped into the back without hesitation.

He scrambled through the console area and yanked a side compartment open to retrieve an M-14 automatic. Clips and another Glock greeted him from a section beneath the headliner. His hand unconsciously strapped a knife to his forearm.

"Hey there," Patrick answered.

"Shots fired. Somebody just tried to take Ashley out. Call it in."

"Where?"

"Outside. Back of the house. By the BMW. I'm going after him."

"Who?"

"Don't know. But he had a red dot sight."

Patrick grunted. "On my way."

"I'll leave Ashley secured here in the BMW. She'll have my phone. You know my code."

"Yeah."

Mark hated saying the next words, but they had to be said. "Don't play hero Patrick. You can't move like you used to. Stay with Ashley."

"Got it. Go get the bastard."

"He's not leaving this property as long as I've got a breath left in me." Mark ended the call and tossed his phone to her.

Ashley touched his arm, and he jerked away. Pushed her down.

"What'd the note say?" he growled.

"It was for you. Something about seeing your face. Said you'd know what it felt like to lose someone."

He rammed the clip in the automatic as his boot rammed the side panel. "You stay right here. Flat against the side. Don't get out until me or Patrick open the door again. Understand?"

"Yes." The apprehension on her face said she knew what was happening. The strength in the set of her expression said she'd do whatever he said. But the slight tremble of her body said she was scared.

And he had no one but himself to blame for what was happening. He should have never sat down beside her at the Kennedy Center. Never.

"The BMW's bulletproof. You'll be safe." Soundproof, too. Maybe she wouldn't hear everything that went down.

The perp had zeroed in on one spot in the rear security glass ever since they'd got inside. Doubtful, but sooner or later, the bullet might make it through. Mark couldn't wait for backup. He had to go. Now.

She crouched in the floor bed between the passenger and back seat, her hands clutched tightly together. For one swift moment, he covered hers with his, then turned away. Weapons ready. He cracked the door, set the code, and rolled to the ground. The BMW sealed closed.

Time to live or die.

Ashley couldn't tell how long it had been since Mark left the BMW. Seemed like hours. Probably closer to five or six minutes. At least the dull ping on the back glass had ended when he rolled out the door. Her mind flooded with all the images of things that could be happening. And she prayed.

A shadow of light filled the encroaching dusk for a moment, then disappeared. Or had she only imagined it? His phone rang, and she screamed in surprise.

"Hello?" she whispered.

"It's Patrick. Don't worry, I'm parked next to you on the driver's side."

"Okay."

"Help should be here any minute."

Within seconds, the steady overhead *thrump, thrump, thrump* of helicopter rotor blades vibrated above the BMW. Bright lights splayed from side to side, then drifted away. Ashley chanced a peek out the window. The chopper hovered in the center of the property, spotlighting the yard from side to side, and front to rear.

"I'm going to hang up for now," Patrick said. "You do exactly what Mark told you to do. Understand?"

"Yes, I understand."

She ended the call, hunkered back down, and clutched the phone against her as the moments passed. Seconds. Minutes. On and on and on. Where was Mark? What was taking so long? Something must have happened. Had he put a Kevlar vest on? She couldn't remember. Her breaths came in short bursts. No other sounds, only herself.

The door opposite her swung open. Mark stood there in the glow of the BMW's dome lights. She crawled to his waiting arms and clawed to hold him closer as tears washed her face. Her insides burned with adrenaline, and she couldn't stop kissing his cheeks, his lips, his hair. There were blurs of other men surrounding her patio, his BMW, them, but all she saw was Mark.

"Shhhhh, I'm okay. You're okay."

Still the *thrump, thrump, thrump* of the chopper filled the air, along with bright lights tracing the back meadow and surrounding pines.

He lifted her out of the hatch opening and steered her inside through the back door, then upstairs to the living room sofa. The jacket he wore now read "CIA" on the back.

"Are you hurt?" she asked.

He kissed her lightly, zipped the jacket tighter. Scraped the sleeve across his face. "No."

"Is it over?"

"They've got him in custody. He won't bother us again."

"Mark, you're needed out back," Patrick yelled from the bottom of the stairs. "Evidently, the guy never met the man who hired him."

She grabbed the front of his jacket. "You're not leaving, are you?"

"Only for a second. I'll be right back." His lips brushed her forehead before he headed outside. "Close the curtains, Ashley."

The door to the deck still stood open. Cold air pouring in. She started to close the door, but voices from the patio below floated up to her. She paused.

"What does he mean he never met the guy?" Mark asked angrily. "A hit job didn't just fall in his lap one day."

"Says everything was done through the internet. Zeroed in on facial recognition using your photo from the computer leak. Got your real name and tracked you from there."

"Then we'll follow the damn links all the way back to the man who paid him. This isn't over."

Patrick coughed in the cold air. "State Trooper Wheat McIntosh just found a gray truck parked a quarter mile down the road from here. Same plates as the ones he ran the day the man stopped at Red's Corner Market while you and I were out of town."

Her breath hitched as she remembered that day at the grocery. The man. The questions. The photo. Without knowing why, she'd lied to protect Mark. Now, she realized how close the man had been to finding his target even back then. But Mark was still alive. And she could breathe easier.

Their voices faded as Mark and Patrick walked across the yard. The chopper, now hovering above the pines, turned and flew away.

She slid the door closed, then pushed the remote and watched the curtains slide into place. No need to worry, Mark would be back inside soon. She and Cocoa settled into their usual spot on the sofa. Huddled beneath the afghan, the two of them waited for almost an hour before she heard his footsteps on the stairs.

He glanced in her direction, carrying his tote bag. "I'm going to take a shower."

She nodded as he disappeared into the bedroom. Thirty minutes later, the *thrump, thrump, thrump* of a chopper caught her attention once again. She pulled back the curtain and looked outside. A different type of helicopter buzzed the back yard. And this one landed.

She tapped on the door to the master bathroom.

"Mark?"

"Yeah."

Pushing the door open, she found him dressed in jeans and socks, his hands braced against the edge of the counter. Head down, the veins on his arms still pumped large with adrenaline. Water glistened across his shoulders. His hair dark and wet and rumpled. The knuckles on his hands scraped and bleeding.

She walked up behind him, placing her fingers on his back. He flinched, but as she caressed his shoulders, he eased. Her lips brushed the tense muscles, and he relaxed even more. She'd already seen the scars that were long since healed. None appeared new from this time. None on the outside, at least.

When he turned to face her, she gasped at what he'd endured. His face had already swelled with the marks of a hand-to-hand battle. The scrape of a skin-breaking blow to his cheekbone. Two fist-sized bruises already turning black on his sides.

"I'm sorry, Ashley. I'm really sorry." Sadness floated in his eyes as he took her in his arms. "By coming here, I've put you in danger. I need to leave."

Leave? She couldn't be hearing him right. "No."

He rummaged in his tote, coming up with a shirt, which he tossed on, then carried his boots to the chair in the corner of the bedroom. "I'll put word out that you were nothing but a few nights of pleasure. You'll be safe that way."

"This is not how it has to be. I'm not afraid. I've

never been afraid with you." She rested her palm against his cheek. "Sure, I was frightened with that guy shooting at me, but I wasn't afraid. Because I've always known you'll be here to protect me."

"Don't you see? By me leaving. That *is* protecting you." He finished tying his boot laces and stood. "If I can't put an end to whoever is targeting us, then I won't ever come back here. Not. Ever. To Nature's Crossing."

She pulled his head down, and her mouth covered his words, long and tight. What was he saying? That's not how this was supposed to work. She'd steeled herself to times he'd leave on an assignment. Had visualized what she'd do during those times. How nice his coming home would be. This. This leaving was not an option.

"I love you too much to risk your life, Ashley." His voice cracked as he grabbed her against him. His hold strengthened and then loosed enough for him to look into her eyes. "I love you too much."

She clutched the front of his shirt with both her hands. Kissed the hollow of his throat, his cheek, his lips. "No, I won't let you go. I won't let you do this."

Lightly, he loosened her handhold from his shirt. "This is who I am, Ashley. This is the life I live. The danger I bring with me. I've made too many enemies in my line of work. Too many years. I should have known it was too late for me to have a normal life."

"Isn't this just because of the computer hack? The leak?"

"No! The leak and my photo on the dark web were how this guy found me. But this is deeper. This is tied to the CIA. And me. And something so personal to someone that it's become revenge."

He walked past her, shoved his dirty clothes into the tote, and zipped it closed. Then walked through the living room, picking up his coat from the sofa, and started down the stairs. She followed. Close behind. All the way to the back door.

Tugging on his hand, she tried to make him step in the direction of staying. "It's been a long night, Mark. Let's just go to bed. Get some sleep. We can talk about this in the morning." She recognized the leaving in his expression. The set of his jaw. The force of stubbornness in his eyes. "No. We can't end this way. No. I'm not going to let it happen. I love you too much to ever let you go."

CHAPTER THIRTY-NINE

MARK HAD ALWAYS realized how hard this would be every time he left on an assignment. But this time was different. Now, the high price of parting was ripping him apart. Love had felt a lot better when he walked in the house on New Year's Eve than walking out now. One thing he knew, though, Ashley was worth the price. Whatever it might be.

She slid into his arms and kissed the tip of his chin before she rested against his chest. "Please... please, don't leave. At least not forever."

In turn, he rested his cheek on her soft auburn hair. "I have to go now. Believe me when I say, walking out this door is one of the hardest things I've ever had to do in my life." He searched her face for strength. "But I need to find this guy. He's not about terrorism or my assignments. For some reason, he's made this a retaliation. For what, I don't know. But it's personal to him. And I will not put you in that danger. Do you understand?"

Slowly, she nodded, regaining control of her tears. And they stood that way for what seemed like a lifetime. In reality, less than a minute.

Stepping back to see her face, he lifted her chin. "I moved the BMW to the parking spaces behind the garage. Leave it parked there while I'm gone. The keys are on the kitchen counter. Tomorrow, Patrick will have a security system installed here at the house. But if you ever feel threatened, you get inside the BMW and push the security button. You'll be safe. Okay?"

She nodded again. "You will be back. Yes?"

"There are only two reasons I won't be back. One, I'm dead on the ground." He pressed her to him as her hold tightened. "Or…I never find the guy."

"What does that mean?"

"Until we can live our life in peace, I won't be back. Pure and simple."

"How long will that be?" She stumbled over her words as the reality of what was happening seemed to grab her.

He had no idea. No way of knowing where this would take him. All he knew was that this had to be done. But she'd asked a question. She needed an answer. And, only yesterday, he'd made her a promise. One he hoped he could keep.

"A week at most." He swallowed the lump in his throat. "Now, help me leave, Ashley. Help me."

They embraced each other tenderly. Their goodbye complete, he stepped aside. Rapidly, she blinked away tears forming in her eyes and lifted her chin, swallowing hard. Her hand trembled when she lightly brushed his hand as he opened the door. There wasn't a name for the agony he felt.

"I'll work on setting up our antique shop while you're gone. That way…everything will be ready… when you return." Her chin quivered, and she bit the side of her lip, but in her voice, she managed a tiny smile. "Don't ever forget I love you. Forever."

He smiled while the scent of magnolias etched into his senses, one last time. Felt the touch of her skin beneath his fingers as he touched her cheek, one last time. Kissed her long and hard and deep. One last time.

"I love you, too."

He stepped out the back door and walked straight toward the chopper, reaching in his pocket for his gloves. Not there. He checked the other pocket. No gloves.

But his fingers brushed against something smooth and cool. He didn't have to see it to know the feel of Ashley's piece of blue sea glass that she'd bought in Washington. The one in the hotel bedroom the first time they made love. The one she'd told him was her luck. The one he'd rubbed between his fingers as she trailed her kisses down his chest only last night. The one he'd warmed in his hand and palmed across the smooth skin of her back.

She must have slipped it into his pocket earlier today, before she'd handed him his coat on the way to the BMW. Before all hell had broken loose. His gloves were evidently still on the sofa where he'd tossed them and his coat as he'd run out the patio door to the deck. No way would he turn around now. He clutched the sea glass as if his life depended on it. Climbed in the chopper, closed the door, and didn't look back.

The hit man had provided very little information, but there'd been enough for Mark to figure the trail started in Chicago.

His phone rang. "Yeah?"

"I heard you might need some help," Mitchell, the agent he'd been training, said amid background noise of clinking glasses, raucous laughter, and loud base-beat music.

"Who told you that?" The chopper lifted off.

"Patrick called."

Should have known he'd put the word out. Partners watched for partners. Especially when they couldn't be there themselves. "Did he mention this is not part of our assignment?"

"We'll just say you owe me one. Besides, I got nothing better to do. Where should I meet you?"

A few hours later, the two men met on the street corner in front of the hotel where he'd stayed twice before. This would be the first time Mitchell and him would work together. But the past few weeks training alongside each other for the upcoming work with DHS, had showed Mitchell was a top-of-the-line agent.

Where his own specialty had always been his speed and tracking, Mitchell's was firearms and camouflage. The man could disappear into his surroundings faster than a blink. They met in a forearm shake and brotherly hug.

"Sounded like I yanked you away from a fun night," Mark joked.

Mitchell shrugged, "You know how it is. Just another night."

"Yeah. Just another night."

He remembered those times years ago. Nights you were wound so tight, you just needed loud and people and a few drinks. As the years passed, that had been replaced with serious assignments, no-nonsense downtime, and minimal trust...of anyone.

Ashley was different. He'd trust her no matter what. Hell, he'd already told her his life story. At least all he could tell without breaking his security clearances. Even shared how he still searched for the last part of his dad's last conversation.

Brenner, the local police, and other CIA/FBI contacts had emailed him leads. Photos of a couple men high on their suspect list. Places to look. Places not to look. Places they'd deny even knowing.

He pointed at the hotel. "My instincts say we'll find a connection here."

"Sounds good." Mark walked beside him. "With a little luck, this will all be wrapped up in a couple of days."

Luck had never been much of a friend to him through the years. Why should things change now?

Winter had been long, but today's sunshine and warmth felt like spring, and Ashley had retreated to the deck with her afghan, a cup of tea, and Cocoa. The BMW still sat where Mark had moved it the night he left. She'd watched it through high winds and rain and sub-zero temperatures. Snowfall after snowfall. Even an ice storm.

At least the glimmer of sun reflecting off the SUV's hood today gave her hope. The past twelve weeks had been long and lonely, but she'd stayed busy. The builder had broken ground on the two shops she was having built on the Peabody lots. And the two temporary shops she planned to open by the end of April, in the historic row of block buildings, were taking shape. Plus, she'd placed lots of orders online with items to stock. Next year, she'd attend one of the gift merchandise marts in a major city.

All in all, she stayed busy. The nights were the hardest.

The little she'd learned about Mark's whereabouts had been the rare times one of Patrick's contacts had relayed a rumor to him. Last they'd heard, Mark and Mitchell were in South America.

She had only herself to blame. The man she'd fallen in love with had turned out to be the exact opposite of a nine-to-five. Or a man who worked in a small cubicle all day. Her insides were breaking. Good thing she trusted him.

Her phone rang with Janie's ringtone.

Ashley sipped her tea. "Hi. What's up?"

"I called to see if you want me to pick you on my way to the Town Council meeting tonight?" Janie said. "Say about a quarter to seven?"

"Oh, my gosh. I totally forgot." Ashley scratched Cocoa beneath her chin and received tail wags in return. "Thanks, I'll be ready and waiting."

That evening's Town Council voted to allow the planned community development on the Haney property at the edge of town. The one proposed by the man from her backyard, Taylor Randolph, who'd ended up being an environment-friendly real estate developer. He'd learned not to trust Chase Andrews. And convinced Nature's Crossing and the surrounding county that he intended to do his best to keep the area pristine. Data and recommendations from his previous developments around the United States were more than enough reassurance he was a man of his word.

Even Peabody and Chadwick had come to an understanding, thanks to her. The entire town was in awe that she had the two men talking again.

"Now, we come to the business of needing a replacement for Lloyd Gregory on the Town Council," Peabody said from his seat on the front row of the ones present. "As most of you already know, Dot and Lloyd have sold their property to Ashley Lanovan and moved to Florida permanently."

Ms. Lavender tapped the gavel, while the other three Council members present stared at the group. "Do we have any volunteers to be on the ballot?"

None.

"This would only be until the end of Lloyd's term, which is September."

Again, no one volunteered from the nineteen people present.

Peabody stood. "I would like to nominate Ashley Lanovan for the position.

She gasped. Shook her head.

"As you can see, I had not talked to her about this idea."

Lorna Horton seconded the nomination, while Gus nodded in agreement.

"Did you know about this?" Ashley whispered to Janie.

She quickly shook her head, but the pursed-lip, I'm-not-going-to-smile look said otherwise. And when Ashley looked at Patrick sitting in front as one of the Council members, he gave his stoic look and stared right in her direction.

Ms. Lavender tapped the gavel again. "Are there any other nominations?"

None.

"All in favor of Ashley Lanovan taking over the empty Lloyd Gregory, Town Council position say aye."

The ayes were unanimous except for one nay.

"Ms. Lanovan, would you like to say a few words?" Ms. Lavender asked.

Slowly, Ashley stood and looked around the room. She'd chosen this community when she bought the Gregory property. And if she wanted to see Nature's Crossing become prosperous again, if she wanted to keep someone like Chase from destroying the town, and if she was willing to do everything she could to make everyone feel like this town was worth their time, then she needed to start with herself.

She glanced around the room. "First, I want to thank everyone for their vote of confidence. But second, I just want to say, I think I was set up." She pointed her finger at Peabody, Janie, and others. The room laughed. "But I love this town, and I'll do my very best to make this a place people want to visit. A place they want to live. And a place they want to start their business."

The room cheered, and she sat down. How had this happened? All she'd done was come to the meeting instead of staying home, wallowing in self-pity. Of course, all she'd done in the first place was come to visit the Gregorys, and look how that had turned out. She smiled at all the good things that losing her newscaster job had brought her.

Once the meeting ended, everyone pitched in to clean up. She finished her notes and packed the briefcase the Council had given her with all the town files she'd need to get started. And they gave her the job of heading the committee for further research on improving Nature's Crossing events.

Taylor leaned toward her chair. "Would you like to have dinner with me sometime?"

"Thank you, but no."

"Is there someone else?"

"Yes."

"I'd heard as much but hadn't seen him around. The dinner offer still stands if you get tired of waiting. I'm not asking for anything more. Just dinner."

"Mark will be home soon." Ashley's eyes drifted to the front table where moments ago the Town Council had sat. She could wait forever if need be.

Taylor glanced out the window into the darkness,

his gaze forlorn and detached. "I know how it feels to lose someone you love. My wife was killed in an accident a few years ago. It's hard to deal with… lonely."

She looked to the floor, avoiding the conversation. Lonely. Mark would be back. Life without him was unimaginable. As much as she thought dinner was all he wanted, she couldn't do that.

But realizing Taylor also needed comfort, she turned back to their conversation. "I'm sorry. I didn't know about your wife."

He cleared his throat as he grabbed a bottled water from the vending machine. "Tell me about Mark. This man you love."

"What's to tell?" She felt the smile on her face. "I love him. And that's enough."

Twenty minutes later, back at her house, she immediately changed into her jammies. She grabbed the book she'd been reading from her nightstand and headed to the kitchen for something to nibble on with Cocoa padding behind her.

Patrick's ringtone shattered the quiet.

"Yes." She always tensed with his calls. Of course, she never had long to wait once she answered. He was always straight, concise, and to the point. "Rumor is that Mitchell had to leave for an assignment. Mark's still following the trail."

Her eye twitched. Breathing intensified as she struggled to hold her tears at bay. "Where?"

"Los Angeles."

"Alone?"

CHAPTER FORTY

MARK STARED AT the stats monitor by his bed as if hypnotized. Yesterday had been a rude awakening. At least the part about being shot. A fitting end to his career with the CIA. And somewhere along the way to the hospital in the ambulance, in pain, in and out of consciousness, he'd finally remembered the entire last conversation between his dad and him.

Now the walk with his dad danced through Mark's thoughts once again. As long as it had taken him to remember its entirety, now that was all he could think about. The Washington Memorial, the ice cream, the conversation. "Your grandfather, great-grandfather, even further back, fought for freedom. But I've already paid the bill in full for our family, son. Done and seen things no man should. Don't ever think you need to follow in my footsteps. I'll give enough for you and your sons."

Had his dad known his next assignment would be his last? What else could he have meant? Mark moaned with the thought. Listened again for his memory. "Remember, I love you. And that you can do whatever you want with your life, Mark. Whatever you want, son...whatever you want."

He'd only been thirteen that last time they talked. And he'd never remembered the complete conversation before now. Mark lolled his head to the rock beside him.

Why had he banished that independence from his mind all these years? Why had he chosen to follow the same path? If not out of obligation, then why?

The nurse walked in to check his vitals. Efficiently, she updated his digital chart on the mobile electronic health record workstation.

"You have any kids?" Mark asked.

Glancing up, she smiled. "Sure do. My little boy is almost three. And his older sister is seven, going on thirty, if you know what I mean. How about you?"

"No. Never wanted any." He stared out the window.

"That's okay. Everybody has to make their own decision."

"Yeah, guess so." He stared out the window. "But the woman I've been seeing, she wants children."

"So how did she take that you couldn't have children?"

He pinched his eyebrows together. "What?"

"Well, if you don't want any kids, I assume you've had a vasectomy."

"Nope. Never had one."

The nurse slowed her movements. Erased the board on the wall. Took her slow time in rewriting the exact same thing that had been there in the first place.

He knew she was waiting to see if he wanted to talk any more. "I scheduled one a few different times. Even made it all the way to the waiting room once. But never had the surgery."

She straightened the covers on the end of the bed. "Nothing to be ashamed of. Lots of men are leery of the surgery."

"I'm not afraid of anything."

"By the way, is your lady friend named Ashley?"

He brightened at the mention of her name, felt himself smile. "Yeah. How'd you know?"

"When you first arrived on the floor, you were still coming out of anesthesia. You kept calling for Ashley. She must be quite a woman from the things you said." The nurse started out the door. "Anything else I can get you?"

"Did Doc say how long I'll be here?" He tried not to grunt as he rearranged himself in bed. And he damn well wouldn't ask for any pain meds. All he wanted was to be out of the hospital.

She blew out a heavy sigh. "There's no change since an hour ago when I told you the doctor will be by on his evening rounds. He'll make his decision then."

The nurse walked on out of his room, letting the door close behind her. He'd only been in the hospital since about eleven last night, but every second was one too many. Reaching in the drawer of the bed table, Mark pulled out his phone and dialed his boss's number.

Brenner answered on the second ring. From everything his boss said, their ploy of Mitchell leaving and Mark appearing to be alone, had worked perfectly. The guy had made himself known. Mark had felt the prickle on the back of his neck. Mitchell had taken the guy out the instant he saw the flash from the shooter's rifle.

"Who was the guy you'd been tracking?" Brenner asked.

"Someone I never met. Never even knew existed. Blamed me for recruiting his brother to help us in the Middle East. Said I got him killed." Mark's voice sounded deep, hoarse, weary, even to himself. He remembered the brother. A good man, who'd longed for peace and freedom.

"That's a lie."

"Well, this guy believed it to the end. Thankfully, Mitchell hit the guy spot on." Mark realized just how important that shot had been. "Ends up, this had nothing to do with my name being leaked from the CIA list."

At least the man he'd been trailing had missed chest center and hit Mark in the arm. Of course, as luck would have it, the bullet hit a bone, fragmented and nicked an artery. Would take longer to heal. Maybe physical therapy. But he was alive.

Mark sighed, long and hard. Thought of what he wanted to share. If anyone would understand, it would be his boss. Brenner had always understood how his field agents felt because he'd been one himself years ago.

"You let us know the minute you need a ride

to the airport," Brenner said. "Let's get you back home to heal. You need anything else?"

Another person asking if he needed anything. Before, he'd always shrugged things like that off. This time, other people's concern was what he needed more than anything else. Almost anything else. He needed Ashley in his arms to feel complete again.

He cleared his throat. "Yeah. You know how you're always pushing for the agents to talk to one of the agency shrinks?"

"Yep. I've talked to them myself."

"Well, if you'll send one over to the hospital, I'll take you up on that offer while I'm here."

"Consider it done."

"Have you ever talked to one?"

"Once. Needed to put some things in perspective. You know how it is."

There they were again, those old standby words—you know how it is. Whether his boss had or hadn't didn't really matter. Just the fact Brenner had accepted the idea as okay was all Mark needed. There was very little he'd miss in his new job with the Parks Service. Brenner was one of them.

"Yeah. In the ambulance on the way to the hospital, I kept going in and out of consciousness. But during one of those times, I remembered my dad's conversation. All of it. Now I need to figure out why the hell I've kept doing this thankless job my entire life."

Could it be as simple as the fact he chose his life because he wanted to follow that path? Maybe.

Maybe not. His once simple life had changed in the past months. Ashley had made him ponder who he was and what he wanted in the future. One thing for sure, he wanted her. Needed her. She filled a void he didn't even know existed.

Hours later, after Doc had told him he'd be in the hospital a couple days, and the agency shrink Brenner sent had stopped by, the nurse made her nightly med rounds. She insisted Mark sit in the chair as she changed his bed, then helped him settle in again. He insisted she angle the stats monitor for him to see. Dimming the lights on her way out, Mark asked the nurse to leave the door cracked a few inches. He wanted the lights and sounds of safety there when he woke up later.

Then he laid there staring at the stats as if hypnotized. Watching his breaths in numbers—oxygen levels in percentages—beats of his heart in jagged lines on the screen. He'd survived. Lying there between crisp, clean sheets, he finally felt some serenity and optimism as he clutched the cool fragment of blue sea glass. The one he'd carried in his pocket ever since the day he left Nature's Crossing.

That was enough until he got his body healed. His mind straight. His future planned. Enough until he held Ashley in his arms again.

CHAPTER FORTY-ONE

THE REMODELERS HAD been right on schedule when they told Ashley they'd have the two storefronts she'd chosen, combined and finished out by the beginning of April. Now Janie and a few other friends from around Nature's Crossing helped her as she feverously worked to be ready for the grand opening in two weeks.

And thanks to others seeing the potential for the row of block buildings, she wouldn't be the only one doing business by summertime. Eloise, along with a couple of energized moms in town, would be opening a bakery in the two shops on Ashley's left. And on the right, a yarn shop was in the works. Besides which, Lorna and Gus had decided to open a barbeque shop a block or so away and were working out the logistics to be open by Memorial Day.

Ashley reached for the pendulum mantel clock from the crate on the floor, thankful her new shop was taking on the flavor of quaintness she'd envisioned. With only a few days left, half the gift items still hadn't arrived, but plenty of antiques absorbed the space. The adjoining coffee house section would be ready by opening day. At least she hoped.

Smiling, she admired the red and gold letters on the front window—*Serendipity Forever—Gifts, Antiques & Coffee.*

"Where's Patrick?" Ashley asked.

Janie paused from dusting a pitcher. "Said he was going for a walk. Did you notice he doesn't use the cane near as much?"

"I sure appreciate everything he did to move the builders along. Without him, I wouldn't be able to open this soon."

"He enjoyed it. In fact, he seems to like everything the last few days. I was beginning to worry about him after Mark disappeared. He was really down and…" Janie looked at the floor. "I'm sorry. I shouldn't have said anything."

"Don't worry. I'm fine." Ashley gave her a shoulder-hug and swallowed the sudden lump in her throat. Tissues stuffed in her pocket were always available, but she batted her eyelids instead.

A tap on the front glass caused them both to jump, and Ashley's gaze flew to the window. She still hoped Mark would return, but the last update Patrick had given her said Mark was still in Los Angeles.

Janie rushed to open the door for Patrick. "Where do you want this? It's the last one on the trailer?" he asked.

Ashley pointed to the corner. "Thanks a lot. I don't know what I'd have done without your help."

"Any time. Janie, we better get going, my Town Council committee has a meeting tonight." He disappeared out the door with a let's-get-going hand jerk.

"Paddy, wait for me," Janie called.

Ashley laughed. "You better run, before he leaves you here to walk home."

"He better not. I'll see you tomorrow about two. Maybe there'll be more deliveries by then." Janie scurried out the door, pulling it closed behind her.

"Hope so," Ashley shouted.

She ran to answer the ringing phone behind the counter. The women had been so busy, there hadn't been time to tell Janie about the deer by the apple tree that morning. She grabbed the phone, then pulled out her paperwork to verify amounts ordered from the supplier on the line. The items were already late, so at this point, she'd take whatever she could get.

Finishing up the call, she surveyed her surroundings. Displays of antique furniture were grouped with what few gift arrangements had arrived. Antique wood scents filled the air with the fresh aroma of lemon oil and a patina of age. Silver items were polished to perfection or tarnished with age, depending on the feeling each piece shared with her. She smiled at the little shop's invitation for happiness.

She stacked a few remaining Styrofoam filled boxes on the counter, one on top of the other, then shuffled the box tower to her arms and headed to the storeroom in back. The bell above the front door jingled, and she realized she'd forgot to lock the door once Janie left.

A trickle of fear zipped through her mind. That was foolish. This was a shop, and someone thought the store was open. Focused on the box tower balanced in front of her, she couldn't turn to look even when the door clicked closed.

"I'm sorry, we're not open," she shouted over her shoulder.

"I thought maybe you could make an exception," Mark replied.

She gasped at the sound of his voice. Bumped the counter. And the boxes tumbled to the floor. White Styrofoam peanuts sprinkled like falling snow as she turned around.

There he was. The love of her life leaning against the front counter. He looked like it was his usual spot to stand in the store. His right forearm braced against the counter, the left supported in a black sling, his eyes looked weary. His face thinner. But he still held his head high. And looked sexy as ever.

His two-finger salute caught her off guard, and she couldn't breathe. "I see you're still running into things." He stepped in her direction as the tiny quirk of his lips became a full smile.

"Mark. My beautiful Mark." The whisper of her voice made everything real.

Ashley dashed across the floor and encircled him with her arms, covering his face with kisses. There was nothing and no one else in the world but them. Unwilling to relinquish the feeling, she clung to the moment. To him.

"Are you really here? Please, don't be a dream. Please."

"I'm real." Mark pulled her closer, gathering her into his embrace with his right arm. "I'll take this as a sign you're glad to see me."

"I was beginning to think you were—"

His mouth covered hers before she could voice the word. His hold firm and secure. The insistence of his kiss, tender yet demanding. Her lips parted, allowing him in. They'd survived.

Ashley laid her cheek against him, accepting his touch as he melded their bodies together. She pushed to be closer, rested her head against his chest. He flinched. Grunted.

"You're hurt," she said.

"I'll heal."

Drawing her nearer, they stood heart-to-heart, holding on to each other. This was all she needed. She fell into the temptation of his clear, blue eyes. Melted as his fingers tangled through her hair, his lips caressing her neck, finding her tender spot. A whimper escaped her lips an instant before his firm, urgent kisses demanded her mouth again. More and more. Each one of them slow and deep and strong, erupted within her—again and again and again.

Mark paused but kept her close. "I listened to your messages on my answering service. You sounded desperate, pretty lady."

Struggling to return to his lips, she remembered the first time she'd left a message. The phone might have been smashed, but his answering service still worked. She'd hoped he'd listen. And if he didn't, at least she'd felt a contact. Some days that was all that kept her going.

He slid his hand up her sides. "Felt nice to keep hearing you say you loved me."

"I just wanted to make sure you knew my feelings." She loved the touch of his fingers.

"I knew, but it was better hearing you say it."

Her gaze held his. "Then I'll say it every day. I love you, Mark Garmund. I love you."

"What about those curse words you used when you begged me to come back?"

"I didn't beg."

He flipped her around and pinned her to the counter. Face to face. Body to body. Pressing. The look she loved filled his face. One that left her breathless. Reeled her in and ignited her soul. He was back, thank goodness… He was back.

"Oh, yeah, Ashley. You begged." He guided her even closer, rolling her hips back and forth against him. Hot and suggestive, he winked before his lips eased to her neck, nipping and tasting the tender spots along the path to her ear. He blew a long, slow, steady breath of heat against her lobe, her hair, her neck. The feel of his fingers as they inched their way under her sweater, circling against her skin and gliding upward, pushed her over the edge.

"You never know what a little begging will get you," he whispered, hoarse and ragged.

"Mmmmmm." There was barely space to breathe between them. No imagination needed. "Well, I just wanted to make sure I had your complete attention."

"Lady, you've had my attention for a long, long time." Mark eased his hold, then outlined her cheek to the tip of her chin. "By the way, do you happen to know of someone I could stay with around here? Forever?"

Had he asked her…forever? Forever. Ashley tilted her head and smiled. "What about Washington?"

"We'll have two homes."

"We? That sounds like a proposal," she said.

Grinning, he nodded and brushed her hair back. "So, what's your answer?"

That was all she needed. No need to ask about his job. He'd keep them safe, no matter what. No need to ask about the past few months. Whether he'd found the guy or not. She figured he had and knew he'd share what he could. And she'd listen. She'd hold him. She'd understand.

The future? What would be would be. He rested his chin on top of her head for a moment before he gazed into her eyes. But his expression made her feel as if this would last for eternity.

She whimpered, ecstatic with the moment. "Well, I could take you in on a trial basis. You'd have to run my bath and keep me warm and… anything else I might need."

His laughter filled the air for a moment. Then, his expression turned serious as he slipped the bit of smooth blue sea glass into her palm. "I love you, Ashley."

"I love you, too."

"I'm still waiting for your answer." His lips

skimmed hers, his gaze questioned. "Will you marry me? Be my lady forever?"

"Yes. Yes forever."

He smiled. "Good. By the way, what do you think about having two children?"

Stunned, she couldn't believe her ears. What had happened in the last few months? What had changed his thinking? Made him want to have a family? Didn't matter. Evidently, he'd found himself. And she'd be forever grateful that she'd found him.

Linking her hand in his, her insides fluttered with happy what-ifs as she kissed his cheek. "I think two would be perfect. Just like you."

She folded the fingers of her other hand around their lucky piece of blue sea glass, slipping it carefully in her pocket. Then smiled. She'd waited for her blue-eyed man to return. And he had.

Thank you for reading
A WEEK AT MOST

The Nature's Crossing series continues with
TIME TO GROW

TIME TO GROW
(Nature's Crossing Series, Book 2)

CHAPTER ONE

A few things New York CEO Taylor Randolph had learned during the time he'd spent serving as an Army Ranger were how to hear the lies. See the trepidation. Smell the fear. Long since out of the military, those same instincts now guided him in his position as head of T-Randolph Environmental Development (TRED). And the man he'd just fired had dinged every one of those tells.

Taylor walked to the door of his office and braced his hands against the side doorjamb. Watching the hastily retreating back of the ex-employee charging down the hallway, he briefly glanced in the direction of his executive assistant's desk located outside his office.

"Mrs. Parker, call front door security. Tell them Chase Andrews no longer works here. Have them relieve him of his company credit card, phone, keys, and anything else he was issued when he came on board."

"Should I also contact our site in Nature's

Crossing?" She reached for the phone.

"Yes. Jake will know what to do on that end." He turned his attention back to Chase just in time to see the angry man shoulder-shove a woman out of his way.

She stumbled, slamming against the wall before bumping her head. Her arm collided with the table lamp, knocking it to the floor as her briefcase fell from her fingers. The satchel landed with a thud, spewing pens, notebooks, and a pink cell phone across the carpet.

Reactively, Taylor rushed to help the blonde-haired woman trying to regain her balance. She rubbed her shoulder as she kicked her phone from beneath a chair, then grimaced with the move. Hurt? That was all he needed to make this day one perfect disaster.

"Darn it, darn it," she mumbled in clear exasperation. "Double dang darn it!"

"I'm sorry. What did you say?" Taylor asked.

Kneeling on both knees now, she reached under the side chair, trying to grab her pens. "I said darn it." She glanced up at him. "Got a problem with that?"

"Nope. No problem." The touch of a Southern accent made him inwardly smile. And her eyes—the color of melted caramel—took his breath away.

He prided himself on trying to know every employee in the office, but he'd never seen this woman before. Maybe she was a new hire or lost on her way to Human Resources. Moving closer, he offered his hand to assist her in standing. "Here, let me help you up. Are you okay?"

"Yes, I'm fine. Thank you kindly." She barely glanced at his offer of assistance. "I don't need any help."

In one fluid motion, she nudged back on her high heels and flexed upward. Trying to avoid contact, he stepped to the side as she tugged her suit into place. Brushing her skirt smooth, she blew out a soft sigh and lifted the corners of her mouth in a half-smile.

He took in the trim navy suit cropped above the knees, showing only the business-proper amount of skin. Long legs that flowed into conservative heels. And what looked like blonde hair. Hard to tell with the way her hair was twisted up tight on her head like some high fashion model.

"Human Resources is down the hall." Taylor jerked his hand to the left and pointed. He'd had enough disruption to his day. "Be sure to tell them you fell after being pushed by Chase Andrews. They can help you fill out the proper paperwork. Get you medical attention."

"There's no need for that. I'm fine. I just—"

"Fine now, but you could wake up tomorrow with a concussion." Yeah, he knew he sounded over-reactive. But, damn it, he didn't like anyone getting hurt on his watch.

She didn't budge. "I don't need to fill out paperwork."

"Human Resources." He pointed to the left again. "Fill out the paperwork. See the nurse."

"Oh, excuse me." She stooped to pick up a pen

lying by his foot. Her fingers lightly touched the side of his arm as she steadied herself when she rose, then blushed and stepped back. "Sorry."

His mouth dried like sand in a high noon desert sun. The warmth of her touch lingered on his skin, shocking him with the unexpected sensation. He glanced at his forearm then felt the heat travel all the way to his core.

He needed this reaction like he needed to be called up on active duty again. Thankfully, he'd never been attracted to an employee, and he sure as hell didn't plan to start now. He gulped in a breath of air a moment before he focused on her face and opened his mouth to speak.

She stop-signed him with the palm of her hand. "Okay…okay…okay. If it makes you happy, I'll fill out paperwork."

"Good." He had things to do. People to see. The past to get past. He half-turned away. "Keep a copy for yourself, too."

"Why not? In fact, maybe there'll be a hundred pages." The woman pushed wisps of her hair that had loosened in the altercation back in place. "I'm sure the world won't mind losing a tree for the tiny bump on my head."

Sass? She'd sassed him? "Do you know who I am?"

"Does it matter?"

"Yes, it matters."

"Why?" She stared into his eyes. Didn't blink. Didn't smile. Didn't appear intimidated in the least. "Why is knowing who you are so important?"

"Because…because I said so." That even sounded childish to himself. He inwardly winced at the wrinkling of his forehead as his eyebrows pinched together. The woman had turned him into a babbling idiot. Exasperating. That's what she was.

Struggling to keep his reactions in check, he braced his hands on his waist. "As I was saying. Do you know—"

Behind him, he heard Mrs. Parker laugh along with a fake clearing of her throat.

He knew full well her cleared throat was his clue to calm down. Don't overreact. They'd worked together long enough to have their signals. But the laugh? The laugh was new. "Mrs. Parker, is there something funny?"

"No, sir." The middle-aged woman shuffled papers on her desk. "Not a thing."

He focused back on the long-legged blonde who'd defied him. She met his gaze, confident and unapologetic. Then, as if everything was her idea, she turned and walked down the hallway toward Human Resources.

Unable to drag his eyes away, he watched the way her jacket hugged her waist. The glide of the skirt skimming her hips. Her slender ankles as they balanced safe and secure with every step she took until she turned the corner. With any luck, he wouldn't run into her again.

Although, if he wanted to, he could find out her name from Human Resources. See which department she worked in. Check on her progress and… Nope, one of his rules was don't mix business and pleasure.

Besides, this was the first woman in a very long time who'd stoked his fire the moment he laid eyes on her. Didn't mean a thing. Just an already rough day, sharpening a dull edge.

He'd made himself a promise years ago. The day his life had shattered in a barrage of bullets halfway around the world. Loss was always hard. But failing so many people he'd cared about, all in one day, had changed his outlook on life forever. Some days he wished he could just move to Nature's Crossing permanently, instead of being stuck here at his office in Kansas City part of the week. At least this setup had allowed him to move out of New York.

He rolled his shirtsleeves down and buttoned the cuffs before turning toward his own office. Time to focus on his next appointment. He lifted a couple of butterscotch candies from the dish on the corner of his assistant's desk. "Guess I got a little absorbed for a second."

"I don't know what you're talking about, Mr. Randolph." Mrs. Parker held out a folder. "Here's the extra info you requested earlier today."

Some days, Mrs. Parker knew him better than he knew himself even if she did try to mother him, telling him what she thought he should do. How he should move on with his life. He let her. Only her. Others knew to keep their thoughts to themselves.

"Thanks. You know, I think I'll keep you around." Taylor grinned and tossed a candy in his mouth, remembering the day almost three years ago that he'd inherited Mrs. Parker along with the chair his dad used to sit in as the head of TRED.

"Oh, that's such a relief, sir." She patted her heart in mock thankfulness at his remark. "You don't know how worried I was about that."

Trim, professional, and somewhere in her late fifties, she'd let him know she expected to be treated with the same respect that she'd always garnered from his father. Part of which meant he'd call her Mrs. Parker, and she'd call him Mr. Randolph. He smiled to himself. And any comments about her prematurely gray hair or dangly earrings would not be tolerated. That part he'd learned the hard way.

He pocketed another piece of candy, then walked across the hall to the executive conference room. The room and the view always seemed to center him. Today was no different.

Thinking about his upcoming meeting with Crawford Enterprises, he wished his old college buddy Mathew Crawford was the one coming. But today's meeting would be with a company representative instead. Years ago, Mathew had mentioned his brother and him planning a business after college. Maybe that's who was coming. But for the life of him, he couldn't remember the brother's name.

If today's deal worked out the way he hoped, he and Mathew would have plenty of time to hash over college times. They'd only been friends in passing, but they'd kept in touch occasionally after graduation, then less and less. In fact, he hadn't heard from him since about the time his own life had been hurtling out of control. Life had been one giant blur of business since then.

Taylor left the calming atmosphere of the conference room and headed back to his office. The image of the long-legged blonde flitted through his thoughts. Had she found her way to Human Resources? Before he left for the day, he'd make a call to see if she filled out the paperwork or if she'd simply ignored him once she turned out of sight.

"Anything else you need for your meeting?" Mrs. Parker asked as he passed her desk.

"Yeah. I can't believe I'm saying this, but…" he laughed at himself, "I've completely forgotten the name of the man I'm meeting from Crawford Enterprises."

"Rylie…Rylie Crawford."

Bridgette Rylie Crawford walked a few steps down the hall toward Human Resources and pretended to be rummaging in the side of her briefcase. She didn't need to fill out paperwork. She wasn't hurt. Sooner or later, Taylor Randolph would go back in his office, then she could introduce herself to his assistant. She'd already swallowed a ton of nerves when he reached out to help her up from the floor.

Then he'd asked if she knew who he was. Of course, she knew. But right then had not seemed like a good time to introduce herself. Especially when less than a minute before she'd been kneeling

on the floor in front of him, searching for pens and
her composure.

And the story continues . . .
TIME TO GROW
http://claudiasheltonauthor.com/

ACKNOWLEDGEMENTS

The manuscript for A WEEK AT MOST has had a long journey to find its way into print. You might be interested to know that this is the first full-length novel that I ever wrote. Of course, between when this was completed in 2008 and now, I've done plenty of rewrites, reworks and revising as I've grown in my writing. But all this time, and through all the other books I've published since then, this story, setting and series kept calling me back.

So here I am, hoping you've enjoyed reading A WEEK AT MOST (formerly titled Freedom & Magnolias). And I hope the Nature's Crossing series is one that calls you back, also.

There have also been a lot of changes in my life during this time. The day I completed the manuscript back in 2008, my husband and I laughed and smiled and hugged celebrating my accomplishment. He was always so proud and supportive of my writing. A few months later my husband passed away, but he's always with me and I'm sure he's happy that this story has completed its journey.

I'm blessed to have my sons, daughter-in-law and grandsons' energy and excitement urging me along in my writing, also. They make my life so much brighter! And they will probably recognize some sections throughout the book that reflect places I've been, things I care about, and foods, sights and scents that I love.

Thank you to Jeff, at Fan Favorite Digital, for designing the book cover for A WEEK AT MOST, while at the same time reworking my website, social media banners, and more for release day. I truly appreciate how you gave me multiple choices when I really had no idea, or words to convey, what I wanted done.

Thank you to my content/copy editor Tera Cuskaden, who helped me find the starting point of the book and guided me through altering a storyline. Yet at the same time, she allowed me to tell the story within my own guidelines, not preconceived ones in publishing. And thank you to my proofreader Susan Panak, who offers word changes every so often besides finding those pesky missing quotation marks.

And what can I say about my critique group The Cosmos (Linda Gilman, Suzie T. Roos, Michelle Sharp)? They rock! They're always there with laughter, support, and words of wisdom regarding my characters and scenes. And, as a group, we are super extraordinaire on writing blurbs!

Thank you to all my readers, beta reader and ARC readers. And to everyone who follows me on my various social media sites or subscribes to my newsletter. You are the reason for my stories! Hope you enjoy the Nature's Crossing series with its small-town setting and everyday characters. Maybe this story, and others I'm working on, will call to you as much as they have to me.

Smiles,

Claudia Shelton

Books by CLAUDIA SHELTON...

CONTEMPORARY ROMANCE

Nature's Crossing Series
A Week at Most
Time to Grow

An Awesome Christmas Book
Cocoa for Two

ROMANTIC SUSPENSE

Shades of Leverage Series
Slater's Revenge
Dangerous Lies

Risk Series
Risk of a Lifetime

ABOUT THE AUTHOR

Award winning author Claudia Shelton has already proven herself a contender in romantic suspense books that cross over into the mystery-suspense-thriller genre. Whether sexy protector agents or small-town family settings, her fast-paced stories keep the reader guessing all the way to the end.

Now, with the release of the first book in her new Nature's Crossing series, she's entering the contemporary mainstream romance genre (a crossover between contemporary romance and women's fiction). The ongoing small-town saga is nestled in south-central Missouri, somewhere between Lake of the Ozarks, Table Rock Lake and Mark Twain National Forest.

Claudia is a two-time finalist in the Daphne du Maurier (unpublished) Award for Excellence in mystery and suspense. Her debut book release, Risk of a Lifetime, was voted one of Ebooks Galore's top reads for 2014.

On a personal note, Claudia considers herself a music lover and water person, plus she enjoys anything to do with nature. In fact, the Nature's Crossing series allows her to bring all of those things closer. Her main priority, though, is spending time with family, friends and her two sweet, conniving rescue dogs, Gidget and Daisy.

She enjoys hearing from readers, so stop by her website and drop her a note. While there, sign up for her newsletter or some of the other sites where she keeps everyone informed on her writing shenanigans.

Website & Newsletter Sign-up:
http://claudiasheltonauthor.com/

THANK YOU IN ADVANCE FOR LEAVING
A REVIEW
ON THE BOOKSELLER'S SITE—
IT'S TRULY APPRECIATED

Made in the USA
Coppell, TX
16 May 2021